DATE DUE

MY 07			
7/5/10			
FEB - - 2011			
5/10/14			

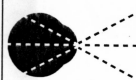

This Large Print Book carries the
Seal of Approval of N.A.V.H.

THE OUTCAST: RED MESA

LUKE CYPHER

WHEELER PUBLISHING
A part of Gale, Cengage Learning

GALE
CENGAGE Learning

Detroit • New York • San Francisco • New Haven, Conn • Waterville, Maine • London

GALE
CENGAGE Learning

Wheeler Publishing Large Print Western.
The text of this Large Print edition is unabridged.
Other aspects of the book may vary from the original edition.
Set in 16 pt. Plantin.
Printed on permanent paper.

LIBRARY OF CONGRESS CATALOGING-IN-PUBLICATION DATA

Cypher, Luke.
    The outcast. Red Mesa / by Luke Cypher.
      p. cm. — (Wheeler Publishing large print western)
    ISBN-13: 978-1-59722-796-4 (pbk. : alk. paper)
    ISBN-10: 1-59722-796-X (pbk. : alk. paper)
    1. Clergy — Fiction. 2. Widows — Fiction. 3. Ranching — Fiction. 4. Large type books. I. Title. II. Title: Red Mesa.
    PS3555.I23O987 2008
    813'.54—dc22   2008016837

Published in 2008 by arrangement with The Berkley Publishing Group, a member of Penguin Group (USA) Inc.

08-23-16
Wheeler
(Gale)
09/08
$24.95

Printed in the United States of America
1 2 3 4 5 6 7 12 11 10 09 08

I will not turn away
the punishment thereof;
because they have sold
the righteous for silver.
— Amos 2:6

And there was war in heaven:
Michael and his angels
fought against the dragon;
and the dragon fought and his angels.
— Revelation 12:7

And they covenanted with him for
thirty pieces of silver.
— Matthew 26:15

Oh, God, You who know the frailty of man and what he is and what he would be, lift this burden from my shoulders, from my soul, and guide me on the path You chose for me so long ago. Let me walk beside the cool waters and feel the light of Your forgiveness upon my shoulders. Let me not fall into the abyss from which I came. Heal my wounded spirit and accept me as Your penitent son who grieves for the pain and misery he has inflicted upon Your world. Let me do Your bidding and carry Your word to those places where it has been forgotten and bring them once again into the grace that was bestowed upon David and the wisdom You granted Solomon.

Prayer of Amos Hood

1.

The sky was a hard blue that a nail couldn't scratch as Amos Hood rode slowly down out of the blue hills and began to cross the mesquite flats toward the town of Jericho, New Mexico, nestled against a bloodred mesa. Above the mesa in the distance, dirty dishwater clouds scudded across the sky, making the sun appear like an orange smudge. It was a vast and lonely land, lost except to those few who did not welcome visitors. The smell of mesquite and piñon was heady, and cactus wrens and quail lifted in low flights away from their nests as he drew near. Yet, at the edge of the red mesa, he could see a small slice of green as if cut with a giant's knife, and knew that he was at the edge of an otherwise desolate land where only the most stalwart could eke out a living.

He had spent the night in the ruins of an old Spanish church, roofless, the chancel filled with old ashes of fires and debris and horse apples. A lone buzzard circled overhead when he had risen to ride out in the early morning coolness. Now, however, his gray mare, Sheba, was as tired and dusty as he, with a fine grit covering her coat, but she kept a steady pace, weaving her way through the prickly pear cactus and mesquite bushes, and he could feel the powerful reserve in her between his legs. At his side trotted Sam, a half-grown pet wolf he had rescued as a pup when he had been Tom Cade, the sheriff of Walker, a railhead town back in Kansas. But now, he wore a new name and the clothes of a preacher, and at the bottom of one of his saddlebags, wrapped in oiled leather, rested the ivory-handled Schofield .45 with which he had earned a reputation as a gunfighter. In the other saddlebag was his father's Bible and the silver cross his father always wore when he preached. They had been sent to him by his brother upon his father's death in Tennessee after Tom had gone West to try to avoid a feud with the Johnson clan. But the Johnsons kept coming after him anyway, and to make matters worse, he had befriended Sam Kilian, a known gunfighter, who taught him how to use the pistol. Unfortunately, after Kilian was killed by some of the Hardestys who had been hunting him after he killed one of their relatives, Hood had inherited the Hardesty feud as well when he killed those who had slain Kilian.

Now, as he watched the brooding slate-gray buildings of Jericho draw nearer, he thought about the irony of leaving the Tennessee hills to avoid one feud only to be drawn into the middle of two. But Tom Cade was gone now, and Amos Hood, preacher, had taken his place. Perhaps all the killing had been laid to rest back in Walker. Every night, beside his lonely campfire high in the mountains where the leaves had been a splash of red and orange fall colors, he had read a chapter from the Bible and prayed that his new life would mean an end to the old. That shouldn't be difficult, he reasoned now, as it was a big country, a sprawling country that was just beginning to flex its muscles, and somewhere there had to be a place where he could begin again as Amos Hood.

A roadrunner sped across his path as he rode into Jericho while noting the weathered clapboard sides of the church as he passed it. Tumbleweeds had gathered around the sides of the church and the steps were cracked like old bones. The street had deep

11

ruts cut through it by the spring rains. The air smelled dry like dusty bones in an old tomb. But it was nearly fall now, and the country showed the hard end of a drought. A blacksmith shop and stable, a restaurant, and a general store that also served as a feed store, post office, and stage stop stood so close together, they looked as if they had been built by a carpenter in one long run. Two bat-wing-door saloons stood separately. The sign on the sheriffs office across the street next to the hotel hung from a single hook, and the door was weathered gray and sun-split. A few houses stood on the outskirts of town, most of them well kept. One had well-tended rosebushes and late-blooming desert flowers that had been transplanted in an attempt by its owner to bring some sense of beauty to the harsh land.

Hood turned Sheba into the stable and dismounted stiffly. Sam followed in and sat on his haunches, red tongue lolling as he watched Hood's every movement with wary eyes. The blacksmith laid down his hammer and tongs, wiped his hands on the seat of his pants, and came over. He was balding, but his shoulders were wide and his arms heavily muscled. Blue eyes twinkled merrily from the leathery seams in his face.

"Afternoon," he said pleasantly. "My name's Bert Evans. Something I can do for you?"

"Amos Hood," Hood answered. He indicated Sheba. "I'd like to put up my horse. We've come a long way and we both could use a rest."

"It sure looks like you've come a long way," Evans said, eying Sheba critically. "Twenty-five cents a day and that includes a bait of oats or corn. I have a boy who'll curry her for you if you want."

"Sounds good," Hood said. He reached in his pocket, took out a dollar, and handed it to Evans. He nodded up the street. "That hotel any good?"

Evans shrugged as he took Sheba's reins. She stiffened at the unfamiliar hands on her reins, and Evans waited patiently as she made up her mind whether she would accept his lead or not. He patted her on her shoulder and ran his hand down her side, crooning softly to her. She relaxed.

"Doesn't matter," Evans said. "It's the only one in town. Unless you want to sleep over one of the saloons." He looked Hood up and down, noting his clothes and the lack of a pistol at his side, "But if I were you, I'd take the hotel. You'd rest easier there."

13

Hood smiled faintly. "Sounds like good advice."

He untied the saddlebags behind his saddle and lifted them off. He took from its saddle sheath the Spencer that he had bought in Tennessee when he was young and tucked it under his arm. He'd started to leave when Evans spoke.

"You wouldn't happen to be a preacher, would you, Mr. Hood?" Evans asked. "You don't appear to be a gambler and them ain't clothes a cowhand would wear."

Hood turned and looked intently at Evans. Slowly, he nodded.

"Yes," he said softly. "I'm a preacher." He looked around the town. "And it looks like this town has need of one."

Evans sighed and rubbed a calloused hand over his bald spot.

"Well, won't say that we don't. But preachers don't last long here in Jericho. We been without one for the past eighteen months or so. I wish you luck."

"Thanks," Hood said. He turned to go. "Sam."

The wolf scrambled to his feet and followed at Hood's heels as he headed down the dirt street toward the hotel. A couple of loafers watched him curiously as he passed. One of them called to him.

"Hey! That wolf tame?"

Hood paused and said, "As tame as anyone in this town."

The loafer laughed, uncertain how to take Hood's answer as Hood continued on his way to the hotel.

He entered and stood for a moment, blinking the sunlight out of his eyes. A dusty rose-colored settee showing wear stood on his left next to an old Hitchcock chair, the finish long worn away. Then, he crossed to the desk, where a clerk sat on a stool, reading a newspaper. His shoulders stood up behind his ears like a vulture's wings. He looked up at Hood's approach.

"Something I can do for you?" he asked. He was thin with black hair slicked back. He was neatly dressed with a string tie and his white shirt had been carefully ironed.

"I'd like a room. If the mattress isn't ticky," Hood added.

"They're clean," the clerk said curtly. His eyes slipped down to Sam sitting patiently by Hood's heels.

"We don't let dogs in," he said.

Hood reached for a pen and turned the register around.

"He's not a dog. He's a wolf," he said. "And he stays with me."

The clerk frowned. "We have rules," he

began, but Hood interrupted him, smiling.

"And rules are rules. But they can be overlooked now and then, can't they? After all, he's just a pup."

"Looks to me to be more than a pup," the clerk said. "Dogs tend to take a leak where they want. Don't belong in a hotel."

Hood smiled faintly. "He's trained."

The clerk studied Hood, noting his black hair and long jaw and the blue eyes that pierced his own. His eyes looked over the dusty black coat and pants and the saddlebags hanging from Hood's shoulder. He started to object, but something in Hood's eyes made him reconsider. He shrugged.

"I just work here," he said indifferently. "It's okay with me if you can get the okay of the owner."

"And who might that be?"

"Mr. Barth. Halsey Barth. He also owns The Cattleman's Saloon across the street. You'll find him there."

"All right," Hood answered "But first, I'd like to get settled and cleaned up a bit. That all right with you?"

"All right with me," the clerk said "I'm Howie Statler. You want a bath?" He pushed a key on a brass ring across the counter.

"Yes," Hood said, taking the key. He glanced at the number: four.

16

"Upstairs and to your right," Statler said. He glanced down at Sam. "Sure hope that animal's tame."

"So do I," Hood said.

He turned and climbed the stairs with Sam at his heels. He found his room halfway down the hall and opened the raw wood door. The room looked as if had been furnished from someone's attic, but it was clean and free of dust. The bed had an iron bedstead and was neatly made. A white enameled pitcher and basin stood on a small table below a mirror. A towel hung on a hook at the side of the table. An old wardrobe stood next to it. An overstuffed Belter rosewood chair carved with vines and leaves stood by the window opposite a spindle-backed rocking chair with cyma-curved arms and seat. A small table with curved cabriole legs stood between them with a brass kerosene lantern on it. On the floor was a latch-hooked rug.

"Better than we expected, eh, Sam?" he said softly.

Sam walked in and sat on the rug. Hood closed the door and crossed to the bed, hanging his saddlebags on the back of the Belter chair. He removed his long black coat and looked ruefully at the dust clinging to it.

"We need a full cleaning, I expect," he said.

Sam turned around three times before lying down on the rug, his muzzle propped on his front legs, yellow eyes following Hood's every move.

Hood hung his coat over the door to the wardrobe and rolled up the sleeves of his white shirt. He poured some water in the basin and scrubbed his face, drying himself with the towel. He crossed to the window and looked down into the hardpan street. A feeling of loneliness spread over him.

A knock came at the door, and he turned away from the window and crossed the room to open it. Sam's head came up, ears cocked as he watched. The clerk stood there, holding a large towel with a cake of soap on top. He handed them to Hood.

"Water's being brought up now. Bath's ten cents. I'll just add it to your bill, if that's all right with you."

"That's fine," Hood said, taking the towel and soap.

The clerk's eyes flickered down at Sam. He shook his head.

"Sure hope no problem comes from having that wolf in here," he mumbled.

"I'll talk with Mr. Barth and straighten everything out," Hood promised. "Just a minute."

He collected his coat and brought it back to the clerk.

"Would you mind seeing this gets a good brushing?" he asked.

The clerk took it and shook his head again as he turned away, walking stoop-shouldered down the hall. Hood closed the door behind him, and went to his saddlebags and took out a fresh shirt and pants and his ivory-handled razor. He looked down at Sam.

"You mind your manners while I go bathe," he said.

Sam whined and dropped his head back down on his paws. Hood opened the door and closed it behind him, and walked down the hall to the bathroom. A high-backed tin tub stood in the center of the room. A young boy had just finished pouring the second of two buckets of water into it. He looked up at Hood.

"That be enough, you figure? Or should I haul up some more?" he asked.

"That'll do," Hood said.

The boy nodded and left. Hood gave the key a half turn in the door, locking it, then stripped and stepped into the tub, resting his back gingerly against the cold metal. He sighed with pleasure and began working the soap into a lather.

A town without a preacher, he mused. Maybe the Good Lord had sent him this way after letting him wander for weeks in the wilderness. Might make for a first sermon.

He began washing.

2.

The rain clouds hadn't settled over Jericho as Hood walked across the dried and rutted street spiderwebbed by cracks to The Cattleman's Saloon. Heat lightning flashed over the red mesa, but the smell of dust and dry heat was in the air and Hood sensed that the rain would not be coming.

His long black coat had been brushed, and around his neck he wore a neatly knotted string tie along with the large silver cross on a heavy, silver-link chain that centered the cross on his chest. The moon rose like a large orange planet above the distant blue hills, but the stars were still hidden in the final rays of the sun setting over the red mesa, casting blue shadows of the buildings over the town.

He pushed opened the bat-wing doors of the saloon and entered, nose twitching as he smelled the sour beer and spilled whiskey in the room. Gray smoke hung heavily in the room, and a thin yellow light from a chandelier made the smoke appear hellish. Above the bar between two mirrors hung a painting of a voluptuous nude reclining on a blue velvet settee, hands held provocatively behind her head. Bronze cuspidors had been placed down the side of the mahogany bar for the customers. Tobacco juice spattered the floor around the cuspidors from careless customers who had lost their aim once whiskey visions danced behind their eyes. On the bar stood jars of pickled eggs and slices of dry bread and thinly sliced beef for sandwiches when the drunks felt they needed something in their stomachs to dry up the whiskey and beer they had been swilling.

The poker tables and faro tables were filled. At the back of the room stood a worn green felt–covered table around which well-dressed men sat, engrossed in a poker game where red, blue, and white chips were piled high. A huge man, dressed nattily in a gray coat and white shirt and embroidered blue waistcoat that strained at his broad shoulders, sat with his back to the wall. His flat black eyes stared emotionlessly around the table as he waited for others to consider their bets. A cravat had been tied around his thick throat, the ends tucked neatly beneath his shirt. A diamond stickpin was centered in the cravat. The man held a large black cigar in the fingers of a huge hand more appropriate for a well-digger than a gambler. His eyebrows were black half-moons that looked as if they had been drawn by a charcoal pencil. A thin white scar ran through the left one. His black hair had been freshly barbered, and talcum had been brushed across his neck and around his throat.

Hood let the doors swing shut behind him and walked across the barroom floor past the roulette table. Sam trotted by his side, drawing curious stares. Hood came to a halt in front of the poker table at the back, and waited until the large man lifted his eyes to study him. His eyes flickered over Hood's appearance, holding a moment on his hips as if expecting to see a pistol belt, then rose to meet Hood's.

"The game's closed," he said indifferently in a Texas drawl. He pushed a stack of blue chips out on the table. "Call."

He spread a queen-high heart flush neatly in front of him. The others swore softly and tossed their cards into the deadwood at the right arm of the man who raked in the chips, neatly stacking them in front of him. He gathered the cards and began sorting them, ignoring Hood.

"I don't gamble," Hood said quietly. "Are you Halsey Barth?"

The man glanced up at him, then down at his cards, running his fingers around the gathered deck before expertly riffle-shuffling them. He slid the stack to his right and the man cut them and slid them back. He picked up the cards and began dealing a game of draw poker.

"I might be," he said. "Who wants to know?"

"I'm Amos Hood. I just rode into town and took a room at your hotel across the street."

"Thanks for your patronage," Barth said, concentrating on his dealing. Two of the others laughed.

"I have a small problem. I understand you don't allow dogs in your rooms?"

"That's right," Barth said, placing the stack to his right and gathering his cards to him.

"I would like to keep Sam in my room," Hood said.

Barth glanced down at Sam, sitting on his haunches, his yellow eyes steady on Barth, ears pricked, red tongue lolling to the side of his jaws.

"That's a wolf, I don't miss my guess,"

24

Barth said, picking up his cards.

"Yes, he's a wolf," Hood said quietly, keeping his eyes steady on Barth's face.

"Not much different than a dog," Barth answered.

"There's a lot of difference," Hood explained. "I want to keep him in my room. I'll clean up after him if he makes a mess."

Barth shook his head. "Rules are rules."

Hood felt irritation growing inside him, but forced the feeling away, reminding himself to keep calm.

"He's just a half-grown pup," he said. "He won't hurt anything."

"No," Barth said calmly. He discarded two cards and waited for the others to make up their minds.

"Sorry to hear that. I'll find some other place to live," Hood said, and turned to leave. Barth's voice stopped him and he turned back to the table.

"You a preacher?" Barth asked.

Hood nodded. Barth smiled slightly.

"The last two preachers didn't last long here," Barth said. "Jericho doesn't have much need for one."

Hood turned his head slowly, considering the saloon before looking back at Barth.

"Seems to me that if any town needed one, it's this one. I noticed you have a

25

church."

"It hasn't been used for eighteen months," Barth said, tossing some chips into the pot.

"Maybe it's time the church was resurrected," Hood said calmly. "A man needs a church as much as he needs a saloon."

A man at the table laughed again, and Barth stared coldly at him until the man coughed and high color came into his cheeks. He pretended to study the cards in his hand. Barth lifted his eyes to Hood and placed the cigar in his mouth, drawing on it. He blew a thin stream of smoke across the table toward Hood.

"People become churchgoing, they want to close the saloons down," Barth said. "I can't have that."

"Too bad," Hood said quietly. "I think it's maybe time that it reopened for those who feel that they need it. Personally, I don't have anything against saloons. As long as they don't try to be anything more than what they are."

A tiny smile flickered on Barth's face. His even teeth were small and white. "And what might that be?"

Hood shrugged. "A social gathering where men can relax."

Barth studied him for a moment, then shrugged. "All right. We can give it a try.

26

You can have the church and the wolf can stay with you. Tell Howie I said it would be all right."

He turned his attention to the game. Hood stood for a moment, looking at the play, then thanked Barth and turned and made his way out of the saloon. Barth watched him leave, then turned back to his cards.

"I think that preacher's gonna make trouble for you, Halsey," the man on his left said.

Barth glanced up at him. "We'll see, Jackson," he said, and calmly laid down a full house, treys over fours.

Jackson swore and slammed his cards down on the table. "Damn! A man doesn't have a chance with you, Halsey!" he exclaimed.

The others laughed as Barth raked in the chips.

"It's living a clean, God-fearing life," Barth explained mockingly.

A roar of laughter broke out and ran around the table, and even Jackson grinned as he sat back in his chair, waiting for the new deal.

Outside, Hood heard Halsey's words followed by the laughter, and ignored it as he stared up and down the street, taking in the small town and the worn fronts of the buildings. He bent down and scratched behind Sam's ears. The wolf grumbled with pleasure.

"Looks like we've got our work cut out for us, Sam," Hood said softly.

He slipped the cross from around his neck and placed it in his pocket. Then, he turned and made his way up the street to Mother's Place, which advertised meals.

He walked inside and found that long tables, bleached near-white from many washings, had been set up instead of individual tables. He removed his hat and ran his hand over his black hair, smoothing it into place. He took a seat on a bench in the corner of the room where his back would be against the wall, and laid his hat on the seat beside him. Sam lay down next to him, regarding the others in the room with interest.

A fat, buxom woman with twinkling brown eyes came up to him.

"I'm the owner. Most folks call me Mother. What can I get for you?" she asked. She glanced down at Sam, but ignored his presence.

Hood looked up at her and smiled, suddenly feeling ravenous. "I'd like a steak and whatever you have that would go with it."

"Potatoes and some carrots," she answered promptly. "We're out of peas. But I have fresh apple pie just out of the oven."

"That'll do. And coffee, if you've a mind to that as well."

"I have a mind to it," she said. She glanced down again at Sam. "I also have a bone back there I was going to use for soup. Your dog can have it, if you want."

"He's a wolf," Hood said automatically. "But that would be generous of you," he added.

"I'll be right out," she said, and disappeared into the kitchen.

Hood sighed and stretched his legs out contentedly beneath the table. He rubbed the bridge of his nose with his thumb and dropped his other hand down to ruffle Sam's fur as he glanced curiously at the other diners in the room. A cattleman sat a few seats down from him and looked up after the woman had left. He had a thick, fleshy face and a long handlebar mustache that curved down over thin lips to his square chin. His eyes were bright and hard. He wore a leather coat with a blue and brown checked shirt beneath it.

"Who sent for you?" he demanded harshly.

Hood waited for a second, then shook his head. "Nobody. I go wherever I'm needed."

29

"Well, we don't need you here," the man said rudely. "Move on."

"Who's giving the advice?" Hood asked quietly.

The man's face flushed the color of mottled liver. "I'm Jake McQuade. I own the Box M a few miles out. We don't need your kind here."

Sam sensed the animosity in the man's voice and growled quietly. Hood continued petting him, soothing him.

"And what kind might that be?" he asked.

"You're a man who has the look of trouble about him," McQuade said roughly. "We got enough trouble here without importing any more."

"Sorry," Hood murmured. "Maybe I can help ease the problem a bit."

"Or add to it." McQuade shook his head. "Move on. Or my men will move you."

"I don't think so," Hood said easily. "It appears to me that Jericho has need of a minister."

"A minister?" McQuade's eyes bored into Hood's. "That what you are?"

Hood nodded.

"You don't look like a minister. You got more the look of a gunman."

"I'm a minister," Hood replied softly.

McQuade looked at him uncertainly, then

his jaw hardened. "That might be just as bad. We certainly don't need a minister around here any more than we need another gunman!"

"Aw, Jake! Let the man be. He's a man of peace, not a gunfighter. No one sent for him," one of the other men down the table said. " 'Sides, the town could use a preacher. It might even settle some folks down."

McQuade turned to the man. "He may look to you like a preacher, Hoffman, but there's something about him that tells me different," McQuade said. He turned back to Hood. "You got the look of a hard man about you. I've seen enough of them come up from Mexico and from Mogollon to know. You ever use a gun?"

"You're getting pretty personal," Hood answered calmly. He nodded toward Hoffman. "He's right. I plan on opening the church again."

"Why?" McQuade asked bluntly.

"A town needs a church," Hood said mildly.

McQuade shook his head and rose, throwing a silver dollar down on the table to cover the cost of his meal.

"It may look like we need a preacher around here," he said, "but what we really need is a solution to all our problems and that a preacher can't help with."

He stalked out of the café and Hoffman grinned down at Hood. "You gotta take what McQuade says with a grain of salt. I'm Edgar Hoffman and have the Rafter H on the other side of McQuade. He's not very friendly."

"What's the problem that he's talking about?" Hood asked.

Hoffman became serious. "Well, there's four outfits in the area: mine, McQuade's, the Slash K that's run by the Rawlins brothers, and the Bar S run by a woman who inherited it from an old man who should have known better than to deed it over to her in his will. The Slash K are a hardcase outfit — some say the Rawlinses used to run with the Hash Knife outfit over in the Utah brakes — and they seem to care little about whose mavericks are running on open range." His mouth turned down in a grimace. "Fact is, they don't care much about cows carrying another's brand. Or so it seems."

"I see," Hood said.

"But the problem is the Bar S. Everybody wants it because it holds the water rights to the entire valley. There's a natural lake up in the red mesa country that is on Bar S land, and the streams that come down through the mesa and across the grassland are hers. McQuade needs to have the land as he has pushed his boundary from the east right up against the Bar S, and the Rawlinses are on the west. Both of them are trying to get control of the Bar S."

"What about her men?"

Hoffman smiled grimly. "She ain't got no one but herself. No cowboy wants to work for her. You see, Mary Riley used to be a saloon girl. John Stockton, who used to own the Bar S, took sick and Mary Riley nursed him until he died. But before he died, he willed the ranch — lock, stock, and barrel — to her."

"What about Stockton's relatives? How'd they take that?"

Hoffman shook his head "The judge couldn't find no one, so that left the will clear and proper. Leastways, there was no relatives that old Stockton was willing to claim. No, he did it right proper with a lawyer and land registration over in Trent and everything. She has it ironclad. Right now, the war is between the Box M and the Slash K for Bar S land."

"What about you? Seems to me that you'd want to be on it, too."

Hoffman rubbed a huge, calloused hand across his face. "Well, I won't say that I would, won't say that I wouldn't like it. My land butts up right against hers on the south, but Mary has always been good to me and lets one of the streams run through my place so I have water. Enough to irrigate hay land or water my cattle. I'll admit," he added grimly, "that I've had some trouble with McQuade and the Rawlinses as well, but I don't have the water rights and that's what both McQuade and the Rawlinses want. Whoever controls the water rights controls the valley. It's that simple."

"Doesn't sound simple," Hood said, leaning back as Mother brought his food and busied herself laying out knife, fork, plate, and the coffee in front of him. He noted the huge slab of apple pie with pleasure and gave her a smile. She dropped a bone, dripping with fat and shreds of meat, in front of Sam, who looked at her in surprise before turning his attention to the bone.

She cast a sharp look at Hoffman and glanced at Hood, her eyes shining a warning. He wondered what that was about as she turned and bustled away, and made a mental note to ask her when they were next alone.

"Well, it is and it isn't simple," Hoffman continued, oblivious to Mother's warning glance at Hood. "Mary Riley is an outcast here in town because she was once a saloon girl. The other womenfolk ignore her when she comes to town to get supplies. But she doesn't come often because when she does come in, then that leaves the Bar S unprotected. You see?"

Hood nodded as he began to eat.

"She has no money to hire gunfighters, and I don't think she would even if she had the money. Gamblers are offering odds in The Cattleman's that she won't last six more months on the place before being driven out."

A woman with nerve, Hood thought as he ate. Two outfits, possibly three, wanting one piece of land being held by a woman who sat on the hot seat between major cattle companies. There is strength in such a person who is willing to stand against everyone around the country and in town. Strength, but loneliness as well. It would be hard on her to be constantly on the watch against any encroachment on her land by the other ranchers.

"Well," he said as he finished the steak and pulled the piece of pie in front of him, "it seems to me that she could use a friend."

"She could," Hoffman said, spreading his hands. "But although I can protect my own land, I ain't big enough to have the men to wage a war against McQuade or the Rawlinses. I can hold on only by minding my own business and letting the chips fall where they may. I hope she can keep the Bar S, though. If McQuade or the Rawlinses get her land, I have a hunch that water will be pretty pricey."

He slapped his hands on the table and rose. "Well, I'd better get over to the store and pick up my wagon. It should be loaded by now and I need to be heading back. I don't like crossing the flats in the darkness. Too much can happen then."

He nodded at Hood and left, closing the door behind him. Hood picked up his cup of coffee, sipping. It was good coffee, fresh ground, and he leaned back to enjoy it. He wasn't surprised about the range war that was threatening. Three ranches, and at least two of them wanting the land of the fourth. He wondered if the Box M and the Slash K had land rights registered or if they were ranching open range. That would make a big difference in their attention to water rights owned outright by someone else.

Mother came out of the kitchen, carrying a cup of coffee, and sat down opposite him. She placed the cup on the table in front of her, wrapping her hands around it as she stared at him.

"You be careful," she warned. "Hoffman talks sweetly enough, but there's a hard line in him, too. Some people say that he's in partnership with Halsey Barth and that's why McQuade and the Rawlinses leave him alone. I've seen many men with honey in their mouth and larceny in their soul, and I've got a hunch that Hoffman is just such a man. If Mary Riley decides to sell out, Hoffman will be the first with an offer to buy. And he seems to have a lot of ready cash, despite his whining about being headed for the poorhouse. McQuade and the Rawlinses have money, but it's all tied up in stock."

"Thanks for the warning," Hood said.

She nodded and looked at him closely. "You planning on reopening the church?"

Hood nodded.

She sighed and sipped her coffee. "Well, won't say that we don't need a church here in Jericho, but there are some who don't want one here."

"Why's that?" he asked.

"You bring a church in, you bring in the beginning of civilization," she said. "The next thing you know, you'll have more farmers coming into the valley looking for free land. The Box M and the Slash K depend on open range to run their cattle. The farmers we have here now stay in the lower end of the valley and the ranchers pretty much leave them alone. They don't need their land. But I think that would all change if we get more farmers in. They'll be wanting land and take to crowding the ranchers."

"I take it the Bar S is title-free?"

She nodded. "Yep. John Stockton took special care to ensure that before he died. No one can cut up the Bar S. But the Box M and Slash K now, well, they're something else. A lot of that land depends on who has the guns to hold it. Well, I'd better get back to work. I have a Chinaman back there to do the dishes but if I don't watch him, he'll try and stack some to do in the morning and sneak off. I don't begrudge him that often," she added hurriedly, "but tomorrow's Saturday and we'll have people coming in for supplies and some cooking that don't include ranch beans from the cookhouse. Finish your coffee."

She rose and left while he enjoyed the last of his coffee and watched the night suck the last of the daylight out of the sky.

At last, he rose, feeling content, and called Sam as he left the café. He stood for a moment on the boardwalk and enjoyed the night, watching the stars come out against an ink-black sky. A soft wind came down off the red mesa, smelling of desert flowers, but beneath the soft sweet smell was another that was dry and dusty and reminded him of an old graveyard he had stumbled across back in Tennessee once, while chasing a raccoon on the heels of the dog days of August. He turned and walked down the street back to the hotel, Sam trotting at his heels, the bone, picked clean, hanging out of a corner of his mouth.

3.

The red-streaked morning sky turned the distant hills a deep blue as Hood stepped out from Mother's Place with Sam and made his way down the main street of Jericho. A dampness hung in the air, suggesting the coming of rain. Mauve shadows hung in the alleys he passed as he walked down to the church and stood outside, studying the exterior. The tumbleweeds had blown halfway up the west wall, and one stood caught in the steps. He walked around the church, noting the privy in the back, the door hanging on one hinge, the sides gray and ramshackle. He walked up the steps and opened the church, and stepped hastily aside as a rattlesnake buzzed angrily and slithered swiftly toward him and out the door, disappearing across the hard-baked ground.

Gingerly, he walked inside the church. The interior was gloomy, white paint peeling from the walls. One window was cracked like a spiderweb and dirt clung in the cracks. The floors were dirty and cobwebs draped from the ceiling. The front of the lectern had fallen after the wood had dried enough to loosen the nails. The heavy oak cross that had hung against the front wall had fallen, and the communion rail sagged in the middle, but the pews, although covered with an inch of dust, appeared to be solid. He found the bell rope, stiff from disuse, and pulled it once, listening to the deep, hollow ring of the bell in the steeple. Sam raised his muzzle and howled a reply.

"Easy, Sam," Hood said, grinning. He patted him on the head and walked to a closet. He opened the door and found mice nesting behind a straw broom, and wondered if it was the prospect of the mice that had brought the snake into the church.

He sighed and went back outside and removed his coat. He rolled up his sleeves and began to gingerly pull the tumbleweeds away from the church, bringing them around to the front, where he heaped them together in a pile. Briefly, he felt his father's ghost beside him, but as the sun climbed into the sky and his muscles loosened with his labors, the ghost faded away. The outside of the church badly needed painting, but that would have to wait. He had one day to get the church somewhat presentable for Sunday morning services, although he did not have the slightest idea as to how many would come. Only the townspeople for now, he thought, as word of a new minister probably had not made the rounds of the countryside. But everything had to have a beginning and this would have to do for the moment.

A couple of hours later, he heard a wagon pull up, and went outside to greet whoever had come. He was surprised to see a man and three boys climb down. They were each dressed in clean homespun clothes and wore heavy work boots and wide-brimmed hats against the sun. The man had shoulders the width of an ax handle and a deep chest that strained the buttons on the front of his gray shirt. The back of the wagon was loaded with brooms and rags and several buckets of whitewash. The man came forward, smiling and holding out his hand.

"How do," he said "You the new minister I heard about?"

"Amos Hood," he said, shaking the man's hand. "I guess so, unless another has come in since last night. I wasn't expecting anyone. I'm surprised word got around so fast."

Sam growled and sniffed the man's shoes suspiciously.

"Sam," Hood said, and the wolf moved back reluctantly to stand alertly by Hood's side.

The man laughed. "Looks like you have a guardian."

"He's protective," Hood said.

"I heard about you and him," the man said. "News about a new reverend travels fast in Jericho. Mostly we only get grifters and drifters traveling through. Well, I don't know what brought you to Jericho, but you are certainly welcome. I'm Ezra Tannin and these are my boys Matthew, Mark, and Luke. Their mother and me adhere to the Book. It won't solve all your problems, but it's a great comfort to know it might. Taking your name from it means you carry a piece of it with you every day of your life. We thought you might need a hand and came on in to see what we could do."

"You are most welcome," Hood said warmly. He glanced at the church. "I don't know if I could have gotten it ready in time for Sunday services, but I intended to give it a try."

"Oh, you won't be alone," Tannin said. "There are others who are coming in to get supplies, and they'll stop and lend a hand

43

for a little while before they go back to their places. My wife — Martha — will be up in a little bit. She's down doing some shopping, and we'll swing by the store and pick up our supplies later."

He eyed the outside of the church critically. "I'd suggest we get some ladders and see if we can't slap a coat of whitewash on the outside." He turned to the oldest boy and said, "Matthew, you take the wagon on down to the blacksmith shop and see if he ain't got some ladders we can borrow. Tell him what it's for and you see anyone we know, tell them as well. We just might be able to make this place look a little presentable for tomorrow."

"Yes, Pa," the oldest said, and handed the bucket he'd taken from the back of the wagon to his brother. He climbed into the wagon and clucked to the horses, driving away toward the middle of town.

"Well, boys," Tannin said, rubbing his hands together with relish, "you can at least start on the outside and paint up as far as you can until the ladders get back."

Obediently, the two boys gathered wide-bristled brushes and moved toward the church. Within minutes, they were vigorously slapping paint on the boards, which soaked up the whitewash greedily, while

Sam barked at the brushes. Tannin shook his head.

"Looks like it'll take more than one coat, but we've got all day. Here come some others," he added, pointing down the road away from town.

Hood turned and saw a line of wagons rolling slowly toward the church.

"If'n I don't miss my guess, that wagon in front will be Jim Parks and his family. Parks has a place close to mine. He's a beekeeper, too. He has mostly girls so they won't be doing much fixing, but they'll sure clean up the inside for you. Mrs. Parks — Beth — is a stickler for spit and polish. You watch what she does with a dust rag and some lye soap. Make your eyes water for a while, but you'll be able to eat off the floor after she's done."

"Where are you from, Mr. Tannin?" Hood asked.

Tannin waved his arm to the south. "About twelve miles out. I have a little homestead, but it's good land with two tanks that hold enough water during the rainy season to carry us through with a little irrigation." He made a face. "Of course, there's been some years when we've had to haul water in for our crops, and water's running low now, but we make out. The same with the others. All it takes is a little work."

"I thought that Mary Riley had the only water around," Hood said.

Tannin turned a sunbaked face to him, blue eyes twinkling. "Now, where would you get that notion? No, there's enough water here for a small farmer if he's willing to work for it. It's the big ranchers that need more for their stock."

"They tend to leave you alone?"

A cloud passed over Tannin's face. "Well, now, I wouldn't say that it hasn't been hard. Especially at the beginning when the ranchers tried to keep the homesteaders out. But those of us who stuck to it made out all right, thanks to the courts — and the army from Fort Craig. But what little water we have ain't a drop in the bucket for what the big ranchers need. So, they leave us alone. For now." He shook his head "No one knows what the future holds, though. I 'spect that sooner or later they'll come after us again. Now that the Indians are moved away and all."

He clapped his hands together.

"Now, I'd say we'd better get to work, or those boys will think they can slack off because their elders are standing around shooting the breeze. I got an extra brush. You want to paint or work on the inside?"

"If you got a hammer and some nails in

46

the back of your wagon, I'll get started fixing up on the inside."

"Brought a toolbox," Tannin said. He reached in the back of the wagon and effortlessly swung a wooden box to the ground.

Hood squatted and studied the contents — a handsaw, brace and bits, hammers, nails, pliers — all that was needed to work with. Several spare planks lay in the bed, and when he looked up questioningly, Tannin grinned and pulled at an earlobe.

"We had a barn raising a couple of months ago and these were left over. I figured we might put them to good use here."

"The privy could stand rebuilding," Hood said.

"If I remember that privy right, a new privy would be more in order," Tannin said. He took a shovel from inside the wagon. "So, I reckon while the boys paint and you begin fixing up the inside, I'll just tend to getting that chore started. When Parks gets here, he'll spell me. We'll have a new one up in no time."

He marched purposefully out behind the church, Sam at his heels, ears pricked, tongue lolling out the side of his muzzle.

Hood placed his hands in the small of his back and bent backward, stretching the muscles. Then he bent forward and strained to pick up the heavy toolbox to carry it inside. His heart felt lighter with the friendliness Tannin had shown. He carried the toolbox inside and stood for a second, studying the interior. It would take more than one man to lift that heavy oaken cross back to its place.

"Might as well begin at the front and work back," he said to himself, and walked up to the lectern. He took the pliers and began pulling out the old nails, trying to keep them straight so he could reuse them. By the time he'd finished, other wagons had pulled in front of the church. A thin, raw-boned man with a lantern jaw, followed by a woman with a long, homely face, came down the aisle to greet him. The man wore a battered broad-brimmed hat and faded bib overalls.

"If I'm right, Tannin has already told you who I am so let's just make it official. Jim Parks." He turned and put his hand on the shoulder of the woman, pulling her forward. "This is my wife, Beth. We heard you had come into town yesterday and decided that we'd just make this an extry trip to see if we could lend a hand."

"Amos Hood. And you're mighty welcome," Hood said, taking Parks's hand. He gestured around the church. "I'm afraid this would have been a hard job without some help."

"That's what we're here for," Parks said. "And Sommers and Drabble and Roberts are right behind us. They're bringing their families as well. The women have a lunch that we'll set up later, but I'd say we should get the hard stuff done right now while it's still a bit cool."

"Mr. Tannin's out back digging a new privy," Hood said.

"Well, then, I'll just get a shovel and go right on out and give him a hand. Don't you worry none, Reverend. We'll have this place ready for services before sundown."

"I'll start the dusting," Beth said firmly in a no-nonsense voice. She wiped a finger down the back of a pew and studied it, making clucking notes of disapproval deep in her throat. "It's a shame that a place of God would fall into such disrepair. Reckon it's as much fault of ours as anybody's. But now's the time to put things right."

Hood watched in awe as she walked purposefully out to the wagon and began unloading cleaning supplies. Sam trotted up behind her, then stood looking indecisively back and forth from Beth to Jim as if trying to figure out what was going on. He gave a short bark, then loped off into the brush behind the church.

Hood watched him go, then turned to refitting the front of the lectern back into place. When he'd finished, he looked in wonder at other women working diligently, dust flying like tiny clouds as the women made their way through the church with dust rags and buckets filled with soapy water. They chattered to each other like busy jackdaws. He smiled and turned to repairing the communion rail with a happy heart. He felt as if Jericho had been waiting for him all along.

4.

By the time they had finished, the sun was lowering in the west, casting deep purple shadows over the town. Above the mesa, the sky appeared in gray and pink streaks over a deep red that seemed to bleed onto the mesa. Hood was tired, but happy and satisfied. The church was ready for the morning, and Tannin and Parks had promised to be at the church early for any last-minute touches that might be needed. Hood couldn't think what that might be; the outside of the church had been given four coats of whitewash from exuberant children who made a game of seeing who could cover the largest area; the ladies had driven every speck of dust from the church and the pews glistened with a fresh waxing; the piano had been somewhat tuned by Mrs. Haddorn, who had been the accompanist before the last preacher had "gone south"; and even the bell rope had been replaced when Luke

Tannin had climbed up the ladder and hung a new one.

Now, Hood thought as he walked back to his hotel with Sam, all that remained was for him to come up with a sermon. Maybe it would appear to him as he soaked in a bath.

"Evening, Parson."

He looked up and saw Barth standing outside his hotel, leaning up against a beam, quietly smoking an evening cigar. He wore an ivory coat, a white stock tied neatly tucked around his neck with a pearl pinned neatly in it, and a brocade waistcoat. He wore low-heel boots, odd for the country.

"Good evening, Mr. Barth," Hood said politely.

Barth smiled faintly as he considered Hood's dusty appearance. "It looks like you've had a full day. Church ready for the morrow?"

Hood nodded. "I think so. At least, I hope so."

"You one of those hell-and-damnation preachers?" Barth asked mockingly. "Coming to bring all us sinners within reach of the Pearly Gates?"

Hood paused. Sam dropped down on his haunches and looked keenly at Barth.

"The path to heaven isn't strewn with brimstone," Hood said gently. The words stirred a buried memory in his mind as he thought about his father's quiet ways in the pulpit, giving out hope rather than fear.

Barth laughed quietly. "Here in Jericho, you'll find more brimstone than primroses. Maybe you'd better find another pulpit somewhere if you're going to talk about Solomon's lilies. I have a hunch there's a lot of pulpits in other towns."

"You advising me to move on?" Hood asked, smiling gently.

Barth shook his head. "Nope. Just offering a bit of friendly advice. It hasn't been that long ago since a bunch of Apaches tried to tree the town." He looked off toward the mesa. "Didn't do them much good. We buried a goodly share of them back there afterward." '

"Sounds like Jericho's had some hard times," Hood replied. "Maybe time has come that it can find some peace."

"A lot of people have tried to bring the walls of Jericho down over the years," Barth said. "But they're still standing."

"Meaning?"

"Meaning that you won't change people's ways that fast. Best to take it easy at first and see what is here before you go stomping on what you don't know anything about."

"Good advice," Hood said. "I'll think about it."

"Do more than think about it," Barth said. A harsh note crept into his voice. "There's a lot of hatred here and a lot of prejudice buried within the people. They'll come to your church and listen to what you say, then go out and do what they want anyway." He pointed across the street at his saloon. "And after church, the men will come in there for a drink before heading home. Some may stay for three or four and tempers will come up and we'll have a fight or two to put down." He shrugged "That's the way it's been for years."

"What happened to the preacher before me?" Hood asked.

Barth shook his head. "No one knows. But the one before him was killed on his way back from one of the outlying ranches. Nobody ever found out who did it. His horse brought his buggy into town and there he was, slumped back in the seat, a bullet in his chest. I guess the meek won't inherit the earth after all. Leastways, not here in Jericho."

"You have any ideas?"

Barth laughed loudly. "Well, hell, yes, I

54

have ideas. Everyone has ideas. But no one is going to put a voice to his idea. They don't want to end up like that Reverend Black. The funny thing is that Black was a good man. He just couldn't keep his mind on his own business and kept poking his nose into other people's."

He waved the cigar at Hood. "You just keep to your preaching and let things be in Jericho, Parson, and you'll get along just fine. People will come to your services and go home or down to the river on the Bar S to eat their chicken dinners, and think about how their souls have received exoneration for another week. But that still won't change anything. Monday rises a new day and brings with it the same routine in lives."

He took a step down onto the dusty street, then turned back to Hood. "You know, a church is kind of like a circus where a person can go and break the humdrum of his life for a moment or two. But after that moment passes, his life slips back into ordinary time. It's called human nature, Hood. Human nature."

He sauntered across the street and disappeared through the bat-wing doors of his saloon. Hood stood for a long moment, considering Barth's words, then turned and entered the hotel, asking the clerk to have hot water brought up to the bathroom on his floor. He walked into his room and stared at his reflection in the wavy glass above the washbasin. His eyes were red-rimmed, and tired circles hung under them. He looked down at his hands, noticing the dirt under his nails and the calluses worn smooth on the palms from where he had wielded the hammer. His shoulders ached, and Barth's words kept running through his mind.

He sighed, and went and sat in the Belter chair. Sam dropped on the braided rug at the side of the chair. Hood bent forward and patted him, then reached for his saddle-bags lying on the small table in front of him. He began removing the contents, one by one, setting them aside. At the bottom of one, he found the black cartridge belt and holster and Schofield still wrapped in a soft, oiled cloth. Slowly, he unwrapped it and looked at the metal shining ominously in the lamplight. His hand curved around the butt and he swung the weapon up, automatically aiming at various points in the room. It seemed to fit his hand as an extension, comfortable, deadly. A coldness settled in his stomach, and the old familiar calmness buttressing a deadly awareness crept over him. He felt the Schofield drawing him to it, making him want to belt the gun around his waist. A darkness began to move through him, and he felt the great desire to move into the darkness. He smelled something dank and distasteful, but recognized it was the dark desire within him to go back to the world that he had once known. Hastily, he wrapped the Schofield again and stowed it in the bottom of the saddlebag. He removed his father's Bible and opened it, reading what fell in front of his eyes.

Blessed is the man that walketh not in the counsel of the ungodly, nor standeth in the way of sinners, nor sitteth in the seat of the scornful.

But his delight is in the law of the Lord; and in his law doth he meditate day and night.

And he shall be like a tree planted by the rivers of water, that bringeth forth his fruit in his season; his leaf also shall not wither; and whatsoever he doeth shall prosper.

The ungodly are not so: but are like the chaff which the wind driveth away.

Therefore the ungodly shall not stand in the judgment, nor sinners in the congregation of the righteous.

For the Lord knoweth the way of the

righteous: but the way of the ungodly shall perish.

A concise, poetic contrast of godliness and wickedness, Hood thought. *I wonder if that would be appropriate for the first sermon for Jericho. There seems to be a balance in the town between the two, but I wonder how delicate is that balance. Will the people understand me or will I simply be whistling in the wind?*

He tapped his fingers on the small table as he stared down into the growing dusk of the street. Faintly, he heard music playing from across the street in The Cattleman's, and he wondered which of those who were gaming and drinking would be sitting in his church in the morning, a slight pounding in their heads, their eyes glazed from the play of the night before, seeking forgiveness for their dalliance in the hall of the wicked.

He grinned sourly. *You're beginning to sound like your father,* he thought. *But is that all bad?*

He pulled pen and inkwell and paper to him and began writing. The night deepened as he wrote, and moths flickered around the flame of the lantern. He paused to watch as they snapped against the hot glass, recognizing in them a metaphor for man, who flirted with the fires of heaven and the flames of hell, not recognizing one from the other, but reacting to the light that he wanted to get close to.

As he wrote, time fell away from him and he felt himself back in the Tennessee hills, seeing the trees change to russet browns and deep gold in the Indian summer, the cold clear water rushing down through the millrace, and the smoky change in the season readying itself for winter. He laid down the pen and read again what he had written. A pang of loneliness swept through him. He leaned forward and picked up the pen, dipped it in the inkwell, and began writing again. The words seemed to come easily to him.

5.

Sunday came up crisp and cool and Hood rose, washed, and dressed carefully. Around his neck he placed a Wesley collar and the silver cross. He picked up his father's watch and grinned at Sam.

"Well, boy, this is it," he said wryly.

Sam rose and crossed to the door, waiting patiently. Hood opened the door and walked down the stairs and outside. He glanced to his right toward the mesa, and noted the deep purple shadows streaking down the side of the mesa. He looked toward the east. The sun was rising, striking the steeple of the church into shadow. He smelled dust in the air, and watched thunderclouds beginning to bunch and form like the fists of giants in the south. Flash lightning flickered along the fingers of the clouds. The golden leaves of the cottonwood trees above the wash south of town moved gently in the soft wind. Out of habit, he touched his side where the Schofield once hung daily, then admonished himself for the gesture.

Placing his hands behind his back, he walked slowly toward the church, lost in his thoughts. He didn't see the man step out from the shadows and stand in his way until Sam offered a low growl of warning. Hood looked up and noticed the cowboy dressed in a pearl-gray shirt and black pants with silver conchos sewn down the outside of each leg. Huge Mexican rowels were strapped onto his black boots. A well-oiled cartridge belt hung around his waist, the holster tied around the man's thigh. The walnut pistol handle was well polished from use, and the hammer strap had been slipped from his Colt, hanging down against the holster. He was lean, his cheeks high and well formed in a face that had a hardness to it that suggested a man used to getting his way among others.

"Yes?" Hood asked pleasantly. "May I do something for you?"

"You the new preacher man?" the man drawled lazily. His eyes danced with a lighted madness.

"I suppose I am," Hood said.

"I'm Rollie Rawlins," the man said. "Me and my brother own the Slash K."

"I'm happy for you," Hood said. "It's the

mark of a good man who keeps himself employed in these times."

A tiny frown twitched between Rawlins's eyes, then slipped away. "The problem is that certain, ah, 'employment' has a tendency of slipping away from a man when a preacher comes into town. Jericho don't need a preacher. My advice is to seek a church elsewhere before you come to bad doings."

Sam let out a low growl.

"Hush, Sam," Hood said softly. He smiled gently at Rawlins. "I just follow where the Good Lord leads me. Nothing more. Apparently, He thought Jericho needed a minister here for the good of His flock. So, I'm here."

Rawlins tapped the walnut handle of his pistol significantly. "That could be a short time," he said.

"Or a long one," Hood said coolly. "It all depends on how one counts the time." He looked around the street. "Where's your brother?"

"Minding the stock with the rest of the boys," Rawlins said. "I thought I'd come in early for some supplies."

Hood glanced over at the store. "I think you have a little wait ahead of you. I don't think the store is going to open for another hour or so. Why don't you join us for services? It's as good a way of passing the time as any other and better than some."

Rawlins reached inside his shirt pocket and removed the makings and began to build a cigarette. "You don't seem to understand what I'm telling you," he began.

"I think I do," Hood said quietly. "A preacher brings a sense of order to a town. Like a sheriff, in a way."

"We haven't had a sheriff longer than a preacher," Rawlins said with a short laugh. "Neither one lasts long in Jericho."

"Then, there must be a need for one or both," Hood answered.

"Depends upon what sort of man each is," Rawlins said, lighting his cigarette. He blew a cloud of dirty gray smoke toward Hood. "But that's a never-mind. Best thing to do is just to have such a man move on before trouble begins."

"You planning on trouble?" Hood asked. His muscles began to tighten along his back and a coldness settled in his stomach.

Rawlins smiled mockingly. "Me? Nope. I'm the one who nips the trouble in the bud before it gets a chance to grow. Much easier that way and keeps things simpler."

"Well, Mr. Rawlins, such thinking can sometimes prove unhealthy," Hood said.

"Maybe it would be better if you'd just accept the coming of the times. I suggest that you read the first chapter of Ecclesiastes. That might help explain some things to you."

Rawlins made a small dismissive gesture with his left hand, keeping his right near the handle of his pistol, the threat subtle but not meant to be taken lightly.

"I can see that you ain't the type to take a suggestion," Rawlins said.

Hood shrugged. "Nobody knows if he is a wise man or a fool. I take all suggestions and consider them. But then I remember also that a man of God is one who seeks out all things done under heaven that good men should do with their lives."

He looked at Rawlins's pistol. "Some things are the result of vanity. You might give some thought to that as well. Now, if you'll excuse me, I have my work to do. Again, you are welcome in the church. Just leave your pistol in the vestibule. Guns do not belong in the house of the Lord."

Rawlins studied him for a long moment, then gave a curt laugh and moved away. "You've been warned, Preacher. Don't stay in Jericho. We don't need you here."

"I think you do," Hood said, and continued down the street, Sam hanging close to his right leg and looking over his shoulder as he trotted beside his master.

Hood glanced down at him. "Well, Sam, I think we're going to have our work cut out for us here."

Sam rubbed his head briefly against Hood's leg as they made their way down the street to the church.

Buggies were already ground-hitched to flatirons while people in their Sunday finest milled around in small groups, talking quietly about crops and cattle, watching Hood's approach.

Tannin stepped out from one of the groups to greet Hood. They shook hands and Tannin raised his head to look down the street.

"I see you've already met Rollie Rawlins," he said in a low voice.

"Yes," Hood said. He looked back the way he had come. "He's a troubled spirit."

"He's also a killer," Tannin said dryly. "He's the gunman with the Slash K. They must really be worried about you if they sent him into town. He killed two men in a shoot-out over Durango way. Some say even Clay Allison walked away from him, but I don't know about that. I hear Allison shoots anyone who comes against him. Word is Allison's crazy, but Rawlins seems to be in possession of his senses. I don't think he's one to go up against Allison. Of course, I could be wrong. Some men like to build a reputation with a gun and do dumb things."

"People have a lot to say about a lot of things," Hood said. "And stories grow with each telling. It would do mankind a big service if people would remember the truth of what happened instead of building the truth into a legend. But" — he clapped Tannin on the shoulder — "that's the way of man. Someone always has a different perspective on what was and what he thinks was. We cannot control what others feel or think."

For a moment, Tannin looked puzzled, then he smiled. "Dang if you haven't put a finger on it. But I can tell you that Rollie Rawlins is bad news and it's always a good bet to walk softly around him."

"If trouble is avoided by the righteous, then that trouble will be magnified for the next man who encounters it," Hood said. "Sometimes, it's best to meet trouble head-on and turn it away."

Tannin took a half step back to look at Hood. "If you aren't the strangest preacher I've ever met."

Hood smiled. "No, I'm just a man like any other. Shall we begin? I see the others are getting a bit restless."

"Missus Haddorn's been warming up for the better part of a half hour," Tannin said, stepping aside. "Maybe we'd better get in there before she wears her fingers out. She ain't as young as she once was, but she can sure play when she wants to. Wish we had an organ, though," he added wistfully as they moved toward the church door. "An organ always seems to make things better."

"Jesus had no organ and His message was not lost upon those who listened to Him," Hood said philosophically. "But I agree: There's something soothing about an organ. Maybe in time, we'll be able to afford to have one brought in."

Tannin slapped Hood on the shoulder, driving him forward. "I do like a man who thinks about the future," he said with a laugh. But he still glanced over his shoulder back toward the center of the town, where Rawlins leaned against a post in front of the store, smoking and watching.

Hood greeted everybody, then stepped into the church and made his way up to the pulpit. The people watched curiously as Sam followed Hood and curled up beside the pulpit, staring out at the congregation. Hood noticed their attention and smiled.

"I notice that my friend has drawn your

attention. Do not be concerned. He has been my companion since I found him on the prairie beside his dead mother. He reminds me constantly of my duty to look into the hearts of men and beware of the wolf that might be lingering there."

A laugh spread across the congregation. Hood took the moment to nod at Mrs. Haddorn, who gave him a half smile, then turned back to the piano and began playing 'The Old Rugged Cross."

No hymnals were needed as the congregation's voices rose enthusiastically with the verses, and Hood's heart filled with gladness as he joined in with the familiar song that had been one of his father's favorites, his voice rising in a rich baritone. A warm feeling spread over him during the hymn, and he felt his father's spirit smiling happily at him.

After the hymn was finished, the congregation took their seats and looked up at Hood expectantly.

"Good morning," he said, and waited as several answered his greeting. "My name is Amos Hood, for those of you who were not here yesterday to lend a hand in readying the church for this day of worship. I'm from Tennessee and my grandfather and father were both ministers. I don't know how much of them rubbed off on me, but I expect quite a bit. The fruit doesn't fall far from the tree, and in my family, the ministry has deep roots."

A small sound of laughter tittered through the congregation.

"We have a lot of building to do," he said, "and I'm not talking about this house of the Lord, but that building which lies waiting for a carpenter in each and every one of you. I hope I can bring you that peace and contentment that you have been waiting for."

Smiles appeared on the faces of the congregation as Hood opened his father's Bible and began reading:

"Blessed is the man that walketh not in the counsel of the ungodly, nor standeth in the way of sinners . . ."

6.

After services, Hood stood outside, accepting the thanks of the congregation and listening to the plans of Mrs. Parks, who wanted to reorganize the women into a circle to help benefit the church and provide a Sunday school for the children. He felt warm and good with the reception he received after his first sermon, and when the last family had climbed into their buckboard and departed, he heaved a contented sigh and glanced down at Sam.

"What do you say, boy? Should we take Sheba out for a little exercise? It would do us all some good to see the lay of the country."

Sam barked excitedly, and Hood laughed and walked down to the stables with Sam hard on his heels. Sheba grunted at being left so long without Hood's attention when he entered the stables.

"I know, old girl," Hood said soothingly,

running his hand down her mane and shoulder. She shook her head and shuffled her feet. "I've been a bit neglectful, but we're going out for a Sunday ride together now."

She tossed her head again, and turned to nuzzle his arm. He laughed and collected his saddle, blanket, and bridle, and led her out of the stables into the bright sunlight. He glanced at the black clouds in the south, moving ponderously away from Jericho, and shook his head.

"I don't think it will be a long one, girl, but we'll get a bit of exercise just the same before the heat becomes intolerable," he said.

He mounted in one smooth motion and felt Sheba's muscles bunch beneath his legs. She crow-hopped a little to show her annoyance at being left alone, then settled down as he nudged her sides with his heels and turned her head toward the road leading west out of town.

Soon, they were loping through the small hills leading up to the mesa. Hood enjoyed the feel of the mare beneath his legs, and settled back in the saddle while Sam ranged in a large circle around them. He rode up into the mesa country, into wilder and wilder regions. Great canyon walls towered

71

above them and he drank deeply of their coolness. He came out upon a high plateau where the wind was strong and carried with it the hint of heavy rain that came across the lonely stretches of open land, and he smelled the mesquite and sage and sego lilies that hadn't given up yet for the fall.

He reined in and sat for a long time, staring out over the wild land. In the distance, he could see the deep blue broken lines of canyons running off into all directions, and wondered if any were inhabited by men who kept by themselves, disdaining the company of others.

On impulse, he rode toward one, and soon found himself in a long canyon where deep grass grew and the sides of the canyon were covered with tall ponderosa pines. The air smelled clean and fresh here and the wilderness made his spirit soar.

He rode slowly, watching the game move warily away from his approach. Deer stood frozen in the deep shadows of the pines, and occasionally sage hens flew away from him.

He followed the canyon down to its end, and discovered a faint trail leading up out of the canyon. He turned Sheba onto the trail, and leaned forward as she gingerly began to climb.

At that moment, something whipped past him, followed a moment later by the echo of a gunshot.

Sheba twisted like a cat on the trail and ran back down. He turned her into the trees as another bullet whapped the tree beside them. He kicked his feet free from the stirrups and dropped down into the tall grass on her off side. He heard another shot, and crawled rapidly to a deadfall and slipped behind it. Sheba ducked into a thick stand of pines on the other side of the small clearing and stood still, nervously pawing the ground. He felt rather than saw Sam slip in beside him and hug the ground, whining.

Hood placed his hand on Sam's head, soothing him, as he searched carefully through the dead limbs. But he saw nothing. Still, he waited, making himself as comfortable as possible behind the deadfall, searching the places where a man with a rifle might be waiting. Time ticked by, and beads of sweat began to trickle down his face. Still, he remained unmoving. Then, Sam relaxed and settled down. Hood glanced over toward Sheba, and saw the mare beginning to graze on the thick grass around her.

Cautiously, he started to rise, then remembered the heavy silver cross around his neck.

Light would be reflected from it. Carefully, he slipped it off and placed it in a pocket of his coat. He glanced behind him and noted the deep shadows. If he moved slowly, his black clothes might blend in with the shadows.

He worked his way back on hands and knees until he was well within the pines, then rose cautiously and began slipping through the pines on a small detour until he came up behind Sheba.

"Easy, girl," he murmured.

Sheba's head came up, then bent to graze again.

The shooter's probably gone, Hood thought, but he didn't take any chances. He slowly gathered Sheba's reins and led her deep into the pines. At first, she resisted, reluctant to leave the fresh grass, but Sam growled at her heels and she moved forward, following Hood's lead.

When he was well within the pines, he mounted and rode south, putting distance between himself and the shooter before swinging back toward Jericho. His hands were slick on the reins and he felt a hollowness in the pit of his stomach. He kept a sharp watch for any movement, but saw nothing as he came again to the trail leading back into the canyon. He let Sheba have her head, and relaxed in the saddle as she made her way gingerly down the trail.

At the bottom, he lifted her into a canter and rode back to Jericho, his mind working on who had shot at him, but most importantly, why.

7.

The muscles in his back felt rigid as he came into Jericho, glancing right and left, remembering men and faces as he had once as Tom Cade, sheriff of Walker in Kansas. *Old habits die hard,* he thought sourly. Then, he noticed a sorrel gelding standing head-down, well lathered from being ridden hard, in front of The Cattleman's Saloon. He reined in Sheba and sat for a moment, considering the horse, then rode over and hitched Sheba next to the horse. He ran his hand down the sides of the sorrel, flicking the warm lather off onto the ground. Then, he noticed pine needles caught in the horse's mane. Anger flushed through him, and he forced himself to draw several deep breaths.

He lifted the saddle skirt, smiled grimly, then mounted the steps to The Cattleman's and pushed his way gently through the bat-wing doors, Sam close on his heels. He moved automatically to his left to place his back against the wall, and looked casually over the crowd in the saloon. In the back, Halsey Barth, a glass of whiskey at his elbow, held sway over the poker game that never seemed to quit. Hood recognized some of the faces in the game as those who had been in the game the first time he had encountered Barth.

He glanced along the bar and noticed Rollie Rawlins leaning on his elbows on the mahogany bar, one foot propped on the brass foot rail. Sweat showed in the armpits of his pearl-gray shirt and slid down the right side of his face in two trickles. A layer of dust clung to his clothes. His hat was pushed back off his forehead, and showed fresh salt stains along the brim and up the side.

Hood felt a tiny grin tug at his lips as his eyes met Rollie's mocking stare in the mirror behind the bar. He cleared his throat and raised his voice.

"Anybody in here belong to a sorrel out front? He's been ridden hard and needs some care."

He knew that such a statement would bring concern to all in the room. A man's horse was special in the West. A man cared for his horse before he cared for himself, and to leave a lathered horse standing at a hitching post in town while his owner was refreshing himself with a beer or whiskey pull was unforgivable.

A burly man at the faro table on his left looked up, angry glints showing in his eyes.

"You claim there's a hoss out there needing care?"

Hood nodded solemnly. "Yes, I do. That horse's been ridden hard and still flecked with lather. He's in a pretty bad way."

The burly man shoved away from the faro table and walked purposefully to the door, his boot heels thudding hard on the planked floor.

"I'll be damned! He's right!"

He turned to the room and glared around it. "Now, what low-life sumbitch would do that to a horse? That horse ain't cooled down soon, I'd say that he won't be worth a plugged nickel by morning. The rider in here?"

"He's in here," Hood said. He nodded toward Rawlins. "Aren't you, Mr. Rawlins?"

Rollie smiled lazily and turned around, hooking one boot heel over the foot rail. He leaned back on his elbows.

"You saying that hoss out there is mine?" he asked arrogantly.

"That sorrel's sweating; so are you. Both

of you look like you've been ridden hard. But you've put yourself up while leaving that animal out there to suffer," Hood said.

Tiny lights danced and flickered in Rollie's eyes.

"Why, I don't know what you're talking about," Rollie said lightly. "I've been in here the better part of an hour." He glanced over at Barth. "Right, Halsey?"

Barth shrugged. "Yeah, I'd say the better part of an hour," he answered.

"Any other Slash K riders in here?" Hood asked casually.

Rollie made a pretense of glancing around, then shook his head. "Don't see any."

"Strange. That's a Slash K horse out there," Hood answered. "And your initials are burned under the saddle skirts. I'd say that sort of narrows it down some, wouldn't you?"

A low murmur ran around the room as Rollie's eyes narrowed to pinpoints of anger. Hood smiled gently.

"And I noticed that the horse has pine needles in its mane," he added.

"So? What the hell does that have to do with anything?" Rollie asked edgily.

"Nothing," Hood said. "Except someone tried to dry-gulch me up in one of the canyons off the mesa about three, maybe four hours ago. Mind if I have a look at your rifle?"

"Hell, yes!" Rollie said angrily. "You accusing me of trying to shoot you?"

"Yes, I am," Hood said calmly. He turned to the burly man. "Would you mind bringing in the Winchester that's in the scabbard on the horse?"

"Don't mind if I do," the burly man said. He paused to run a thumb and forefinger down the sides of his handlebar mustache. He looked over at Rawlins. "It takes a pretty low-down sumbitch to ride a horse like that and leave him tied up, let alone take a shot at someone unarmed."

Rollie stepped suddenly away from the bar, hunched slightly from the waist, his hand poised over the handle of his revolver.

"Mister, you make one move toward my horse and I'll put a bullet in you," he said angrily.

Hood smiled gently and stepped between the two. "Go get the Winchester," he said. "If Mr. Rawlins wants to shoot an unarmed man, I expect that there'll be some consequences." He glanced at Barth. "Even in Jericho."

Barth smiled faintly and lifted his glass of whiskey in salute to Hood.

The burly man slipped outside, and was

back in a moment with Rawlins's Winchester. He handed it to Hood.

"It's been fired recently," the man said soberly.

Hood worked the lever to open the breech, nodded, and closed the action. He eased the hammer down with his thumb.

Rawlins shrugged "So what? I tried to shoot a deer on the way in and missed. Guess it wasn't my lucky day."

"Uh-huh," Hood said, handing the Winchester back to the burly man. "But that doesn't explain what you were doing up in the mesa country if your ranch is to the south."

Rawlins laughed. "Hunting. What else?"

"Maybe," Hood said, his eyes boring into Rawlins. "But I think you're a liar."

Silence fell across the saloon like a shroud. A slow smile began to spread over Rawlins's face.

"Tall talk for a man who doesn't go heeled," he said.

Hood smiled and spread his hands in front of him. "I simply tell things the way I see them."

A deep flush turned Rawlins's face the color of spoiled liver as an excited murmur ran around the saloon. Barth leaned back in his chair, holding his glass of whiskey.

He looked with interest at both Hood and Rawlins. A wide space opened between the two men as others looked on expectantly.

"Heel yourself then!" Rawlins said thickly. His hand twitched above the butt of his pistol.

Hood opened his coat, showing that he was unarmed. "Shoot now, and you'll be committing murder in front of witnesses this time, Rollie."

Someone laughed, and tiny fires began to burn deep within Rawlins's eyes. For a moment, Hood felt that he was gazing into the fires of hell; then a deep calm came over him and he smiled at Rawlins.

"Goddamn you!" Rawlins said viciously. He tugged at the buckle of his gun belt, then flung it on top of the bar. "All right, then. Make good your words."

He slapped his hat on top of the bar next to his gun belt and hunched over, bringing up his fists. He started stalking around Hood, his spurs jingling on his scuffed boots.

A bemused look came over Hood's face as he stood in front of Rawlins, his hands hanging loosely at his sides, turning slightly as the cowboy shuffled around and around in a circle.

"Leave it alone, Rawlins," Hood said quietly.

Rawlins straightened, contempt showing in his face. He dropped his hands and took a step closer to Hood.

"You won't fight?" he said. He glanced around at the solemn faces of the others in the saloon, watching.

"What kind of a man won't back up his words?" he demanded, swinging around to face Hood again.

"He's a preacher," a man said quietly from his place at the bar.

"A preacher, eh? Well, then." Rawlins took a step forward and slapped Hood across his face.

A low murmur of disgust rolled around the room, but Rawlins ignored it.

"Then you should turn the other cheek," Rawlins said, and backhanded Hood, who rocked back on his heels from the blow.

Sam growled and crouched, hair bristling. Rawlins looked at him uneasily, but Hood quieted Sam with a word.

"Leave it alone, Rawlins," Hood said again, this time an edge to his words. But Rawlins was strung as tight as barbed wire and the words, this time a warning, didn't register with him.

"Turn the other cheek," he taunted, and

swung again.

This time, however, Hood took a step back and caught Rawlins's fist in his hand. He twisted and turned, throwing Rawlins with a rolling hip-lock. Rawlins landed hard on the floor and slid through a puddle of beer to slam up against the side of the bar.

A sigh came from the room as Rawlins lay propped against the bar, stunned for a second at what had happened to him. Then, he pushed himself erect, let out a bellow of rage, and came at Hood, fists swinging wildly.

Hood had grown up in rough-and-tumble fights in the Tennessee hills, and slipped away from Rawlins. He slapped Rawlins hard on his shoulder as he went by, staggering him. His arms windmilled as he tried to regain his balance before he crashed on top of a poker table, overturning it.

"I'll be damned," someone said softly as Rawlins pushed himself up again.

"I told you: 'Leave it alone,' " Hood said.

"Like hell," Rawlins said thickly.

He brought his hands up and this time approached Hood warily. Rawlins feinted with his left and crossed with his right, but Hood slipped away from the blow and dug his left fist deep into Rawlins's stomach.

The air left Rawlins's lungs with a loud

whoosh! and he started to fold at the waist. Hood brought up the heel of his hand under Rawlins's chin, raking upward. It was a brutal blow that snapped Rawlins's head back and popped his nose. A bright splotch of red appeared in the center of his face.

"I don't want this," Hood said warningly.

Rawlins swung blindly, and Hood slipped the punch and landed a quick right-left combination against Rawlins's jaw. The cowboy's eyes glazed; he wobbled for a moment, then toppled forward, landing facedown over a cuspidor.

"God's judgment shall be final and unrelenting," Hood said solemnly.

A hushed silence fell over the saloon. Hood glanced around at the men standing by the bar and sitting at the poker tables. His eyes lit upon Halsey Barth sitting quietly in his usual place. A small smile came over Barth's face.

"You all would do well to attend church services," Hood announced. He nodded at Barth, who inclined his head slightly in mocking salute.

"I said it once," Barth said. He took a small sip of his whiskey, rolled it around in his cheek, then swallowed. "You're a strange man for a minister,"

"God works in mysterious ways," Hood

answered.

"That He does," Barth said. "It's a strange habit He has."

"You also said that Rawlins had been in here for an hour. I think that's strange as well."

Barth's eyes narrowed, but he held on to his smile as Hood turned on his heel and walked quietly from the saloon, pushing the bat-winged doors open to slip out. He walked to Sheba and untied her, leading her down to the stables, Sam trotting by his side.

8.

When Hood stepped out of the hotel in the early morning, the sun was flushing the sky with pale streaks of pink light. While he stood, already feeling the promise of heat folding around him, the eastern sky began to turn a deeper red color like blood seeping up into the hard blue. Dampness began to creep down his side beneath his shirt and Sam began to pant at his side, tongue lolling. Hood thought about breakfast, then dismissed the thought as the heat made his stomach feel tight. He sighed and walked diagonally across the street to the store. The owner was already out with a broom, sweeping dust from the boardwalk in front of the store. He'd moved an old oak barrel outside snug against the store's front. Shovels and hoes blossomed from the barrel.

"Morning," he said as Hood walked up. "Looks like another hot one."

His face had a whiskey bloat to it. His eyes

were red-rimmed.

"Good morning," Hood answered. "It doesn't look like rain will be coming. I'm Amos Hood."

"John Peterson," he said, offering his hand. The palm felt dry like old leather when Hood took it. "I was at church yesterday. A fine sermon."

"Thank you," Hood said, smiling. "I hope you continue to like them."

Peterson grimaced. "I hope you stay around for a while. Preachers have a tendency of moving on pretty quick around here. Especially when the cowboys get to hoorawing them. Mainly, it's the Slash K, but the Box M riders have taken part in the past as well. I heard about your run-in with Rollie yesterday. I think that's already made the rounds."

"I understand one of my predecessors was murdered," Hood said. "Black?"

Peterson's lips tightened. "Ayuh, that was his name. Sheldon Black. A fine man. Worked hard at trying to bring in more members to the congregation. He kept going out to the ranches despite being warned to stay away from them. I guess he was doing his job, but sometimes a man would be better off listening to reason instead of following a set course of thinking." He

88

shrugged, "I don't know. They never found his killer."

"Any ideas about who could have done it?"

"Not a one," Peterson answered. "Well, maybe that's not quite right. If I was to take a guess, I'd say it was one of the Rawlinses. Probably Rollie. But I'm sure not going to accuse him. No, sir. He takes such things personal and I don't want to find myself lying down dead behind the counter or in the street. He's a mean one. Hell on wheels with that pistol of his. People say he's killed a dozen or so men, but he doesn't count Mexicans or Indians. I'd stay away from him if I was you. No good will come out of trying to save him. I figure his soul's already owned by the devil."

"What about this Mary Riley I've been hearing about?" Hood asked.

"Now, there's a sorry story," Peterson said. "Most folks hereabout think she's trash who bilked Old Man Stockton out of his ranch. But she's never done any harm to anyone that I know. Always pleasant when she comes into the store — when she can," he added grimly. "She has to stay pretty close to home, but I expect you've heard about that by now."

"Yes," Hood said. "I thought I might ride

out today for a visit and welcome her to come on in and attend church on Sundays."

"That might make her feel good," Peterson said. "But don't get your hopes up. She knows how most of the citizens around here feel about her. A person can only take so much snubbing and back-talking and she's had more than her share."

"Maybe we can change that," Hood said.

Peterson shook his head. "People have narrow minds with their own sense of sanctity. Sometimes, it's all I can do to wait on some of them. Set my teeth on edge with their pious talking. Like Missus Haddorn. Tongue like acid. The wives are the worst, although I've seen their husbands on a toot now and then down at The Cattleman's and never hear a word about that. There's even been talk about what you did to Rollie. Some don't think that was what a reverend should do. There's a lot of hypocrisy here. You'll run into it as time passes. Hope you can change it, but I won't be holding my breath."

"Sometimes, people just need to be shown the error of their ways," Hood observed.

Peterson looked closely at him, noting his easy manner, his steady eyes that didn't flinch from his own, the shoulders broad and heavy with muscle, his deep chest.

"Maybe you are the one to show them."

"Where can I find Mary Riley's place?" Hood asked.

"Ride west toward the mesa. Take the third trail to the north that winds along the side of the mesa. You'll come to a canyon with a year-round stream flowing out of it. Go on up the canyon and you won't miss it. The Bar S is the whole canyon and the land alongside the mesa."

Hood thanked him, and went into the store and bought two blue work shirts and a pair of heavy pants to wear when he worked on the church. He had Peterson hold them and walked out of the store, heading down the street toward the blacksmith and stable. He moved easily as heat hammered down upon the town.

As he was passing The Cattleman's, the doors swung open and Halsey Barth stepped out, carrying a glass of whiskey with an egg broken into it. He was neatly dressed in a gray suit with a blue shirt. Onyx cuff links gleamed.

"Morning, Parson," he said laconically.

"A little early for that, don't you think?" Hood replied, gesturing at the glass.

Barth took a swallow and smiled. "Readies me for the day. Most men gulp their whiskey. They don't take time to enjoy the finer things in life," he drawled, Texas accent more noticeable than usual.

"A man could get the same feeling with a morning ride," Hood answered.

Barth shook his head. "I leave that for the cowboys. There's little profit in riding."

"You can't serve Mammon all the time," Hood said.

"You going out?" Barth asked, ignoring Hood's words.

"I thought I'd visit some folks who weren't in church yesterday."

"The more folks in church, the larger the collection plate, that it? Sounds as if there's not much difference between us after all. I just take my wages across the table."

"A man has to make his own choices. But not all choices are right for the man."

Barth took another drink. "Depends on the man. I'm content."

"Maybe. Right now, I'd better start working for my wages."

"Stop in when you get back," Barth said, finishing the whiskey. "You might find some more souls to save in this den of iniquity."

"I might do that," Hood said.

He continued on down to the blacksmith shop, and paused to exchange pleasantries with Bert, then saddled Sheba and rode out of town, letting the gray mare stretch her muscles in a lope. Sam trotted beside them as they followed the trail toward the mesa.

An hour later, Hood came upon the trail Peterson had described and turned up it. Within minutes, he was riding along the edge of a green pasture heavy with uncut hay. Cottonwoods skirted the pasture along with some sycamore and pin oaks. Twice he saw deer moving along the edge of the stream, and occasionally some fat cattle grazing lazily through the deep grass. The mesa wall towered to his left for about three miles; then a deep canyon came up, cut in the wall of the mesa. A much-used trail ran up the middle, but a sifting of dust lay upon the trail, showing that it had been some time since anyone had come down it.

"This must be it," he said to Sheba, and turned her up the trail.

The great walls of the canyon towered over him as he rode. He breathed deeply of the coolness within the canyon, and welcomed the soft breeze that blew into his face. The floor of the canyon was green and sego lilies grew in patches. Birds sang in the trees, and the air was fresh with the scent of piñon and pine and cedar.

Sheba slowed to a walk, and Sam disappeared for a few minutes before reappearing with a rabbit in his jaws. Hood grinned.

"A regular Eden, isn't it, boy?" he said.

Sam ran ahead, and slipped into the shade of a piñon and began working with relish on the rabbit.

The canyon widened into a small pasture with a freshwater pond in the middle. Four longhorn steers stood in the middle of the pasture, staring at him. At the end of the pasture, a rambling house with a wide porch had been built up against the wall. Corrals lay to its left next to a barn. Three horses, two sorrels and a bay, were in the corral next to the barn. A well stood between the house and the barn and a large cottonwood provided shade for the house. Hood nodded approvingly. The house was well protected, as anyone trying to come up to the rear of the house would have to come down the steep canyon wall behind it, and the approach from the front was wide and free of cover.

He reined in and sat on his horse, waiting patiently. Given what he had heard about the Bar S, he knew better than to ride up to the house without an invitation. There was no sense in taking a chance on being shot by the wary owner. Sam came up and sat beside them. His muzzle was wet from drinking at the pond. A woman's voice came down to him from the house.

"All right! I see you! Now, what do you want?"

"I came calling," Hood said, raising his voice. "I'm the new minister in town. My name's Amos Hood."

The door opened and a woman came out, holding a Winchester repeating rifle in front of her. She stayed close to the open door, deep within the shadow of the porch. But Hood could see she wore a man's clothes, boots, work pants, and shirt.

"I haven't heard of any new minister," she said suspiciously.

"I've only been in Jericho three days now," Hood replied. "But we had services yesterday. A lot of folks came in. The Tannins and the Parks and quite a number of others. I'm unarmed," he added.

"If you're a minister, I would think you would be," she said drily. "All right, come on up. Slow now."

Obediently, Hood nudged Sheba with his heels and rode up to the house, keeping his hands in plain sight. He halted in front of the steps leading up to the porch and sat, studying the woman. Her black hair had been pulled back and wrapped in a tight bun. Her eyes were huge and violet, her figure shapely with small breasts pushing against the front of her shirt. Her face, with prominent cheekbones, had been tanned by the sun. Her mouth was set into a hard line.

"You must be Mary Riley," he said politely.

"Who else?" she challenged.

"You look like you could use some help around here," he said, ignoring her words. He nodded at the corrals and barn. "They could use a little carpentering, and you've got a lot of hay that needs to be put up down in your pasture."

"And I've got cattle that are fat and ready for the market. But I can't move them either," she said. "Well, you're here and it looks like you're not going to be any trouble. Climb down. I've got fresh coffee on the stove."

"That would be nice," Hood said, swinging down from his saddle. He walked Sheba under the shade of the cottonwood and tethered him to a porch post. He turned to Sam.

"Stay," he said, and Sam moved up onto the porch and sprawled out, resting his head on his paws.

Hood walked up onto the porch and removed his hat. She pursed her lips, nodding, then said, "Come on in."

He followed her into the house, standing just inside the door, blinking in the shadow of the room. A small kitchen stood in an alcove off to his left, opening up into the large central room in front of him. Bookshelves filled with books ran along the back of the room to the stone fireplace in the corner. On the other side of the fireplace stood a gun cabinet filled with rifles and shotguns. A hooked scatter rug lay on the floor in front of a leather chair. A small table with a kerosene lamp on it was next to the chair. The windows were curtainless. A straight-backed rocker rested a short distance from the chair. It was a comfortable room, built for a bachelor, and spotless.

"Nice place," he said pleasantly.

"I like it," she said defensively, setting mugs out on the plain wood table and filling them with coffee.

Hood took the mug from her and sipped cautiously. "You make a good cup," he said.

"Lots of practice. I don't get many visitors. But I'm getting to like the solitude. Have a seat."

She gestured at the leather chair, taking the rocker opposite. "I don't mean that I don't appreciate you coming to call; I guess I just don't know how to handle friendly visitors anymore."

He caught the emphasis and smiled gently at her. "Some people find it difficult to get to know someone else. It doesn't necessarily mean that they don't want to get to know someone. They just find it hard to do."

"Maybe," she said, then laughed derisively. "But most of the folks in Jericho already know me for what I was. I suppose you've heard that story once or twice."

"People also like to gossip," he said vaguely.

"Yes, I'll just bet they do. I'm not going to say that there wasn't something to what they told you. There was. But sometimes, people just have no choice but to be something that they don't want to be."

"True," Hood said, remembering Walker and the past he had left behind. "But like you say, people can change. Or *try* to change. Sometimes, a person just has to leave the old and move on to a new place and begin again."

"You suggesting I sell and move on?" she flared, her eyes snapping with anger.

"I was thinking of myself," he said. "I wasn't born a minister. Fact is, I'm sort of new at this. There are things in my past I'd just as soon forget as well."

"I'll bet you weren't a saloon girl, though," she said. Her eyes began to shine with tears.

"No," he said gently. "I wasn't a saloon girl. But there are some things that are

98

worse. And some things that can't be solved by moving on because they are always with you. You just have to learn to live with them and refuse to bend to the past despite what others think. The only person you have to live with is yourself, and although that might be something that makes you uncomfortable and hateful at times, you have to learn to live with it. Feeling sorry for yourself doesn't solve anything. Once you begin to feel sorry for yourself, then you live in the past all the time and you don't become anything other than what you once were. I don't know if that makes any sense or not, but that's one way of looking at it. Tomorrow's always a new day and we don't know what it will bring."

She heeled the wetness from her eyes and smiled at him. "You are an optimist."

"Well, today maybe. Sometimes, though, it's hard to practice what I preach," he said ruefully.

She laughed, this time deeply, and leaned back in her chair, her face glowing with happiness for the first time. "Right now, I've got a problem that's more important than what others think of me. I've got cattle ready for market and no way of moving them." She made a face. "Fact is, I need new stock. My calves are in the herds of others and if I try to sell the ready stock, I'll have to leave the home place. The minute I do, McQuade or the Rawlins boys will move in and I won't be able to get them off. I suppose you've heard about them during your time in town?"

He nodded, leaning back in the chair and rubbing his hand over his chin. "Yes, I've heard about them. But there might be another way. What about trading off with your stock? Taking in yearlings for what's ready for market? You'll lose some cash, but you might be able to get two yearlings for every steer ready for market. That way you won't have to leave here and you'll have stock that will be ready for growth. You could build up and maybe things would be better by the time they're ready to sell. You've got good grass, good natural irrigation, and that would be one way of increasing your herd right now." He nodded toward the open door. "Of course, I don't know about those longhorns out there. They look pretty old to me."

"They're the last of the cattle that John brought in when he first settled here. They're pets." She shook her head. "Well, your proposition is interesting, but I increase the herd, I've got to have someone to help out, and getting someone to work here is another story," she said. The blackness seemed to be gathering around her again. Her lips tightened and hard lines began to reappear in her face.

Hood studied her for a moment, then shook his head. "That might not be as hard as you think. And until you can find someone, I'll be willing to give you a hand. It wouldn't be steady. After all, I do have some obligations that I have to fulfill, but Jericho doesn't have a large enough congregation yet to demand my full time."

"You ever work cattle?" she asked, hope beginning to shine in her eyes.

"I'm from Tennessee and I've spent some time in Kansas," he said, vaguely skirting the issue. "I think I could help out. It's not that far from town."

She studied him for a moment, then said, "You could stay in the barn. There's a room next to the tack room where a hired hand used to stay when Mr. Stockton ran this place before he died. But I should warn you. The hand who was around then was driven off by the Rawlins boys. They caught him in town when he went in for supplies and beat him hard enough that he came back only to get his belongings. You'd be putting yourself in a pretty bad situation here. *And,*" she emphasized, "there'll be talk among the proper folk in town."

He smiled. "Well, people are going to talk anyway. I'm bound to make some folks upset one way or the other. This way is just as good as any other."

"You are a strange man, Amos Hood," she said.

"People keep telling me that," he said.

9.

The afternoon sun was just above the canyon rim, and sunlight laddered through the branches of the trees as Hood made his way back down the canyon from his visit. Songbirds called to each other among the pines as they chased gray squirrels from their nests, and rabbits scampered away from him, their tail tufts flickering whitely like cotton puffs. Deer moved cautiously back into the shadows of the pines and stood still, watching Hood's passing.

He felt relaxed in the saddle, enjoying the peace of the canyon, the richness of the grass, padded with brown pine needles beneath the trees, and the stream bubbling merrily across gravel. In a way, the canyon reminded him of the Tennessee hills, and he let his thoughts roam, remembering the pleasures of his youth and remarking on how he had not realized how happy he had been at the time. *Youth,* he thought, *is a rest-*

less time in a man's life, and he wants more than he has, not realizing that what he has is good and all he'll want again as he grows older. But by then, it's too late and the only thing left for a man to do is try and rebuild what he had in the hopes that he will be able to give that to his sons and daughters. Then, he has to watch as the wheel of time turns once again, and his sons and daughters come to feel closed in by the life the man has created for them, and they feel the need to break out and set their own lives in motion according to their own wishes.

It isn't youth that is wasted on the young, he observed. *It's wisdom.*

He glanced at the trail as he neared the end of the canyon, then reined Sheba to a halt. He frowned as he studied the ground. New tracks made by a shoed horse lay over his, coming partway up the canyon before they turned back. The tracks were deep-set, made by a horse with a heavy rider.

He frowned and turned to look uneasily back up the canyon. Then, he carefully studied the land around him. It had been a long time since anyone other than himself had gone up the canyon, and the thought made him shift nervously in the saddle. He remembered Mary telling him that he had been the first in a long time to come calling, and matters concerning her had been made pretty clear by the people in town. So, who could have been riding up this way? A drifter looking for a handout? If so, why had he not come farther up the canyon? Why turn back at this point?

Impulsively, Hood followed the track the rest of the way down the canyon, and saw where the rider had followed his trail up from the turnoff and then ridden back and gone on north. Hood sat for a moment, thinking, then started following the man's trail along the edge of the thick grass.

He rode for about an hour, crossing no fence line, then saw where the trail led up into a fissure in the mesa wall. Cautiously, he rode into the fissure, feeling the walls close in on him as he moved along the other's trail. Granite and mica had intruded into the walls, the mica sparkling like diamonds even in the shadows. Heat radiated off the mesa walls and pressed heavily against his chest. Within minutes, his shirt was a sodden mass that clung wetly to his back and chest. Sheba grumbled and shook her head as she picked her way over the narrow stony trail. Then, the walls opened into a small canyon like an amphitheater, but instead of grass and water, only greasewood and mesquite grew in the clearing studded by black boulders shaped like huge walnuts. The trail led across the amphitheater, and Hood could tell that it had been traveled more than once, hooves of horses beating the ground almost hard. On the south wall of the cliff, an old Indian pueblo, now deserted, had been built under an overhang a hundred feet above the floor.

Hood frowned. What would bring a man into such a place? It was obvious no game ran in the canyon to hunt and no forage grew for cattle other than beans off the mesquite when they were in season, but that was sorry fare for cattle, given the land outside the mesa.

For the first time, he regretted that he had left his Spencer behind at the hotel, and remembered the shots that had been fired at him during his last ride out of town. He felt naked and vulnerable. Even Sheba shuffled her hooves nervously, and Sam stood, ears alert, staring across the space as if he sensed the evil that seemed to pervade the rocks and canyon walls.

Light glinted from something metallic, and Hood warily backed Sheba around behind a large igneous boulder that had broken free from the cliff wall. He dismounted and crept forward, flattening himself against the rock as he peered around it. The light was gone, then suddenly it showed again.

He squatted on his heels, studying the trail the man had followed. The right hind horseshoe had a twist to it that he would be able to recognize again. The prints were deep, as if the horse had been carrying a heavy load. An old arrowhead lay beside the print. He picked it up, frowning. It was long and fluted like none he had ever seen before. He slipped it into his pocket and eased back around the rock and mounted Sheba, turning her tightly as he made his way back the way he had come.

He would have to wait to find out what the man was doing. The ground offered no cover for a rider crossing the floor of the amphitheater. He didn't know what had caused the gleaming, but it could have been a rifle barrel or glasses. Far better, he thought, to bide one's time. But it was a curious thing to ponder.

When they came out of the mesa opening, the air felt cooler, although a hot breeze had come up from the south. Sheba snorted and lifted her head against the reins, wanting to move faster away from the fissure. Sam trotted eagerly ahead of them. Something had spooked them as well, he thought. Whatever it was, there was something about that break that weighed ominously upon any who entered.

Or *most* who entered, he amended.

He glanced up at the sun beginning to slant over the mesa. Too late to be calling on anyone else, he reasoned. Best to ride back to town and gather some supplies to take out to the Bar S tomorrow. By then, evening shadows would be beginning to fall.

He eased the reins on Sheba and sat, content to let her pick her own pace back to town.

A heavy blanket of stifling heat wrapped Jericho as Hood rode in. No one moved on the street. Two sorrels and a buckskin were tied to the hitching rail in front of The Cattleman's Saloon, their heads hanging in the heat. Two dogs stood in the middle of the street, tongues lolling out the sides of their mouths. They crimped awkwardly sideways as he rode past. A drummer sat dozing in a chair under the wooden awning in front of the hotel, a forgotten cigar dangling loosely between two fingers. But Mrs. Haddorn was working in her flower garden in front of her house on the edge of town, carefully trimming her rosebushes with a large pair of black-handled shears. Her calico dress was clean and neat, and she wore a bonnet against the harsh sunlight. On impulse, he walked Sheba over to the white picket fence in front of her house. She looked up at his approach. White hair peeked out from around the bonnet and her face was tanned and seamed with age.

"Good afternoon, Missus Haddorn," he said, touching the brim of his hat. "Hot enough for you?"

"Always hot enough," she said, straightening. She placed her hands in the middle of her back and stretched. "But it's worse this year. We need rain bad. Don't know how the farmers and ranchers are going to make out if they don't get some soon. I hear the water holes are drying up. How about some lemonade?"

He looked in surprise at her. "You have some lemons?"

She motioned toward her house. "I have some trees in back. Clem, my husband, put them in before he died. This may look like a desert, Reverend, but things will grow here if you're willing to take the time with them. I have a couple of lemon trees and apple trees and some grapes growing along the edge of my property. I put them up when they ripen. My preserves used to be pretty popular when we had church picnics here. That stopped when things began to change in this town."

"I could use a glass," he said, dismounting. He draped the reins over the fence. Sam slipped in the gate when he opened it, and loped over to the shade next to the house and plopped down, tongue lolling.

"Come on up to the porch," she said. "I won't be a minute."

She gathered some roses, bloodred and yellow, and carried them into the house as Hood stepped up onto the porch and took a seat in one of the two wooden rockers placed back away from the sunlight. He sighed and took off his hat and laid it on the porch beside the rocker. He removed a handkerchief from a pocket and wiped his face, carefully folding and returning it to the pocket as she emerged from the house with two glasses of lemonade.

"I have a deep well and pump in the kitchen," she explained as she handed a glass to him, the sides of the glass dripping with condensation. "The water's always cool despite the heat."

He took a large swallow of the lemonade and sighed. "Good. Takes the heat away."

"Have a long ride?" she asked, sitting in the other rocker. She sipped from her glass.

"A piece," he said, taking another swallow of the lemonade.

"Up to see Mary Riley, I hear," Mrs. Haddorn said. Her words had a severe, disapproving ring to them. "People are going to talk when they hear about that. And a saloon fight on Sunday." She shook her head. "That doesn't set well with folks."

He smiled gently at her. "Isn't it a minister's work to bring sinners back in the fold?" he countered. "Where would I find them, if not in a saloon?"

"It's what you did when you went into The Cattleman's," she said, fixing him with her pale blue eyes. "Brawling isn't bringing sinners to account."

"Jesus whipped the money changers out of the temple, Missus Haddorn. Sometimes, you have to kick a mule to get it to move where you want it to go. Some people are like money changers and mules. You have to point them in the right direction. When Samson went among the Philistines, he went in peace, but had to smite them hip and thigh when they turned upon him."

She sniffed and clucked her tongue. "And what about turning the other cheek?"

He sighed, knowing that he was caught in the vise of hypocrisy. Resigned, he drank the rest of his lemonade and handed the glass to her.

"That works only once. But if someone

doesn't understand the meaning of the gesture, then it's time to revert to the old ways. Remember, Missus Haddorn, that God Himself has an avenging angel to unleash against those who would violate His commandments. His name is Michael. Thank you for the lemonade," he said, gathering his hat and rising. "But I'd better get Sheba out of the sun."

She rose with him, sour-faced and mouth pursed primly. "I hope you don't keep on smiting people, Reverend Hood. Some of the lambs among your flock may not care for that."

"Would they be the same lambs who have been turning against Mary Riley?" he asked. "Or would they be wolves in sheep's clothing? There's a difference between attending church and doing the Lord's work. We know ourselves by how we behave toward others. Or," he added with emphasis, "others know us by our deeds. Good afternoon."

He placed his hat on his head and walked down the path to where Sheba stood in the sun. He mounted and rode toward the blacksmith's, Sam staying close by his side.

Well, he thought, *it's begun. How long will I have before people see me as another Mary Riley?*

The thought darkened his mood and saddened him as he led Sheba into the stable behind the blacksmith shop.

Sunday was cool and for a few hours, the people of Jericho hoped that the gray clouds over the red mesa would bring rain to the parched land. But by the time church was ready to begin, the sun had burned the clouds away and heat waves were rising from the desert.

Hood made his way slowly down the street to the church, noting that several families had already arrived in their wagons and Sunday best. He smiled as he came up to them, and then noticed with surprise that Mary Riley was waiting off alone from the others. Her face lit up when she saw him. He smiled and made his way toward her, stopping to greet the others. She wore a gray dress split for riding and with a high white collar. She held a wide-brimmed hat in her hand, slapping it gently against one leg.

"Morning," he said. "It's good to see you came in."

"I'm nervous," she said. She waved at the others watching them. "Not only about them, but I hope I don't have unexpected visitors when I get back to the ranch."

"I can ride home with you, if you wish," he said.

"That would be nice," she said gratefully. "I'll fix dinner."

"How about a picnic?" Hood asked. "We can stop along the way. Mother will put up something for us."

She nodded eagerly. "It's been a long time since I've enjoyed a picnic."

"Well, come on then," Hood said, offering an arm. "We'll go after services."

She took his arm hesitantly, then lifted her head and offered a tentative smile at the others at they walked toward the front door of the church. Quiet murmurs followed them, but Tannin offered her a big smile when they came up to him.

"Morning," he said, tipping his hat. Martha smiled at her and gestured toward their children.

"Pleased to meet you," Martha said. "This is Matthew, Mark, and Luke. Would you like to join us for services?"

"Yes, thank you," Mary said, her cheeks turning red. "That would be nice."

Tannin nodded and addressed her. "I'm sorry that we haven't got out to visit you, Miss Riley." He flushed beneath the dark tan of his face. "But you are quite a ways out and we've been . . . busy," he finished lamely.

"I understand," Mary said blandly. "Crops

and all."

"Uh, yes," he said. "But we'd be pleased if you'd join us for services."

Hood patted her arm. "It'll be all right. After, we'll go on that picnic."

He looked at Tannin and his family. "Perhaps you'd care to join us? We were thinking of getting Mother to put up a lunch and ride out to the Bar S. It'll be cooler in the canyon out there and it is the Lord's day," he added significantly.

Tannin glanced quickly at Martha. She gave a slight nod and he turned back, a big smile wreathing his homely face. He tugged at his ear. "I think we'd like that."

"Then let's do it," Hood answered. He turned and glanced at the rest of the congregation waiting behind them, eying them openly now with interest. "It looks like everyone is ready."

He saw Mrs. Haddorn in the front of the others, her face pinched, lips drawn together in a tight, disapproving grimace. He smiled and raised his voice.

"Shall we enter God's house and prepare ourselves for our devotion to the One who has made all things good and possible?"

Tannin grinned and turned to escort Martha up the stairs. He nodded at Hood.

Hood led the way into the church. Mrs.

Haddorn made her way to the front of the church and sat on the piano bench, her back rigid. She placed music on the small stand on the piano, took a deep breath, and began to play "Amazing Grace." Hood gave the others a quiet smile as he walked to the front of the church and stepped behind the pulpit. He took a deep breath and led the entering congregation in the first verse.

"Today," he began when the hymn was finished, "I'd like to talk a bit about man's duty to his fellow creatures. We all are aware of the trials that Job went through to prove his devotion to God. Of course, Job did have his doubts when Satan began to unleash punishments fit for a sinner against him. Why, at one time, Job even despaired of his own existence in the face of all his difficulties. Needlessly, I might add, for Job had forgotten, for the moment, that man is nothing if not for his friends." He opened his Bible to the passage he'd marked and read, "A despairing man should have the devotion of his friends, even though he forsakes the fear of the Almighty." He closed the book and stood straight, looking levelly at the others before him. "These are honest words of a man who had been taken to his limit by Satan but still acknowledged that God was his hope and salvation. Is it right that we should do less than Job for the unfortunate ones who are among us and are suffering despite all that they do to try and live a life devoted to God?" He leaned forward, resting his elbows on the lectern. "Relent in your prejudices and your petty securities that you think make you a better person than others who have been forced to suffer the trials of Job. Like Job, perhaps their insecurities are not of their doing. We are all creatures of fate, and what fate hands us at any moment we have to live with. Remember what Christ said to his followers, all of whom had led sinful lives at one point or another. 'Love others as you love yourselves and do unto them that which you would have done unto you.' " He straightened again. "I wonder. How many of you are without sin that you can cast the first stone?"

And while he spoke, sheepish looks began to replace the hard and stern faces of many in the congregation. But not all. Hood saw that as well, and a great sadness filled him for he realized at that moment that despite all that he said, there would be some who would see the sins of other individuals as unforgivable. But if Christ can forgive others while suffering the pain of His cross . . .

117

■ ■ ■ ■

After the service, Hood watched Mrs. Haddorn stalk by, her music and Bible clutched tightly to her bosom as if she were using the word of God as a shield against Hood and those who stood in a tiny gathering around him. Parks and his family were there, the Tannins, a couple of others, but for the most part, the people of Jericho walked by, faces averted.

"I don't think that you struck many chords with your sermon, Parson," Tannin said sourly.

"Unless it was a dis-chord," Parks said.

The others shook their heads in mock dismay.

"I didn't think it went all that bad," Hood protested. "But I guess I was wrong. Some people just don't want to hear about their shortcomings, I guess."

Mary hugged herself, looking down at the ground between herself and Hood.

"You know," she said in a small voice, "I really think that I'd just as soon go home and forget about the picnic, if you don't mind."

Tannin and Hood exchanged glances. Hood leaned forward, trying to look under the wide-brimmed hat that she had slipped on when they came out of the church.

"You can't let others dictate your life to you, Mary," he said.

She gave a brittle laugh. "It looks like I don't have to. They've already taken care of that. With the exception of you folks," she added, looking up at the others. "But I really don't feel much like a picnic right now. Please? Besides, I'm worried about the ranch."

"All right," Hood said, straightening. "I'll get Sheba and ride on out with you."

"You don't have to do that," she said defensively. "I've been managing by myself for quite a spell now."

"Sheba could use a little exercise," Hood said. He nodded at the others. "I appreciate your thoughts, though."

"Yes, that was nice," Mary said. "Thank you."

"You don't worry about what the others might say or how they might behave," Beth Parks said to Mary, looking severely at the departing backs of the rest of the congregation. "Most of them are just Sunday-morning Christians. They'll show up because it's the social thing to do. The rest of the time, they'll slip back into their old ways until the next Sunday. Then, they'll start all over again."

"That's not all bad," Hood said "Maybe sometime they'll get something out of it. You have to look at what is possible, not what is."

"Uh-huh," Beth grumbled. "But you ask me, most of them just need a quick kick in the seat of the pants to wake 'em up to what they are doing to others. And themselves, if you want to think some good of them."

The others laughed, and even Mary managed a small smile at the older woman's ferocity. They separated, Tannin and Parks promising that they'd bring their wives out to visit sometime in the near future.

Hood and Mary walked down to the stable, Mary leading her horse by its reins. She held her head high, although Hood knew she felt the eyes of the town upon her, and in that moment, a flood of pride in her strength flowed through him.

I wonder if I ever had the strength of this woman, he thought. *All I've done is run away from the problems when they became too big for me to handle. First, the problems back in Tennessee, then Walker after —* But he couldn't bring himself to think about Amy, so he deliberately forced his thoughts away from what he had been and now focused on the present. He smiled down at Mary.

"I'll just be a minute," he said, stepping into the shade of the stable. Sheba nickered when she saw Hood, and shifted her feet impatiently in the straw around her while he saddled her. Sam sat on his haunches, tongue panting as he watched Hood.

"You two are the most impatient souls I know," Hood said.

Sam raised a paw and ran the crook of it down his nose as if wiping his eyes. Sheba tossed her head. Hood laughed.

"All right. You win. It's all my fault."

He led Sheba out of the stable, Sam trotting close on his heels. Mary looked at the three of them and gave a small smile.

"That wolf of yours always gives me a turn," she said.

"Why's that?" Hood asked, swinging up on Sheba's back. He steadied her with a firm hand on the reins as she stepped briskly to the side.

"I guess it's because I didn't figure on seeing any lamb lie down with the wolves," she said. Hood's eyebrows raised and she laughed, climbing into the saddle. "Even the devil can quote Scripture, Amos Hood. Surely you know that."

"Certainly," Hood answered. "The question, though, is whether you're a devil or a saint."

She gave a slow look around the town and shook her head. "You mean, you haven't figured that out yet, when most of the rest of Jericho has already analyzed and categorized me?"

"Some things come hard for some men," he said, turning Sheba's head. "My pa always said I was a stubborn one."

She laughed and touched her heels to the sides of her horse. They rode out of Jericho together, Sam working the ground in a wide arc in front of them, searching for a foolish rabbit.

"Something's wrong," Hood exclaimed, drawing rein as they rode into the canyon mouth leading up to the home place.

"What is it?" Mary asked, alarmed She drew her mare to a halt beside Hood, her eyes looking rapidly around them.

Hood pointed to a small group of vultures circling lazily ahead of them. Mary's lips thinned and she slapped her heels hard against the mare's sides. The mare broke into a gallop up the trail. Hood rode rapidly after her, slipping the Spencer from its saddle sheath as Sheba galloped hard on the mare's heels.

They came up to the home pasture and Mary drew rein, pulling the mare to a stop.

In the middle of the pasture lay the four longhorn steers, all dead.

Her shoulders slumped. "I knew I shouldn't have gone in to church."

"I'm sorry," Hood said, staring at the longhorns. "It's always hard to lose something."

She wiped tears from her eyes with the back of her hand. "Yes. They were the last that John brought in. They meant an awful lot to him. But now . . ."

"I know what you're thinking," Hood said. "But you're wrong. It's not the longhorns that Mr. Stockton left you, it's the land. He made the land what it is. The longhorns were just a symbol of what he had done. But the land is everlasting. It will endure forever. That's what he left you."

She drew a shaky breath and tried to smile. "You always seem to have the right words."

Hood shrugged. "That doesn't mean that this wasn't a dirty deed. It was. And sooner or later, someone will be called to account for it."

"I needed that, too," Mary said.

They turned, touched heels to the sides of their horses, and rode in silence up to the ranch house.

10.

The sun rose like molten steel as Hood rode across the desert toward Mary's place. He could feel the promise of heat in the day beneath his brown trousers and a blue chambray work shirt. He had his Spencer rifle tucked into its saddle sheath beneath his leg. A new lariat, coiled and ready, hung on one side of his saddle's pommel, while an old flour sack, filled with small sacks of dried beans, Arbuckle's coffee, flour and sugar, and a side of bacon, hung from the other side. He had left the Schofield tucked deep in his saddlebags back in his room, although he still felt the desire to draw it out and buckle it once again around his waist and give himself over to the darkness that had once almost consumed him.

Sam ranged far ahead, slipping like a shadow around mesquite bushes, pausing now and then to investigate a lizard, then casting a backward glance at Hood before loping on. A covey of quail leaped up at his approach and flew a safe distance away from Sam, who paused, marking where they landed before continuing on.

Hood came to the turnoff to the Bar S and rode up it, his eyes moving ceaselessly as he watched for early morning riders. In the distance, he saw one pull up his horse, a skewbald, and knew that he had been seen, but he kept Sheba at a steady pace as he rode on. One of McQuade's riders, he figured. About as subtle as face warts.

He whistled for Sam as he turned into the canyon leading up to the ranch house, then sat back, drinking in the coolness of the canyon yet untouched by the morning sun. Jays sang in the trees over the gentle rill of the stream as squirrels foraged beneath the trees. Sheba's hooves were muffled in the heavy dust of the trail.

Mary saw him coming, and waited for him on the porch as he came up to the house. She wore a man's blue and white checked shirt and canvas pants, the cuffs rolled down over scuffed boots. Her eyes lit up with relief as he reined in.

"I wasn't sure if you'd come," she said.

"I told you I would," he said, stepping down and taking the flour sack from the pommel.

"Yeah, but a lot of men say one thing and do the other when the trail gets a bit rough," she answered drily.

"I brought some supplies," he said, hefting the sack. "I thought your larder might be getting a little low."

"It's low," she admitted. "Been that way for a spell now. I've got coffee on. You want a cup?"

"That'd go down nicely. I rode out as soon as it was light to keep the noses out of speculating where I was going."

He followed her inside, and lifted the flour sack up on the table and began setting the contents to the side. She glanced at them and gave him a warm smile.

"It's not much," he said ruefully, "but it'll fill in around the edges. I'll bring more on the next trip out."

She filled two mugs with coffee and set them on the table. He pulled out a chair, sitting while he took the mug she'd placed in front of him. He blew across the surface and sipped cautiously.

"Good. You make a good pot," he said.

She shrugged. "I've had plenty of practice out here. I've got eggs. You want some?"

He shook his head. "Coffee's enough for now. I thought I'd gather what cattle I can and put them in the lower pasture. We need to get a count and brand what calves and yearlings that we can find."

She made a face. "I don't know what we'll find — the other ranchers are a bit free with their ropes on mavericks."

"Then, I'd better collect a couple of irons and throw a brand on what I can find before I move them," he said. "As soon as I get a count, I'm going to see what I can do with a trade to a couple of ranchers or farmers who might be willing to take on some feeders for market. But," he added, "I don't know if you should ride out. I saw a rider as I came in. I figure him for a McQuade man. It might be a good idea for one of us to stay close to the home place."

"I'm pretty handy with a rope," she said. "Or I can handle hot iron. With two of us working, we might finish up quicker."

"There's that," he said thoughtfully, finishing his coffee. "There'll be some risk."

She laughed curtly. "You forget. I've been alone here for a while now. I'm used to risk."

"All right. We'll round up what we can and bring them into the lower pasture. Then, I'll dally the calves and you can run the irons on them. In the lower pasture, we'll be close enough to the house to discourage any takeover."

She rinsed their mugs and placed them to

127

dry on a drain board as Hood went out to saddle a deep-chested claybank that looked as if it had bottom, and moved his saddle from Sheba to a grulla that looked like it had worked cattle. Sheba shook her head at being freed, then moved into deep grass and began to graze.

It was still false light in the canyon, but the sun was beginning to peep over the canyon rim when Mary and Hood rode down the trail and began working the side canyons running off into the red mesa. Within an hour, they were covered with dust as they pushed reluctant cattle out of the canyons and into the lower pasture, where the cattle settled down to grazing the lush grass. They managed to gather three hundred head and a hundred ten calves before they decided to end the drive for the day and brand the calves and a few yearlings that had somehow slipped the nooses of rustlers and ranchers.

A dry wind blew up when the sun began to slip over the mesa, filling the air with fine dust and changing the light to the color of butternut squash as they rode their weary horses back up the trail to the ranch house. When they came into view of the house, they saw three saddled horses tied in the shade of the spreading cottonwood tree.

Gray smoke curled up from the chimney.

"Looks like you were right," Mary said bitterly, reining in. "Apparently, someone was waiting for us to leave before making themselves right at home."

"We'll reason with them," Hood said quietly. He loosened the Spencer in its sheath before nudging the grulla with his heels.

"Reason?" Mary gave a short bark of laughter. "Those folk won't be willing to listen to reason."

"You never can tell," Hood said. "Sometimes, the Lord gives folks insight as to what's right from wrong."

"Right doesn't have anything to do with it now," she said, a hard edge to her voice. "And there's three of them."

"More of a chance for a cool head among them," Hood observed.

They rode up to the house, reining in to the side of the porch. Hood glanced at the Box M brands on the horses, then shifted his attention to the three men as they stepped out onto the porch, grinning at the dusty riders. Sam crouched beside the grulla, hackles raised, a rumbling growl coming up from his throat.

"Easy, Sam," Hood said softly.

"You're trespassing," Mary said flatly.

One of the men stepped forward, broad-shouldered, hands scarred from rope burns, thumb tucked into his gun belt, an insolent grin on his hard-boned face.

"Reckon that's a matter of which one's trespassing," he said mockingly. "Seems like we've got the house. Found it abandoned."

"You're a liar," Mary said.

He shook his head. "Now, that's not friendly, ma'am. But I'm a forgiving man and will just put that down to a contrary nature."

The two men beside him smiled. Hood took them in with a single glance: cowmen, but willing to shoot for the brand they rode for if need came to it. One, a short, lanky man with jet-black hair and a pinched face, seemed vaguely familiar, but he couldn't place the man's name.

"Normally, we'd invite you to sit down a spell, but you appear too downright unfriendly, so I guess we're just gonna have to ask you to ride on." The first man shook his head. "That goes against the grain, being the sort who don't turn people away without a plate of beans or something to fill their bellies, but I don't think much would come of any visit anyway. Do you?"

"This is Bar S land," Hood said quietly.

The man looked up at him. "You'd be that

new parson we hear talk about, wouldn't you? I'm Charlie Daniels."

"Amos Hood," Hood replied. "And yes, I'm the new minister. Now, I think it'd be a nice gesture on the part of you all to mount up and ride on out." He gestured at the chimney. "I see you've already made yourself at home and presume you've had your coffee, so there's nothing here to keep you."

Daniels laughed. "Well, me and Josh Slade" — he jerked his thumb at the dark-haired man — "and Billy Richards here, well, we just don't see things that way."

"I see," Hood said mildly. He sighed and looped the reins around the pommel of his saddle. With his left hand, he pushed his hat back on his head, drawing their attention while he slipped the Spencer from its sheath in one smooth gesture and thumbed the hammer back.

Smiles slipped off the cowboys' faces as they stared into the Spencer's big bore.

"Now," Hood said, "I'd appreciate it if you would step down easy from the porch and move out into the yard a bit where I can keep my eye on all of you. As you say, I'm the new preacher and might accidentally slip the trigger. We wouldn't want a tragic accident here, now would we?"

Silently, the three men stepped down from

the porch, keeping their hands wide and away from their holstered pistols.

"Thank you," Hood said politely. "Now, Mary, why don't you get on down and go into the house while I reason with these gentlemen a little."

Hood kept his attention on the men as Mary silently dismounted and walked up on the porch, disappearing into the house. He smiled.

"Now, if you'll just shuck your gun belts, why, I think everyone will breathe a little easier."

"Be damned if I will!" Slade said hotly. His eyes snapped black fire and his hand trembled over the butt of his pistol.

"You will be if you don't," Hood warned. "But the choice is yours. God gave every man free will. Even fools."

"Do what he says," Daniels said, his left hand unbuckling his gun belt. He let it drop in the dust and stared hard at Hood. "You sure act strange for a parson."

"Even Samson had to use the jawbone of an ass on those who wouldn't listen," Hood said. "I don't mind reading from the Good Book to those who need it, but it would be better if you just came to church on Sunday to learn the error of your ways. Now, step away from your guns."

The others followed Daniels's lead, moving slowly so they wouldn't draw any hasty fire from Hood.

"Good," Hood said. "Now you're being neighborly."

He slipped from his saddle and kept an eye on the cowboys as he picked up their gun belts and tossed them up on the porch.

"I'll leave your pistols at The Cattleman's in town. You can pick them up from the bartender the next time you're in."

"You talk mighty big with that big-bore holding on us," Daniels said. "What would you do without it?"

Hood shrugged. "This just seems the easy way to do things," he said. "But you're right. I don't think I'll need this anymore."

He let the hammer down on the Spencer and slipped it back into its sheath. He smiled at Daniels. "There. Now we can all be friends."

"You just made a big mistake," Daniels said.

He balled his hands into fists and came toward Hood, swinging. Hood slipped away and snapped a left into Daniels's face that halted the cowboy in his tracks and forced him to stagger back a step.

Slade made a move toward the porch and the pistols, but a blur went by Hood's vision as Sam launched himself, slamming into Slade's chest and flattening him on the ground. Sam planted both front feet on Slade's chest; teeth bared as he snarled inches from Slade's throat.

"Jesus! Help! Get this wolf off me!"

Billy ignored Slade's cries and came toward Hood, but Mary stepped out of the house and ran down the steps, swinging a cast-iron frying pan with both hands. The frying pan bounced with a loud *thhhwunk* off Billy's head. He stood for a moment, cross-eyed, then collapsed, unconscious, over Slade as Sam leaped aside.

Hood took the moment to step in, swinging low with both hands into Daniels's stomach. Air left the big cowboy's lungs in a loud *whoosh* and he doubled over, only to meet Hood's right coming up from his hip. The blow landed with a wicked *splat!* on his nose and he reeled back, blood spurting. He swung blindly as Hood came in, but Hood slapped the blow aside with his left hand and came over with a hard right that landed on Daniels's eye. The cowboy dropped, stunned, into the dirt. Hood moved back, watching warily, but the fight was out of Daniels and he waved Hood off.

"Enough," he mumbled through swollen lips.

"You've worn out your welcome," Hood said, standing easily, chest rising and falling gently with his breath. "Now, for the last time, mount up and ride on out or I'll tie you across your saddles and let your horses find their own way back home. And tell McQuade to keep his riders off Bar S land. It would be the peaceable thing to do."

Daniels pulled himself to his feet, dragging a dirty bandanna from a hip pocket and wadding it against his nose as Slade squirmed out from under Billy and stepped quickly away as Sam growled threateningly.

"Keep that wolf off me!" he said.

"Sam," Hood said. "Down."

Obediently, Sam lowered himself to the ground, ready to spring if Slade made the wrong move.

"Pick up your friend and put him on his horse," Hood said.

The three climbed on their horses and rode quietly away, slumped in their saddles, without a backward glance. Hood stayed near the grulla and the Spencer until the riders disappeared down the trail. Then, he looked at Mary and smiled.

"You all right?" he asked solicitously.

"Sure," she said, raising a trembling hand to brush a lock of hair from across her forehead. "Where did you learn all that?"

"I told you I came from Tennessee," Hood said. "You grow up as a minister's boy, you learn to take care of yourself quickly. Boys always have to test themselves, and a minister's son is fair game."

"Well, you certainly learned!" Mary said. She glanced down at the frying pan dangling in one hand. "I just grabbed the first thing at hand when I saw them starting to jump you."

"You evened things up," Hood said. "I'm grateful. Things might have gone differently if you waited."

"And Sam," Mary said. The wolf looked up at his name. "You were wonderful, too, boy." Sam dropped his head down onto his front paws. "I've got an old soup bone for you."

She looked at Hood. "Wash up. I'll fix us a bite to eat."

"I could eat," Hood admitted, walking to the washstand at the end of the porch. Sam rose and followed him as Mary climbed the stairs and disappeared into the house.

11.

Silver moonlight ran down the canyon from the house as Hood came out onto the porch, a final cup of coffee in his hand. He took a deep breath and sighed heavily, enjoying the night air filled with the scent of cedar and pine. A hint of dust hung in the air — dust would always hang in the air until a rain finally came to settle it — and the heat of the day still clung suggestively to the night, reminding him that the morning would bring the full blast of heat upon them. He felt tired, but it was a good feeling, this slight ache in his muscles, and he looked forward to arriving back at the hotel and a long soak in a hot tub. Providing, he reflected, that he could get hot water carried up to his floor this late at night.

He glanced at the barn and wondered if he should spend the night, then rejected the thought, remembering the admonishment he'd received from Mrs. Haddorn about helping Mary. All it would take to set the tongues to wagging, like old biddies clucking over a handful of corn, was a suggestion of scandal that would be certain to spread like wildfire over the dry countryside.

He started as a bullbat with a tongue of fire darted out of the blackness, swooping and dancing as it chased insects for its supper. He felt Mary move from the house to stand beside him, and raised his cup of coffee, sipping. He smelled the faint hint of sweat and soap clinging to her, and something else that raised old emotions he'd long thought buried with the impetuosity of the youth he'd left in Tennessee, where a naked swim with Eula Johnson had sent him into the West away from the feuding guns of the Johnson clan.

"A beautiful night," Mary said softly. She stepped close to his shoulder, a scant half foot separating them. Her scent was heady, and Hood took another long swallow from his cup, tasting the grounds on the tip of his tongue.

"It is that," he said, taking a step away from her and sending the dregs of his cup flying into the night with a quick twist of his wrist. He turned toward her, keeping the cup between them as a feeble defense.

Her features looked carved from flawless

marble in the pale moonlight. Her full lips curved into a smile, sending dimples into shadows in her cheeks. Her eyes glittered with promise. She took a step toward him, and he smiled and raised the cup to her.

"I'd better be going," he said.

She paused and took the cup from him. "You don't have to," she said, disappointment in her voice.

"Yes," he answered, "yes, I do. Thank you for the supper."

"There is a place for you in the barn," she began.

"I know. You told me," he said gently. "But it is better if I go now before this becomes something both of us might regret. You are a wonderful woman, Mary, but I'm not the one for you."

He leaned forward and kissed her on the forehead, and stepped back before she could raise her arms. He walked down the steps and took Sheba's reins. Mary laughed, the sound like soft crystal notes coming from the heavens.

"For a moment there, I thought your halo might be slipping, Amos," she said.

"For a moment, it was," he answered, stepping into the saddle. "I'll see you in the morning."

"I'll have the coffee waiting," she called as

139

he turned Sheba and lifted her into a canter.

He turned in the saddle and waved, then sat back, deep in the saddle, moving easily with the rocking motion of the mare. Off to the side, he caught the form of Sam slipping in and out of the darkness as he roamed just ahead of them, A melancholy loneliness slipped down over Hood as he rode through the night, but he recognized the loneliness as a desire to be something other than what he was; perhaps a simple rancher or farmer, sitting on his porch in the evening or in front of a fire with a beautiful wife next to him, content spreading like warm apple pie through his belly.

But that moment had been left behind in Walker after the woman he loved had been killed by a bullet intended for him and after what he had done to the man who'd killed her. Not only had he lost his love, but by his actions he'd lost all possibility for being loved. The night suddenly came alive with his memories, and he slumped in the saddle as he watched them unfold.

"You're wearing your pistol?" Amy asked.

Tom smiled. "I'm still the sheriff. I'll leave it in the vestibule before we go into the church."

"I don't see why you should have to wear a pistol on Sundays," Amy replied. "Isn't Fred

Wilson on duty?"

"He is. But this is the time to take a little precaution," Tom answered.

He opened the door and led her out onto the boardwalk. A great contentedness came over him as they walked slowly toward church, enjoying the Indian summer morning. People greeted them and smiled as if they knew the announcement that was going to be made by Reverend Hancock that morning.

Amy hugged Tom's arm a little closer. "This is a beautiful day, isn't it?"

He smiled down at her. "It is. A very beautiful day."

"I —"

She jerked, and a puzzled look came into her eyes as she clutched his coat.

Tom heard the gun report a fraction later. Then another as a bullet whizzed like a bee past his head.

He whipped his head around and saw Joe Griswald levering another round into his Winchester from the side of the hotel. Tom palmed his pistol and fired two rapid shots. Griswald threw up his arms and fell to the ground as one bullet struck his shoulder and the other his knee. He writhed in pain on the ground.

"Thomas!" Amy said faintly.

Tom holstered his pistol and lowered her to

141

the ground. Blood began spreading rapidly over the front of her dress as a crowd gathered around them. Hawthorne pushed his way through and knelt beside Tom.

Amy lifted her hand and touched Tom's face. "I'm so sorry," she murmured.

Then her eyelids fluttered and closed and her hand fell away.

"Amy!" he shouted sharply. He shook her, but there was no response.

"She's gone, Tom," Hawthorne said in a choking voice. "She's gone."

Gently, Tom lifted her and held her out to Hawthorne.

"Take her home, please," he said softly.

Hawthorne took her from Tom's arms and turned away, tears streaming down his face.

The crowd parted as Tom walked down toward the hotel where Griswald had pulled himself to the side, propping himself up against a rain barrel. He was trying to pull the Winchester to him.

"Griswald!" Tom shouted.

The rancher looked at him, then reached inside his coat and pulled a pistol from a shoulder harness. Tom drew and shot him in the other shoulder, and the pistol flipped away from him. Then, Tom deliberately drew the hammer back and shot him in the leg. Griswald yelled in agony as Tom continued to empty his pistol slowly into Griswald, listening to the man scream as each shot hammered into him.

He paused when he came up to Griswald. Blood was spreading slowly around him. Tom slipped the spent cartridges from the Schofield and methodically reloaded it.

"I — said — I'd — get you," panted Griswald.

"You didn't, though. You killed a woman," Tom said stonily.

"I'm — not — finished yet!" Griswald said through gritted teeth.

"Yes, you are," Tom said. He raised the pistol and put a bullet through Griswald's forehead.

He turned, holding the pistol at his side, and started down the street. He heard another gunshot and turned, dropping to one knee as Bill Devlin stepped out of his hotel, a pistol held in his hand. He raised it and pointed it at Tom. Tom fired rapidly three times, watching Devlin jerk back as each bullet struck him. He fell, slumped against the front of his hotel.

Slowly, Tom rose and looked around. The crowd of people had spread to each side of the street, looking at him strangely as he turned and made his way down to Hawthorne's place, reloading the pistol again as he walked, feeling a darkness come upon him like a torrent, bold and desirable, cloaking him in dead black. He felt himself move into the empty shadows of himself and knew that what had once given him life had gone with Amy's death —

A low growl from Sam jerked Hood back from the black memory of his last days as Tom Cade to the dark night. Automatically, he checked Sheba and lifted slightly in the saddle, senses alert and wary. He glanced at Sam, noticing the wolf crouched, hackles raised, attention riveted forward. Hood slipped from the saddle and crouched beside Sam, hand going gently on Sam's neck, soothing him.

"What is it, boy?" he whispered.

Sam continued to growl, yellow eyes gleaming balefully toward the end of the canyon where it doglegged back with the stream. A small stand of boulders had fallen into the crook of the dogleg, and the stream bent around them before it followed the mesa line down to the homesteaders' valley and disappeared underground. There was something about the boulders that made Hood edgy as he studied them in the light of the half-moon as it slipped in and out of dark purple clouds.

Then, the moonlight glinted off something metallic tucked back in the darkness between two boulders, and a grim smile slipped across Hood's face.

"I see it, Sam," he whispered.

Cautiously, he stood, slipped the Spencer from its sheath, and patted Sheba on her shoulder as he dropped into a crouch and began a small detour along the edge of the creek. He moved quietly, testing the ground in front of him before stepping forward on the balls of his feet. Thick green grass muffled his steps as he made his way to the stand of boulders.

He paused, waiting in the dark, watching the cleft between the two boulders where the gleam had momentarily appeared. He shifted his eyes back and forth, knowing that sometimes things could be discovered in the dark at the edge of one's vision. Dimly, he made out the profile of a hat; then slowly, the outline of someone began to appear. Satisfied, he eased back the hammer on the Spencer, muffling the sound with his hand.

"All right," he said conversationally, "you've got ten seconds to toss your guns out and step into the light before I start bouncing bullets off the rocks. One, two . . ."

A curse came on the heels of his words and he watched the profile waver as the man tried to find where Hood's voice came from.

". . . nine, ten," Hood said, and fired a

shot high between the two boulders. Immediately, he moved to his left as his bullet whined back and forth off the rocks.

A yelp came after his shot.

"Gawddamnit! Hold your fire! You 'most took my head off with that one!"

"Toss your guns out. I won't say it again," Hood ordered.

A Winchester came flying out, followed by a handgun.

"Now, keep your hands high and step out. Slowly," Hood said.

Hood sighed as Slade stepped out, hands held above his head. His eyes glittered at Hood.

"You were lucky," Slade said angrily. "Another few yards and I would've put a bullet in your head."

"That'd be quite a shot in the dark," Hood said mildly.

"I could've made it," Slade said.

"I expect you think that," Hood said. "And maybe you could've. We'll never know, now will we? But I can see that reading the Good Book to you won't get your attention. So I reckon that the next best thing is to show you the error of your ways. Shuck your boots."

"What?" Slade said loudly.

"Then your pants and shirt."

146

"No!"

Hood put a bullet between Slade's legs and Slade dropped quickly to the ground, tugging hard at his boots. He set them aside and looked up at Slade.

"Now your pants and shirt," Hood said.

"What — what are you going to do?" Slade asked anxiously.

"Maybe a little midnight stroll back to McQuade's place will give you pause to think about the error of your ways," Hood said. "Contemplation is good for the soul."

"There's cactus and mesquite out there!" Slade protested, flinging an arm out to indicate the land beyond the canyon.

"You'd better be careful where you step," Hood said. He raised the Spencer, moving the barrel in a tiny circle around Slade's middle. "Now, it's late and you'd better get started if you want to get back to the ranch by morning."

Slade swore, but dropped his pants and slipped out of his shirt, piling them on top of his boots. He started to turn, but Hood stopped him.

"Now the longjohns," Hood said.

"I'll be nekkid!" Slade said.

"That's the idea," Hood said calmly.

Wordlessly, Slade peeled the longjohns off and stood shivering in the moonlight, cupping his hands around himself.

"Now go," Hood said. "And step lively. You've caused enough trouble today to make me just a bit irritated."

Gingerly, Slade started off, moving on tiptoe. Hood put a bullet in the earth behind his heels. Gravel spattered like buckshot against Slade's legs. The effect was terrific and instantaneous. Slade leaped forward like a shot out of a shovel from mucking out the stable, running flat out out of the canyon, arms pumping, and screaming for all he was worth when his bare feet came down upon cactus leaves.

And Hood laughed in the darkness as he watched the naked Slade slipping through the night, moonlight turning him into a pale ghost or will-o'-the-wisp. Hood walked back to Sheba, pausing to pat Sam on the head before stepping into the saddle. His demons had slipped back into memory. He slid the Spencer back into its sheath and nudged the mare to move down the trail. In the distance, he could still hear Slade's yells ringing faintly through the night.

12.

The sun rose slowly, flushing the sky with deep streaks of red like fresh blood, as Hood moved easily in the saddle, letting Sheba pick her own pace toward Ed Hoffman's Rafter H ranch. Tiny clouds of dust rose from her hoofs, and already the promised heat of the day had started to soak through Hood's blue shirt. Overhead, a lone buzzard soared in a lazy, widening circle. Sam loped off to the right, halfheartedly searching for a rabbit or mouse. Occasionally, he would put up a quail or sage hen and watch carefully where the bird would land, but then he'd ignore it and glance over at Hood as if to say, "See what I can do!"

They reached the edge of the mesa where the creek turned and ran down into the lower valley. Here, a small sign had been raised with an arrow pointing under the legend Ĥ. Hood turned Sheba onto the small road, and followed it for a couple of miles before the ranch buildings came in view. By the time he'd ridden up to the ranch house, Ed Hoffman had stepped out onto the porch, a cup of coffee in his hand.

"Howdy!" he said cheerfully. "Have some coffee and sit a spell! It's good to see you, Reverend."

"Thanks," Hood answered, swinging down from Sheba's back. "Don't mind if I do. A cup of coffee would taste good this morning."

Hoffman turned to the doorway and called for another cup, then faced Hood. "You're up mighty early and this ain't even Sunday."

"If it was Sunday, it'd be afternoon before you saw me," Hood said. "Services are in the morning. Speaking of which, I don't recall seeing you there."

A sheepish grin came over Hoffman's face. "Well, you got me there, Reverend. I have to confess that I ain't much for church-going. My ma made certain that her boys attended every camp meeting that came through, and wore out about three birch switches to ensure that we attended every one." He shook his head at the memory. "And Ma was a big woman with a lot of heft in her shoulders. She'd raise a welt on your backside that would last a month!"

Hood grinned. "I know what you mean. Pa wouldn't hit us much for not attending his church, but he had a tongue like an adder that would leave you skulking around out of his sight for days. I don't know which was worse, getting hit with his leather belt or having to listen to his lecture for missing church. I finally realized the best thing to do was to go to church and not take a chance that I could get away with missing it. Most of the time, I couldn't anyway."

A man wearing a clean apron knotted around his waist came out and silently handed Hood a cup of coffee. Hood tasted it and nodded.

"Good," he said. "Mother's coffee is all right, but there's something about a man's coffee that always sets better."

"Sit, sit," Hoffman said, gesturing to two rawhide-seat chairs placed back in the shade of the porch. "How have things been going?"

He took a seat to Hood's right and looked expectantly at Hood. He sipped.

"Good. Well, as good as can be expected, I suppose," Hood added ruefully. "There's some that take a dim view of my ways. But any new preacher is going to run into that. People can't help comparing the new with the old, and most times the new comes out

151

behind expectations."

Hoffman laughed. "If I had to guess, I'd say you ran up against Missus Haddorn. She has a word for any who dispute her as an authority on anything that she puts a mind to. Most folk just turn a deaf ear to her and mumble politely when she gets off on one of her tirades. She offer one of her elixirs? She claims she can cure anything from the colic to the gout and some things that haven't even been given a name yet."

"No, she didn't. All I got from her was some lemonade."

"You're lucky. Her elixirs would gag a pig." He paused, looking shrewdly at Hood. "But, if I don't miss my guess, this isn't just a polite call to try and talk me into coming to church this Sunday."

"You're right," Hood said, laughing ruefully. "You've seen right through me. Although," he added, "I do confess that I planned on trying to talk you into appearing now and then in the congregation."

"I'll keep that in mind," Hoffman said. "What else can I do for you?"

Hood took a deep drink of coffee and placed his cup on the floor next to the leg of his chair. He sighed and removed his hat, running his finger around the sweatband.

"Mary Riley," he said quietly. "She's been

having some trouble with McQuade and Box M riders. She's got a small herd that is ready for market, but no way of getting it there. I thought I might talk you into being neighborly and trading some of your yearlings for market stock. You could make the drive along with whatever you have ready for the market. You'd make money and Mary Riley would have the stock needed to build up her herd for next year. She's got good grass and water and I figure that if I can get a few more folks to help, why, we might throw up a fence to cut down on Box M cattle mixing with Bar S."

"You mean Box M riders branding Bar S mavericks," Hoffman said.

"That, too," Hood agreed. "Fencing her land and establishing a new herd might go well toward stopping a range war."

Hoffman looked at him sharply. "You think we're headed for one?"

Hood nodded slowly. "Yes, this place has all the makings of one brewing. You got McQuade and the Rawlinses both wanting Bar S land, and I would imagine there are probably a few homesteaders who wouldn't mind adding part of the Bar S to their own holdings."

"You forgot me," Hoffman said wryly, grinning. "I wouldn't mind getting Bar S land either."

"I thought of that," Hood admitted. "But it would be right neighborly and Christian of you to put your own wants aside for a spell."

Hoffman nodded. "Well, I'm in no hurry to expand right now. I've got about as much as I can handle right now. I take on anything more, I'd have to hire more hands and that's always a loss for a year or two before things start paying for themselves. Of course, I think the market price is going to go up on cattle in a month or two, and if I can get a herd to the railroad in time, I should be able to hit the market at its high. Of course, this is only guesswork, you know," he said. "What kind of a trade were you looking for?"

"Two for one, Bar S favor," Hood said.

Hoffman shook his head. "Pretty steep. Even if Bar S cattle have hit the best market weight. How many head we talking about?"

"Say two hundred head," Hood said. "There could be a few more, but she's got some heifers with new calves."

"That'd mean four hundred head on my part," Hoffman said. "I don't think I could do that. I'm willing to help, but that's a bit too steep for me. Maybe the Box M could go that, but McQuade is bigger than I am.

How about two seventy-five?"

"Three twenty-five," Hood said promptly.

"Split the difference. Three hundred. At that, I'll throw in twenty calves fresh off the teat."

"I'd say you got a deal," Hood said, stretching his hand out. Hoffman shook hands and laughed.

"Well, I guess I'd better get my men to rounding up my end of the trade. How about you?"

"I think you know we've got the cattle in a holding pasture," Hood said, smiling at the rancher. "I'd say that not much escapes anyone's attention around here."

Hoffman laughed. "Yeah, you're right. I know you got a herd already gathered. Pretty sure of yourself, weren't you?"

"Had to be done. It's easier to hold on to a loaf of bread when it's whole than when it's half-cut," Hood said philosophically. "Riders have an easy time picking up a couple head here and there where no one can see them. In a large herd, it's easier to protect the cattle from outriders. Would you mind driving your stock over and Mary's back?

Hoffman's eyes danced. " 'Mary' is it? You certain this is just a Christian act on your part? She's an almighty pretty woman."

"Blessed is he who has regard for the weak; the Lord delivers him in times of trouble," Hood answered.

Hoffman raised an eyebrow. "You just made that up," he said.

"Psalm Forty-one," Hood said, rising. " 'The Lord will protect him and preserve his life; he will bless him in the land and not surrender him to the desire of his foes.' A good read. Why don't you come to church this Sunday? You might find something good for your soul."

"I'll take your word for it," Hoffman said, rising. He held out his hand. "But I might be moving cattle on that day. I know it's the Lord's day and all, but some things don't necessarily wait on the Lord. He who helps himself helps the Lord. Right?"

"Even the devil can quote Scripture," Hood said, grinning. He took Hoffman's hand, shaking it firmly. "But I thank you for what you're doing. I'll remember you in my prayers."

"I'll take all the help I can get," Hoffman said. "I'll have my men begin rounding up some yearlings to drive over. It'll take a couple of days."

"No hurry," Hood said. "The Bar S cattle will be waiting for you. Thanks for the coffee."

"Any time," Hoffman said, walking to the edge of the porch as Hood stepped down and crossed to Sheba. He gathered her reins and swung up into the saddle. He touched the brim of his hat and, turning her head, rode easily down the trail away from the ranch house.

The smile slowly slipped away from Hoffman's face to be replaced by a thoughtful look. He pursed his lips and, turning, went back into the house.

The day seemed a bit brighter to Hood and when he reached the end of the Rafter H range, he turned Sheba toward the lower valley to make a circuit of the homesteaders before heading back to Jericho. He rode content with the day, enjoying the play of shadows across the land, watching as patches of green began to replace the brown vegetation in the upper valley. By the time he'd ridden down into the mouth of the valley where Ezra Tannin and his neighbors had settled and turned the land into farmland through shallow-ditch irrigation to water their small fields, the land showed rich and verdant. But still, there was a hint of the desert at the edge of the fields where the irrigation stopped and the creek did not flow.

A conflicting country, Hood thought as he rode. *A harsh country, but similar, I expect, to the land given by God to Israel — fertile in part, but rough enough to keep man from taking things for granted.*

As Hood rode up, he found Tannin repairing a harness in the shade of his barn.

"Glad to see you, Reverend Hood," Tannin said, setting the harness aside and rising. He shook hands warmly. "Been wondering when you'd get out this way."

"Call me 'Amos,' " Hood said. " 'Reverend' sounds a bit too formal. How are things going for you?"

Tannin sighed. "Not as well as I'd hoped. I thought this drought would be over by now. Corn is a bit stunted for this late in the year, and we won't get much despite irrigation and hauling water if it don't rain soon. But," he said, flashing a grin, "maybe all we need is a 'rain prayer' from you. God might be listening a little closer to you than he does to us'ns."

Hood laughed. "I don't know about that, but I'll certainly put in a word or two in case it just might help. I'd think that the Lord probably has more things on His mind than to listen to me, though."

"Come on up to the house," Tannin said, gesturing. "My wife's gone, but there's plenty of cool water. And I know where she's hid the molasses cookies."

"Thanks," Hood answered. "I can't stay long, but I'll have a cookie or two before heading back. I do have a favor to ask of you, though."

"What's that?" Tannin asked, leading the way to the porch of his small adobe house.

Hood sighed as they stepped onto the porch and out of the sun. "The Almighty sure does like to test a fellow now and then, doesn't he? I thought that maybe I could talk you and a couple of others into helping me string a fence between the Bar S and the Box M."

Tannin's eyebrows raised. "What brought that about?"

He stepped into the house, drew two glasses of water from the kitchen pump and piled a plate high with cookies he took from an old biscuit tin. He reemerged and handed one of the glasses to Hood, placing the plate on the floor of the porch between them as they sat in the shade on two straight-backed chairs.

Hood took one of the cookies and bit, nodding approval as he chewed. "Good. The best I've had in a long time. It's like this, Ezra. Mary Riley has been working alone, trying to hold on to the Bar S by herself. A lot of her stock has been rustled, but she still has a nice little herd of fat stock ready for market. Now, Hoffman is willing to trade some yearlings for the fat stock and make a drive, but that will only help ease part of the problem. We need to string wire to help keep her cattle from being taken."

Tannin shook his head. "I can see where you might want to help bring some of the sheep back into the fold, Amos, but helping Mary Riley — well, that's gonna cause a lot of talk. For whoever. You know what she was?"

"I don't cast stones," Hood said easily. Tannin flushed, but Hood continued before the farmer could speak. "There's another reason, too. I think we're heading for a range war if something's not done. The Rawlinses, McQuade, and, I think, Hoffman as well, all want the Bar S land. If Mary's forced out, that will put the Bar S up for grabs, and I've got a hunch that all three ranches will claim it. I can't see a three-way division of the land, so there'll be a fight. Probably between the Rawlinses and McQuade at first, but Hoffman will more than likely be dragged into it eventually. You farmers might be caught right in the middle. You've got some water here, as you said, but just because you think that you don't have enough water to draw any interest from the big ranchers doesn't mean that they won't come after your land, too. Combine all your farms into one and there would be enough water to satisfy one or two of the ranches. Being small helps you right now, but once a range war starts, well, you can bet anything you want that you will be drawn into it one way or the other. No one wins in a range war; everyone loses."

Tannin nodded thoughtfully, leaning back against his chair, sipping his water. Hood watched him, remaining silent to let the farmer sort out his thoughts. At last, Tannin slapped his hand against his leg and said, "I can see what you mean. That makes sense. Helping her seems to be the one way to try to avoid a lot of trouble and bloodshed. All right. I'll help. And I'll ride on over to some of the others and see if I can't enlist their help as well."

He grinned ruefully. "This is going to be a hot topic for a couple of days as some of the other womenfolk won't be in favor of us helping. 'Course, that doesn't include Martha or Beth. They been making the air kinda thick around here about how they should've been up to see her before this. But that don't mean that there ain't others who aren't willing to help. It's just that there ain't a man nowhere who can claim to having the last word right out. A man's gotta talk his way around the problem in order to get his woman to agree. Unless," he added, "he wants to spend a few weeks sleeping in the barn."

Hood laughed. "Well, why don't you use me as the scapegoat and say that I asked for your help? I don't have a wife and I figure I can put up with a few miffed women better than their husbands can. At least," he said, eyes twinkling, "I won't have to sleep in the barn."

"Don't worry," Tannin said, "I'll blame you and you can bet the other husbands will as well. But you let me know when you want me up there and I'll bring my boys along, too. Give me enough warning and I'll use my wagon to pick up the wire and bring it on out to the Bar S with me."

"I appreciate that," Hood said. He leaned back in his chair and sighed. "Frankly, I thought it'd take a lot more than that to convince you to help."

Tannin waved his hand in dismissal. "You're welcome. I'll do most anything to keep away bloodshed. Don't believe in guns myself. By the way, I'm surprised that you were able to find Hoffman home."

"Why's that?"

"I was over in Trent" — he gestured to the south — "to pick up a blade for my plow and saw Barth and Hoffman coming out of the assay office on my way back out of town. They seemed mighty pleased with themselves and I got the feeling that they were planning on staying around for a while. They headed into the Blue Bull Saloon and it looked like they were set on a celebration. Of course, that was a few days ago, but I am a bit surprised that Hoffman got back so soon — if him and Barth were doing the kind of celebration that they seemed intent on."

"Interesting," Hood said. "I wonder what took them there."

Tannin shrugged. "Ore samples, I suppose. Or checking on a land survey. The assay office doubles as the survey office in Trent. Fact is, the court is down there, too. Jericho ain't big enough to handle either one."

"Well, I'd better get going. I've got a bit of a ride ahead of me before sundown." Hood stood and shook hands with Tannin. "Should we figure on next Monday for stringing wire? We can make plans this Sunday after church."

"Sounds good to me," Tannin said.

Hood rode away, twisting in his saddle to

wave at Tannin before lifting Sheba into a lope. He was halfway back to Jericho before he suddenly remembered the tracks of the rider that he had followed into the niche of the red mesa. They had been deep and heavy as if the horse had been carrying a rider the size of Halsey Barth.

13.

Mother beamed as Hood walked into her restaurant early the next morning, Sam by his side and looking with interest at her. She came to Hood's table, carrying a thick mug hooked on one meaty finger, a pot of coffee in the other hand. She placed the coffee on the table and filled the cup.

"Haven't seen you in a couple of days," she said, eyeing him shrewdly. "Heard about what you been up to, though."

Hood blew across the surface of the coffee and sipped cautiously before answering. "I expect most folks have heard," he said wryly. "News travels fast in Jericho."

"Uh-huh," Mother said, sniffing in disapproval. "Bad news, that is. People hunger for the dirt on a person more than they do for the good that he does. You'll find that out more and more as time goes by. *If* you last in Jericho, that is."

"You don't think I'll last?" Hood asked.

He sipped again from the mug. Sam whined from his place beside Hood's chair.

Mother looked around, then lowered her voice. "I hear talk in here. A bunch of Box M riders were talking about what you did to Slade." She chuckled. "Wish I could have seen that. Slade's caused some problems around here, but you sure took the crow out of that rooster. The way I heard it, he packed up and left the country like a hound dog slinking off with his tail between his legs." She leaned a bit closer. "*But* the thing about hound dogs is that you have to be careful that they don't turn on you. You whip a dog enough, he'll turn around and make a meal out of you. If he can. And Slade's the type of person who'd do just that. Oh, he won't be coming at you front-on like that Rollie Rawlins will — and mark my words, you'll have to deal with him again — but Slade will come at you anyway he can when you least expect it. He'll have to. Right now, what happened to him will stay close to Jericho, but cowboys travel some and that story is too good not to be told here and there. A man can't live with that. You watch yourself."

"Thanks for the advice," Hood said pleasantly. "I'll keep your words in mind."

She beamed. "Now, how about some

breakfast? This wolf of yours is mumbling something about wanting to be fed and I think I've got just what he wants — some meat scraps I've been saving, figuring you'd be coming in here."

"He's not the only one hungry," Hood said. "I have some riding to do this morning and some work to do for church on Sunday. Looks like this is going to shape up as a busy day."

"Uh-huh," Mother said dryly. "I reckon I know where you're riding, too. Well, can't say that I approve, but can't say that I disapprove either. That young lady's been treated pretty shabby by folks around here. She could use any friend she can get. I hope that's all you're promising her. Mind, I don't care one way or the other, but if'n you ain't careful, folks will say you're fresh from Sodom or Gomorrah. That wouldn't do for a preacher. You be careful, you hear? Now, how about some eggs and steak? I've got some sourdough biscuits just fresh from the oven, too. And some honey butter that Jim Parks brought in. His bees make the best honey."

"I'll take it all," Hood said, mouth watering. "It's been a spell since I had anything like that."

"Coming right up," she said, slapping him

gently on the shoulder. "Now, you just set there a spell and enjoy your coffee. By the time you finish that one, I'll have your breakfast out. Yours, too," she said, looking down at Sam. He whined and his claws made scratching sounds on the wood floor. She laughed and walked into the back as Hood picked up his coffee, sipping.

The door opened and Charlie Daniels walked in. He saw Hood watching him, hesitated, then, lips pressed tightly together, came over to Hood's table, face flushed. He removed his hat and stood awkwardly, looking apprehensively at Sam.

"Something I can do for you?" Hood asked easily.

Daniels shuffled his feet and pulled at an earlobe.

"Thought I should come over and apologize," he mumbled.

"You did?" Hood took another sip of coffee.

"Well, I got to thinking about what we did up at the Bar S and, well, I don't think that's right." He grinned and rubbed his nose with the heel of his hand. "I think the whipping you gave me made me see things a little differently. I ain't been whipped much. Leastways, not since my pa kicked me around our spread up north. My pa's got big feet, too."

"All right," Hood said. "Apology accepted."

"Yeah. Well." He shuffled his feet, then straightened and looked at Hood. "Look. That ain't all. I quit the Box M. Right after Slade came back a-hootin' and a-hollerin', his feet all bloody from cactus and himself cut all over from mesquite. He got what he deserved. I didn't know he was fixing to ambush you out there. You gotta believe me on that. Shooting a man's something I didn't hire on to do. And shooting a man in the back or laying for him goes hard against my grain."

He cleared his throat. "I could use a job," he blurted. "And I don't have anything against working for a woman, like some folk do. I don't mind riding fence either, and you know cowboys don't like fence riding. I'll work for bed and keep until you all sell some stock and then take whatever you think is fair."

"Why are you doing this?" Hood asked, frowning.

Daniels shrugged. "I know the Bar S is up against a loaded deck. And I give it some thought about what my pa would've said if he learned the part I was playing in that. It ain't right. I think I knew that when we went up there to try and force Mary Riley off her place while you two were out gathering stock. I've done a lot of things I'm not proud of, but shoving a woman off her place ain't setting right with me. I don't think it was setting right when we went up there. But it was a job I was ordered to do. And" — he grinned and rubbed his nose again — "I reckon you and her just knocked some sense back into me that I'd misplaced along the way."

"I see," Hood said.

He sat back as Mother came bustling out of the kitchen with a platter in one hand for him and a bowl loaded with scraps for Sam. She gave Daniels a suspicious look as she placed the platter in front of Hood.

"I'll get you some more coffee," she said as she straightened and turned to face Daniels, her hands firm on her hips. Her jaw thrust out dangerously at him. "And what about you? You want something? I don't know if I'm gonna be serving more Box M riders around here after what they did up at that poor girl's place, so you'd better grab what you can while I'm studying on it."

"Yes, ma'am," Daniels said abashed. "I could use a cup of coffee and some breakfast."

"You could," she said, sniffing. She looked down at Hood. "That food to your liking, Reverend?"

"Looks good," Hood said, taking up his knife and fork. He looked back at Daniels. "You might as well sit. We can talk some more while we're eating."

"You certain?" Daniels said, a hopeful look leaping into his eyes.

"Sometimes a man has to learn something the hard way. That don't mean he isn't a good man; he just has to be shown the error of his ways. I've done some things that I'm not too proud of, too. Besides, the Good Book tells us that we should forgive and forget. Turn the other cheek — although I'm not much for doing that more than once," Hood said reflectively. "But I'm willing to give a man a second chance. Long as I think he's sincere about it. Sit down."

"Thanks," Daniels said eagerly, pulling out a stool and straddling it. He looked around uncertainly for a moment, then placed his hat on the floor. "I appreciate this."

"You'd better," Mother said warningly. "You cause any trouble and I'll dent your head with my frying pan. And it's a big 'un. Now, I'll just get you a cup of coffee and your breakfast."

She nodded at Hood and disappeared back into the kitchen. Hood cut a piece of steak and began to chew.

"I can't promise you a job," he said, looking at Daniels. "That'll be up to Miss Riley. But I'll put in a word for you with her. However," he said firmly, "you pull any stunts like you did the other night, and you'll think the whipping you got was a mild scolding after I get through with you. I'm a man of peace, but peacefulness can only be stretched so far."

"I'm with you," Daniels said. "I know I'm coming in on the short end of the stick, but all I'm asking is for a chance."

"You'll get it," Hood promised. He nodded as Mother came out of the kitchen with a cup of coffee and another platter. She plopped it down in front of Daniels, sniffed, gave Hood a warning look, then went back into the kitchen.

"Eat up," Hood said. "We'll ride on up to the Bar S after breakfast and have a little talk with Miss Riley. Then, we'll get some work done. I've got some folk coming in Monday to help string some wire up there between her land and the Box M and the Slash K. Some people don't think that fences make good neighbors, and I'm not certain they're not right. But in some cases,

172

fences can separate a person from possible trouble. At least," he reflected, "for a while anyway."

Mary listened suspiciously as Hood suggested that Daniels come to work for her. Daniels stood meekly at the side, furtively watching as Hood explained Daniels's seeming change of heart. At last, Mary grudgingly gave way and nodded curtly, saying, "All right. I'll give him a chance. On *your* say-so, Amos. But," she added, facing Daniels truculently, "you turn out to be a wolf in sheep's clothing and I'll put a Winchester .45-70 in you. Understand?"

"Yes, ma'am," Daniels said, looking gratefully at Hood. "I won't disappoint you."

"You can bunk in there," she said, nodding at the barn. "There's a room next to the tack room where the hired hand used to sleep. Until," she added acidly, "you Box M riders drove him off."

"Yes, ma'am. And I'm sorry about that, ma'am," he said, stumbling over his words.

"And for Christ's sake, stop calling me 'ma'am,' " she added irritably. "You can call me Miss Riley or Mary. Take your pick. Ma'am-ing me here and there is just going to make things confusing."

"Yes, ma'am, er, Miss Riley," Daniels said.

"I'll try to remember it."

"Well, put your things away and then come on up to the house. I've got some coffee on and we need to talk about what has to be done. Amos?"

"I'll take a cup, Mary," Hood said, looping Sheba's reins around a porch post. He looked at Sam. "You stay here, Sam."

The wolf whined, then turned around three times grudgingly before dropping onto a patch of grass beneath the cottonwood. Hood dusted off his pants with his hat as he mounted the steps and followed Mary into the house.

She turned from the stove with three cups and the coffeepot.

"You certain that he'll be all right?" she asked, staring past him out toward the barn. "He's one of those who tried to push me off this place."

"I think he'll be all right," Hood said, pouring coffee into the cup she placed before him. "But I will keep my eye on him. It'll be good having him here, though. He'll be able to take up the slack when I'm not around."

She looked swiftly at him. "You going somewhere?" she asked, concern in her voice.

He shook his head. "I have a church to

174

manage as well," he said gently. "You know that. I've neglected some of the parishioners this past week. I'll be in and out whenever I can. I promise you that. Sunday, though, is two days after tomorrow and I have to get ready for services. I'll be back out on Monday. I thought we'd lay a fence between the Slash K and the Box M. A fence will serve notice that Box M and Slash K cattle aren't welcome on your land and to your water. That might make things a little easier here — having a definite boundary between those two spreads."

"That might cause some problems," she said doubtfully.

He shook his head. "It might also save some problems. Tomorrow I thought I'd ride on over to Trent and get a copy of the official survey, and use Saturday for getting ready for church. That way, we might be able to begin on Monday."

"That's a lot of work for just the three of us," she said doubtfully.

"There'll be others," he said quietly. "I've arranged for a couple of homesteaders to come in and help. Besides, we have to get that fence up as Hoffman will be bringing some cattle over for trading. He agreed to trade some yearlings for your fat stock. That way, we won't have a drive to make this year and we'll have a fresh bloodline to introduce into your stock for the future."

Her face softened and her eyes grew misty at his words. "I . . . I don't know how to thank you, Amos," she said softly. "You've been very good to me."

"You can thank me by coming in to church again this Sunday," he said. "Daniels can stick behind and watch the place. It's time, Mary, for you to take your permanent place among the rest of the folk."

She looked crestfallen and shook her head. "I don't know —"

"None of us do," he said, interrupting her. He took her hands. "But it's time for you to show the others that you are not afraid of them. And you won't be alone; I'll be there."

She took a deep, ragged breath and laughed. "All right. But don't abandon me when I come in."

"I won't," he promised. He gave her hands a little squeeze before releasing them and picking up his coffee. "Now, I think it would be best if you had Daniels ride down in some of the canyons and make certain that we didn't miss some cattle when we made our sweep. Besides, that will give him a chance to familiarize himself with your holdings. I'm going to ride up north a spell and take a look up there."

"North?" she said, puzzled. "There's nothing up there but broken country."

He shrugged. "It's country that I haven't seen. And who knows? I might find a head or two up there."

14.

Hood rode down the trail to the beginning of the canyon, then took the trail north along the edge. He rode easily, watching his back trail for anyone who might be following, scanning the trail ahead for anyone who might be waiting.

He came to the narrow canyon that branched off from the trail back into the red mesa, and followed it carefully. The trail was littered with rocks of all sizes and shapes, with little vegetation other than tumbled and dried roots that had been washed down from rains over the mesa. Cautiously, he came around the rock that marked the opening into the small amphitheater that held little vegetation other than stunted manzanita and curl-leaf and desert apricot, and that only in sporadic clumps.

He dismounted and studied the trail in front of him. He saw no fresh tracks other than the old tracks that he had followed the first time into the rift and his own, sifted over by fine dust. He started forward, then backed away, frowning. His tracks. If someone had been in the canyon before he entered, they would have seen his tracks coming out.

A lizard lay on a rock in front of him, staring. Its lower lids crept up slowly, its sides panting in the heat reflecting from the sheer walls. Hood made a small gesture with his hand and the lizard scampered away, disappearing into a small hole at the base of the wall. Sweat trickled down Hood's spine and his knees began to cramp, but he ignored the discomfort and stayed still, studying the depression. Sheba tugged nervously at the reins, and he frowned.

Something bothered her; then he realized that he heard no birds singing. Although the canyon was a study in grim and forlorn country, the ancient ruins halfway up the wall on the other side of the canyon were proof enough that life had been there. No matter how many years ago, there still should have been birds, even if only cactus wrens and magpies. But nothing moved and nothing sang.

He gnawed his lip, considering. At last, he rose and took the Spencer from its sheath. He dropped Sheba's reins and told Sam to wait. Sam grumbled and sat, watching while Hood edged around the rock and slipped through the shadows into the depression. He kept close to the large rocks, moving on the balls of his feet, ready to drop at the first sign of trouble. But nothing appeared as he made his way across the floor of the depression to the other side.

The old trail led between two large boulders. Cautiously, he followed it. He emerged in a small saucer-shaped arena. Boulders stood like sentinels on the dried floor, reminding him of Dante's *Inferno,* which his father had made him read as part of his studies. An eerie quiet hung over the canyon and he felt death still lingering, tainting the land. He shivered and shook off the feeling, studying the arena.

On the other side facing him was the opening of an old mine. He straightened and walked to the mine opening. The wood was old and cracked, slivers peeling back from the old beams supporting the sides and roof. How old? he reflected. Certainly older than current memory, if the wood was any indication.

He glanced at his feet and saw a lantern just inside the entrance. He frowned and picked it up, shaking it. Hearing kerosene slosh, he leaned the Spencer against the wall of the mine and lit the lantern with a match he took from his shirt pocket. Then, picking up his Spencer, he moved carefully into the mine, holding the lantern high. A cold wisp seemed to blow over him, chilling him, and an uneasiness settled on him as if ancient spirits were trying to warn him. He looked uneasily at the roof of the mine and the sides. The timbers showed dry rot and appeared to bow in the center, as if the roof was pushing them away from itself. He swallowed and continued on, nerves stretched taut.

He didn't have far to go before light reflected off the walls back to him. Silver. Veins of silver. He wasn't an assayer, but he knew instinctively that the find was rich in ore. And it was on Bar S land, as near as he could tell.

He broke off some chunks of rock and slipped them into his pocket before hastily leaving the mine. He blew the lantern out and replaced it, then moved to the shady side and squatted, removing his hat and wiping his forehead with the sleeve of his shirt. Sweat trickled down his spine and he took a deep breath, steadying his nerves.

This is an old Indian mine, he thought, studying the opening. *But why did they leave*

it after only digging so far? Something hap-
pened, but what? Sickness? Disease? A war
with other tribes?

He shook his head and rose, holding the
Spencer in front of him. He sensed a dor-
mant evil around him and shivered.

He left rapidly, crossing the amphitheater
back to where Sheba and Sam waited. Sam
whined nervously as Hood reappeared and
gathered Sheba's reins. He rubbed his head
against Hood's leg.

"I know, boy," Hood said, bending to give
Sam a quick pat. "I'm just as anxious to
leave as you."

Hood mounted and turned Sheba, riding
back through the narrow opening. He drew
a deep breath when they emerged from the
rift, and let it out slowly. Something was
back there, something evil. He knew it just
as he knew that the ore in his pocket would
test high-grade.

He slipped the Spencer into its sheath and
turned Sheba's head south.

Yes, he knew the ore was valuable, but he
still needed to get it assayed. He might as
well kill two birds with one stone. He
needed to pick up a copy of the land survey
for the Bar S, and that was at the assay office in Trent.

He settled back into the saddle and let

Sheba pick her own pace down the road leading south.

Early afternoon came hot and heavy as Hood rode into Trent. He pulled up at the assay office, draped Sheba's reins over the hitching rail, mounted the steps to the boardwalk, and entered the office. A tiny bell tinkled above the door, and a small, balding man neatly dressed in a white shirt and string tie came from the back and greeted Hood pleasantly.

"Yes, sir. Is there something I can do for you?" he asked.

Hood removed his hat and placed it on the counter separating them. A pair of balance scales stood to his left; a large map of the area had been pinned on the wall to his right.

"Yes," he said. "I'm planning on fencing some land and I'd like a copy of the survey report. I don't want to get on someone else's property," he added.

"Of course," the assayer said. "Where is your land?"

"The Bar S. Up around Jericho," Hood answered. "It isn't my land, but I'm helping the owner."

The assayer frowned "Bar S? That's been pretty popular lately. Yours is the third survey request I've had in the past two weeks."

Hood raised an eyebrow. "The third?"

"Yes, sir," the assayer said, turning to pull a large ledger down from a bookcase behind him and placing it on the counter between Hood and himself. "Seems a lot of folk are interested in that spread. Ah, here we are." He pointed to an entry and took a sheet of paper and a pencil from beneath the counter and began making notations. "It's an easy survey. The marks are pretty stable and the lines are straight. Of course, most of the red mesa is Bar S property as well. Here you are."

He closed the ledger and handed the sheet of paper to Hood.

"I hope this helps you," the assayer said pleasantly.

"What do I owe you?" Hood asked.

"A dollar should do it," the assayer said.

Hood handed him a dollar, hesitated, then took a sample of the ore from his pocket. He placed it on the counter between them.

"What can you tell me about this?" he asked.

The assayer picked it up and took a large magnifying glass from the desk behind him. He gave it a cursory glance, then shook his head.

"I really don't have to assay it," he said. "This looks identical to a piece I did last week. Chloragyrate. Heavy silver-bearing ore." He gave Hood an appraising look. "I'd say that this came from the same place as the other I did."

"It probably did," Hood said. "Who brought the other sample in?"

The assayer shook his head. "Sorry. But I can't tell you that. Assay reports are private."

Hood nodded and took the sample from the assayer's hand. "That's all right. I have a pretty good notion of who it was. I owe you anything more?"

"No, sir. I didn't run a test for you so there's no charge. If you want me to, I could. But I'm pretty certain that the result would be the same as the last one. Might as well save your money."

"Thanks," Hood said, and picked up his hat. He turned to leave, then stopped and looked back at the assayer.

"This assay you did last week, did the person you gave it to file a claim?"

"No, they didn't," the assayer said, frowning. "That's what's so strange. Usually with a sample showing high-grade, you'd think that would be the first thing they did."

Hood nodded and left, closing the door

quietly behind him. He stood for a moment on the boardwalk, deep in thought, then stepped down off the porch and mounted Sheba.

"It looks like we've got ourselves an answer to at least one of the questions," he said softly, turning Sheba's head back the way they had come. "And I can figure the answer to the other is much simpler."

He nudged Sheba with his heels and loped out of Trent, turning back toward Jericho.

15.

The sun was just beginning to touch the rim of the red mesa when Hood rode into Jericho. The streets were free of traffic, but some horses were tied to the rail in front of The Cattleman's. Halsey Barth stood outside the saloon, smoking a cigar. On impulse, Hood rode over and halted in front of him.

"Evening, Parson," Barth said conversationally. He waved his cigar in greeting. "Looks like you've been busy doing the Lord's work."

Hood relaxed, folding his hands on the pommel of his saddle. "He doesn't rest, and that means that His servants have to be busy as well."

"A busy taskmaster," Barth said, a smile turning up on his lips.

"You get out much?" Hood said.

"Riding, you mean?" Barth shook his head, laughing. "No, I gave that up years ago when I decided that it was easier sitting in a chair than in the saddle. And far more profitable. At least," he amended, "I don't ride as much these days. One has to always collect debts, you know."

"And maybe a little sightseeing?" Hood said.

Barth's eyes narrowed fractionally. "There isn't much to see around Jericho."

Hood waved at the mesa. "Well, there's several places back in there where a man can contemplate the wonders of God. Ever go looking?"

Barth considered Hood for a long moment while he took a long puff on his cigar. Slowly, he let smoke trickle from his lips before answering.

"I wouldn't recommend that," he said at last, his words carrying a hint of warning. "Some folks back in the reaches and the brakes take a dim view of strangers coming into their land. I know of a couple of riders who went into the back country and never returned. Nobody knows what happened to them."

He shrugged "I never was that curious to want to ride back in there. Besides" — he grinned bleakly — "I don't like sweat and dust."

"Sounds like you're not interested in

much around Jericho," Hood said easily, his eyes steady upon the gambler.

"Oh, I wouldn't say that," Barth answered. "There are a lot of things around that interest me. All have a price tag on them."

Hood shook his head "There are things on this earth that are more important than wealth."

"And I imagine you could name quite a few," Barth said, blowing a long stream of smoke in Hood's direction. "But I'm a man of limited imagination and simple wants."

"Are you?" Hood asked quietly.

Barth met his stare levelly. "Yes. But what I want, I usually get. One way or the other."

"Sounds dangerous despite what you say."

Barth shrugged and tossed the remains of his cigar into the street in front of Sheba. He gave Hood a faint smile. "The land is full of blood, Parson."

"Yes," Hood said. "And the city full of perverseness. You've read Ezekiel, I see."

"I've read many things, Parson. Many things. And I've seen many things as well." He touched the brim of his hat. "And now, I must get back to work. The devil waits for idle hands."

"And he quotes Scripture," Hood said, touching his own hat brim.

Barth's eyes narrowed and for a moment,

Hood thought he could see the beginning of fires flickering. Then, the gambler drew the veil back over his eyes and laughed gently as he turned and made his way through the swinging doors back into the saloon.

Hood sat for a minute, musing over the brief conversation he'd had with Barth, then turned Sheba and rode down to the blacksmith's shop and stable. He glanced down at Sam.

"If I didn't miss my guess, boy, I'd swear that we'd just been warned."

Sam growled.

"Yes," Hood continued. "I'd say he needs watching. Very carefully. But," he reflected, turning to watch the sun sink bloodred over the mesa, "he has given me an idea for Sunday's sermon."

He smiled grimly in the gathering twilight.

The door of the church had been left open and the windows had been pushed up as far as they would go to encourage whatever breeze might come up to sweep through and cool the people who sat sweating in the pews. But no breeze came and the air seemed to settle over everyone like a stifling cocoon. Children moved restlessly and complained softly of being hot. Mothers shushed them with index fingers pressed against lips while they patted the perspiration from their own foreheads and necks with tiny handkerchiefs. Men waited, suffering stoically in their Sunday best.

Hood eyed the small congregation waiting expectantly for his sermon. His eyes fell on Tannin and a slight smile lifted the corners of the farmer's mouth, and Hood gave him a tiny smile back as he took a deep breath and straightened behind the pulpit.

"Many people think that the Bible should be taken as it stands. Each word is sacred and should be chiseled into the granite walls of our lives. Perhaps it is. But what most folks fail to realize is that those words are there to make folks think about themselves and the world around them."

He waved his hand expansively, indicating not only the congregation but what lay beyond the walls of the church as well.

"You see, some folks seem to think that their own narrow view of the world is what most other folks should cotton to and follow if they want to remain Christian. They build their own walls around themselves and extend those walls to include only those who believe like they do, walk like they do, behave like they do. And that is wrong."

A nervous shuffling of feet followed his

words. Someone cleared his throat. Hood shook his head.

"Think for a minute on the disciples that Jesus chose to follow Him. Now, they could've said no when He told them to give up their lives and go with Him, but they chose to do that on their own. And what a mixture they turned out to be. Folks from every walk of life. Why, some of them were fishermen, some tax collectors, some liked to drink and brawl on Friday nights, others were servants of rich people. And some even doubted what Jesus said now and then. Each of them, however, took what they needed for themselves from Jesus to make their lives richer and fuller.

"That is the nature of man. Now, I don't mean to point a finger at anyone here, but I ask you to think about how you have been behaving toward other people who have been forced to live in a way that you may disagree about. Some of you like to till the ground. Others want to work with animals. Does that make one of you worth more than the other? Most of you women come from good homes, and although you haven't enjoyed riches and been pampered like you might want, you have never gone hungry or been forced to do something you didn't want to do in order to live. Mary Magdalene and others in the Bible had to do things that they didn't want to do. Some of them did what they had to do in order to help their people. Yet, when others find themselves in difficulties here in Jericho, those folks who would consider themselves to be good people throw up walls to keep the unfortunate from tainting them."

He took a deep breath and let his eyes pass over the faces of all in the church as he said, "It's time to take down those walls, my friends. It's time to remember the Golden Rule . . ."

As he spoke, quietly but firmly, he watched the faces change from the grim expressions that had fallen across them at the beginning of his sermon to consternation and guilt. Some, Hood knew, would wonder what he was talking about as their own narrow worlds had walls so thick around them that a hundred trumpets wouldn't crack the walls. He glanced over to where Mrs. Haddorn sat on the piano bench, hands folded primly in her lap, lips pressed tightly together in disapproval of his words. She looked as if someone had given her a heavy dose of alumroot.

He brought his sermon to a close, and Mrs. Haddorn turned back to the piano and played "The Old Rugged Cross" with a heavy hand as the congregation rose and lifted their voices in song.

Afterward, some of the congregation slipped out the door without bothering to shake his hand. Tannin gave him a grin and shook his head.

"I have to give it to you," he said. "You don't mince words when you get a thought."

"It looks like it didn't set well with some," Hood said, nodding at the families who refused to meet his eyes.

"You didn't expect it to, did you?" Tannin said, following Hood's gaze. "But they'll forgive you eventually. Won't forget, mind you, but they'll convince themselves that you didn't mean them and then they'll come back. A lot of folk have long memories, but they don't like to think of themselves as anything other than decent God-fearing people who will be among the chosen when Gabriel blows his trumpet on Judgment Day."

Hood laughed and shook his head. "You're a good man, Ezra. I wish we had more of you around."

Tannin looked embarrassed as he tugged at an earlobe. "Well, I wouldn't say that I'm not much different than most people. Of course, I don't have the ear of a lot of people like some do," he said, watching

Mrs. Haddorn walk past, head held high in disapproval. "But I do believe that the Lord didn't spend most of His time rooting around in rich men's pens. He went down where there were people who needed His help."

Hood laughed and said, "Maybe you ought to start giving the Sunday sermon."

"I've spoken a bit here and there when we haven't had a preacher. Someone's gotta say a few words over a person who's gone to the other side. And I've always believed that a man can't wait until someone does something for him before he helps others out. Which brings me to tomorrow," he added, settling his hat back on his head. "You still want me and the boys out at the Bar S?"

Hood nodded. "If you wouldn't mind. *And* if it wouldn't cause you any problems. I'll have the wire ready at the store if you want to pick it up on your way through."

"No problem. I'll bring the boys to help. Parks said he'd come along as well," Tannin said. He nodded to where his wife stood off to the side, talking with a small group of women. "And Martha and Beth said they'd bring food out so we wouldn't lose any time." He frowned. "I don't know about others, but we'll see."

"That will make seven of us for sure," Hood said. "Charlie Daniels quit the Box M and signed on with the Bar S."

Tannin's eyes narrowed. "You certain? He's not just playing possum, waiting for the right time to do harm?"

"I don't think so," Hood said. "We had a few words the other day."

"Yeah, I heard about your words," Tannin said dryly. "What you did with Slade made the rounds right quick. That didn't set well either with some people." He chuckled. "But I sure liked hearing that gunnie was taken down a peg. He's been walking tall around people with that gun of his ever since McQuade took him on. But you watch yourself," he continued. "Men like him have only their reputation to give them sand around other people. You take that away from them and they become like a cornered wolf." He glanced down to where Sam sat patiently by Hood's heels. "You can expect them to come back at you any way they can to satisfy themselves that they are as tough as they think."

Hood nodded. "I don't think he'd gain much of his reputation back if he shot me. He might come after me, but he'll need to build up his reputation some first. But I'll keep watch," he promised. "Sometimes people will fool you and do the opposite of what you expect."

Tannin nodded. "Well, I'd better collect Martha and the boys. It may be the Lord's day, but stock don't wait to be fed and watered and chores have to be done. I'll see you tomorrow out at the Bar S."

Hood shook his hand and waved at the Parks family as they drove by.

"Well, Sam," he said softly. "I hope that some others think about what I said."

Sam rose and shook himself and set out in front of Hood, walking slowly toward Mother's.

16.

False dawn was just giving light when Hood rose the next morning, dressed, and made his way down to the stable to collect Sheba. Sam grumbled when they walked passed Mother's, and looked longingly at Hood.

"You're on your own today, boy," Hood said. "It's shaping up as a busy day and we have to get started early if we plan on finishing before sundown. But maybe Mary will have something for you."

He saddled Sheba and led her out of the stable and mounted. He glanced over at The Cattleman's and noticed lights still on. He shook his head as he nudged Sheba's sides with his heels.

"Some folk just don't give up on a good time," he muttered.

Sheba began to lope, tugging at the reins, wanting to run. He laughed and relaxed the reins, feeling the mare's muscles begin to bunch as she lengthened her stride until she was running easily.

Hood sat back in the saddle, moving with Sheba's gait, enjoying the early morning as he knew the heat of the day would soon be upon them. To his right, he saw a couple of Box M riders moving a small herd of cattle toward the Bar S and frowned. He reached and loosened the Spencer in its sheath and turned off the road, heading toward the riders. They saw him coming and spread apart, watching his approach cautiously. He recognized Billy Richards, but the dark-haired man with him was a stranger. Richards wore a bandage wrapped around his head under his hat.

"Morning," he said easily, reining in. "You boys are up early."

"We could say the same about you," Richards said curtly.

"No sense in letting the day slip past," Hood replied. He nodded toward the cattle. "You boys moving cattle, I see."

"Anything wrong in that?" the dark-haired one challenged.

"No, as long as you stay on Box M range," Hood said, still smiling. "But you are headed toward Bar S land."

"Uh-huh. Well, reckon that don't matter much, seeing as how this here's open range," the dark-haired one said.

199

Richards moved uneasily, his eyes shifting warily from Hood to Sam and back again.

"Maybe we'd better move the cattle back, Wilson," he said cautiously.

The dark-haired one looked at him. "You heard what McQuade said just the same as I did."

"McQuade isn't here," Hood replied quietly. "And this isn't open range. The land survey shows that the Box M land is a full section away from the creek. You're almost on it now, I'd say."

"I don't know about no land survey," Wilson said harshly.

"You do now," Hood answered. "Move the cattle back away from the Bar S boundary. You won't have to worry about it after a couple of days. Until then, keep the cattle off Bar S land."

Wilson glanced at Richards, frowning. "Why a couple of days?"

"We should have the fence up by then," Hood said, folding his hands and resting them on the pommel of his saddle. "Then, you can let Box M cattle graze where they want."

"What? You're stringing wire? Nobody 'cept a farmer strings wire!" Wilson said, disbelieving.

"Times change and people have to change

with them or become history," Hood said. He touched the brim of his hat. "You have a nice day, now, hear? And keep those cattle off Bar S land."

He reined Sheba around and left, cutting across toward the road leading up to the Bar S ranch house. He held the reins in his left hand, keeping his right close to the stock of the Spencer as he rode, glancing over his shoulder at the cowboys and the cattle until he was out of range. By then, they had turned the cattle and pushed them away from the boundary.

"I reckon it's good that we are stringing that wire now," Hood muttered to himself. "Otherwise, we'd have big trouble from Mc-Quade."

He nudged Sheba into a quicker gait and rode up the canyon to the ranch house. Mary was waiting on the porch and Daniels was hurrying from the barn as Hood reined in and stepped down from the saddle.

"You seem to be in a bit of a hurry this morning," Mary said by way of greeting.

"I thought you were coming in for church yesterday," Hood said.

Mary and Daniels exchanged quick glances and looked away, Mary's cheeks showing the first faint red of a blush. Daniels cleared his throat and stared down at the toes of his boots, then off in the distance.

"I say something?" Hood asked.

"No," Mary said hurriedly. "We just, well, we were busy," she added defensively. "We were riding up in the back reaches, looking for cattle."

"And Mary's horse spooked at something and threw her and I thought I might have to take her into Trent for the doctor, but she wouldn't let me and . . . she's all right now," Daniels said.

"Are you sure?" Hood asked, looking up at her.

She glanced at Daniels and nodded. "Would you like some coffee?"

"Coffee would be good," Hood said, tying Sheba's reins to a porch post.

She nodded and hurried into the house. Daniels hunched his shoulders and shoved his hands into the back pockets of his pants.

"You get some others to help us with stringing wire?" he asked.

Hood nodded. "Tannin said he and his boys would stop by and pick up the wire on their way through town. Parks is coming. Maybe some others. But there should be enough to get the job done. Might be a good idea if we met them down on the flats so they won't have to bring that wagon up

202

the canyon."

"Good idea," Daniels said, moving toward the corral. "I'll saddle up and ride on down. You coming along?"

"After my coffee," Hood said. A grin tugged at the corners of his lips as he watched the cowboy hurry off. Something had happened — he was certain of it. And it was something good. At least, he reflected, he hoped it was something good, and not just a passing fancy that came to a man and a woman out of loneliness and isolation. Mary was vulnerable — he was very aware of that — as she had been forced to live away from other people for quite a spell. And it didn't matter how much she protested that she didn't care for the company of others; being alone too long had a way of settling wrongly with a person who had once been used to the company of others. Even if it was company that she didn't enjoy or necessarily want. There was something about people that drew them together for one reason or another.

Mary came out onto the porch, carrying a cup of coffee. She glanced around.

"Where's Charlie?" she asked.

Mary and Charlie now, Hood thought as he took the cup from her and sipped. Whatever happened had happened quickly.

"Saddling up," Hood said. "One of us needs to ride on down and meet with Tannin so he doesn't have to bring the wagon up the canyon and then back down. Makes sense. I told Daniels that I'd be down in a bit."

She nodded and took a sip of coffee. She sighed, then looked at Hood as if she'd forgotten he was there for a minute.

"Sorry. Woolgathering, I guess," she said. "You find anything on your ride north?"

Hood frowned. "Yes, I did. At least, I think I know one of the reasons why someone is after your place. But who, I don't know."

"I thought it was the water," she said.

"Probably so for some. But I have a suspicion that there's someone else in the game as well," he said. He fished the piece of ore from his pocket and handed it to her. "You have silver on your property. The assayer tells me that this is high-grade and it's exactly like a piece that someone brought in. He wouldn't give me his name, but I have a hunch I know who it is."

"Who?" she asked sharply.

He shook his head. "Not until I'm certain. I don't want to be blackening someone's name on speculation. But it appears as if you're a richer woman than you thought."

She weighed the sample in her hand

thoughtfully, then shook her head. "Right now, I'm more worried about getting this ranch up and running again."

"The silver will help," Hood said gently.

She laughed and said, "I suppose it will. But now isn't the time for worry about that. You can show me where you got this later."

"All right," Hood said. He finished the coffee and handed her the cup. "Right now, I'd better get on down there."

"I'd better saddle up as well," she said.

He started to object, but she spoke over his words.

"We'll be within sight of the canyon most of the time we're stringing fence," she said. "And if I'm down there, that'll give us another pair of hands. There's only one way into this canyon and that's from down there."

He shrugged, recognizing the finality of her words, and gave her a rueful grin. "I guess I'm just not used to a woman competing with a man," he said.

"I'm not competing!" she said hotly, then noticed his smile and flushed deeply.

"This is my ranch," she said. "I need to work it as much as anyone else works their own place. A ranch doesn't run itself."

"Nothing ever does," Hood said, finishing his coffee and flinging the dregs out of the cup with a practiced twist of his wrist. "But then again, maybe it would be good if you stood watch while we worked. There's a stand of boulders down at the mouth of the canyon that would give you a nice view of the country. You'd be able to warn us if McQuade or the Rawlinses and their men decide to come and pay us a little visit."

She gave him a swift look. "Are you expecting trouble?"

He shrugged. "Always expect trouble and you're never surprised when it arrives. That doesn't mean I want it; I just want to be ready when it comes. And, yes, I do think that it will come. Putting a fence up will keep most of it away, but there will be a few hotheads that are bothered by the idea of a fence. Especially one that keeps them away from water."

"That is my water," she said defensively. Then, her shoulders sagged. "You know, Amos," she said softly, "if they would just . . . accept me as one of them, I'd let them have all the water they need. I don't mean to be hard, but there isn't any give to McQuade or the Rawlinses. They want everything." Her lips twisted bitterly. "And me along with it, I think. They can't get over what I was once, I guess."

"Stop that," Hood said gently. He took

his hat off, smoothed his hair, and resettled the hat. "There's no reason to flog yourself with what used to be. No one should live in the past, and as soon as the past is gone, everything should be seen as new. You can't let the past decide your future for you. No one should."

"It must be nice to be so certain about things," she said.

Am I? Hood thought. *Or am I just speaking about things I wish were true for me as well? We both have a lot of baggage, and I'm certainly free with advice for others that I have a hard time following myself. I guess Matthew was right. A prophet has no honor in his own country.*

Aloud, he said, "It's easy to tell others how they should live. In fact, sometimes I think that is the mission of a preacher, don't you?"

She looked at him for a long moment, then broke out in a peal of laughter. "I guess you're right. At least, you've certainly been free with advice since I've known you. And that hasn't been that long."

"Time passes quickly when good news is around," Hood said. "Bad news makes time crawl like an ant through a pool of honey. Seriously, Mary, we really should have someone keeping an eye on things while we're working. A man can't do two things at once and give proper order to both. Although it may look as if I'm trying to push you off to the side, I think it would be prudent to have you up on those rocks where you can keep a sharp eye on everything. Common sense tells me that."

She nodded, the smile still clinging to her lips. "All right, Amos. I agree. I'll go up on the rocks and watch while the rest of you slave in the heat."

"And take along your Winchester," Hood said. "A shot will warn us quicker than you coming down and riding out to where we'll be."

Daniels and Tannin were standing by Tannin's wagon when Hood rode down from the canyon to join them. Tannin smiled and gestured at the wagon bed.

"Brought along the wire as I said I would," he said. "And some tools and a digger." He pointed at Matthew and Mark alternating on digging holes. "You didn't say anything about posts, so I picked some up as well. Told Peterson to put it on my bill and figured you could take care of it when you go into town."

Hood grinned sheepishly. "Yes, well, I guess I did forget about posts," he confessed.

Tannin and Daniels laughed.

"Well, it's good to see that you are human after all," Tannin said. "Parks said he'd be by in a little bit. He had to finish collecting honey before he came."

Hood nodded. "By that time, maybe we can have enough holes dug and posts placed that we can begin stringing." He took the survey paper from his pocket and spread it for the others to see, tracing the Bar S boundary with his forefinger.

"Actually, this is pretty simple here between the Bar S and Box M. We can draw a sightline from the road here directly to the wash and then come over to the north edge of the mesa. From what I can tell here, most of red mesa is on Mary's land north and south."

Tannin gave a low whistle. "Bigger than I expected," he admitted. "That gives her almost sole control of the creek. No wonder the Rawlinses and McQuade are trying to get her out so they can lay claim to the land. Question is, why isn't Hoffman going along with them?"

"He has a couple of tanks on his ranch," Daniels said. "Not much, but enough to keep a modest herd going even through drought — as long as he keeps moving them in shifts so they don't crowd the water. That doesn't mean that he wouldn't like to have Bar S land, but it gives him a little leeway that the Rawlinses and McQuade don't have." He gave a short laugh. "Ol' Mc-Quade and the Rawlinses have been kicking themselves for not proving up on the land when they had a chance. But when Mc-Quade came in, money was a bit tight, I reckon, and he thought it would be better to take sections away from the mesa so he'd have flat land. As for the Rawlinses, well, they like the brakes to the south. Used to it, I hear, from the time they spent with the Hash Knife outfit."

"More hiding places, you mean," Tannin said dryly.

"That, too," Daniels said.

"I figure we can get this fence up in three days if we work together," Hood said. "I'd like to have it ready when Hoffman comes up to trade for Bar S fatted stock. And I'd like to get as much fence up between the Bar S and Box M as possible today. I have a hunch McQuade will be along shortly with some of his riders to put a stop to fencing him off from the water."

Tannin and Daniels gave him a puzzled look, and Hood explained the encounter he'd had earlier on his way out from town.

"Uh-huh, I expect you're right," Tannin

said grimly when Hood finished. "One thing you can always count on from McQuade and that's flying off the handle when told he can't do what he wants. He's the most contrary man I've ever known."

"I agree," Daniels said, removing his hat and running his hand over his hair. He snugged the hat back down, low over his eyebrows. "Fact is, you all don't know the half of it. You should have seen him when Slade got back from his midnight run." He grinned at Hood. "Slade tried to come in the back way, but there's only one door to the bunkhouse and that faces the main house. McQuade just happened to be holding court on the porch with some of the boys and a bottle of Who-flung-John when Slade slunk around the corner of the barn." He shook his head. "McQuade got so mad he came barreling down off that porch with a quirt and started whipping Slade with it. Slade pushed him away, and that was enough for McQuade to order him off the place within the hour. Never even gave him a share of his month's wages. Told him he didn't pay fools and Slade could go to hell in a handbasket before he'd give him another penny."

"I guess he left the country after that," Tannin said.

Daniels shook his head. "I thought that, too. But the other day when I was up in the brakes, looking for cattle, I thought I saw him riding over toward the Rawlinses' place. He might have found a home there. Even though he'd have to put up with some hoo-rawing from some of the boys, it wouldn't be much. For all of what you did to him, Reverend, Slade is pretty handy with a gun. He killed a couple of men down in Nogales before coming up here. Heard tell he wanted to get on with Chisum, but that old brindle wouldn't take him on. Said he had enough guns running around, and I reckon he has. Panhandle Smith rides for the Jingle-Bob brand, you know."

"No, I hadn't heard," Hood said. "I don't know much about him, but I understand that Smith is pretty good with his iron."

"Good enough that he doesn't have to advertise," Daniels said seriously. "There's no flash to him at all."

Hood nodded thoughtfully. "A man to know about." He clapped his hands together. "Well, we'd better get started or prairie dogs will be taking up residence in those holes your boys are digging."

Tannin laughed and took a pair of heavy leather gloves from under the wagon seat. "Guess you're right. After we get ten posts set, I'll lay wire down and you and Charlie can begin stapling."

"Sounds all right with me," Daniels said. "But don't lay more than ten posts at a time. We gotta stretch it."

"Teach your grandmother to suck eggs," Tannin said, grinning. "I've fenced more than my share over the years."

"Never too soon to be certain the other fellow knows what he's doing," Daniels said, shrugging. "Besides, I figure you're more used to walking behind a pair of mules than stringing wire. Might have forgotten the basics."

Tannin laughed and pulled a post from the wagon bed, shouldering it easily as he walked to the first hole and dropped it in.

By late afternoon, the wind, hot as a furnace, had come up and was blowing hard, as if trying to take their souls with its breath. Sand and grit came along with the wind, like a fine curtain with sunlight coming through it hard like an ax driven down. Mary had long given up her post on top of the rocks and gone up to the ranch house with Martha and Beth to help with the food for the men and boys working down on the flat. With the wind coming up as strong as it was, there was no need for her to be watching; no one could see beyond fifty feet or so in the blowing dust and no rider would be out.

Sweat poured down, filling Hood's eyes with salty pools. He gritted his teeth and pulled hard on the last strand of wire until it thrummed like a banjo string. Tannin quickly hammered home a pair of staples, anchoring it to the cedar post, and stepped back.

"Reckon that'll do for the east boundary," Tannin said tiredly, but there was a note of satisfaction to his words that Hood felt also.

Hood released the wire cautiously and straightened, pressing his knuckles against the small of his back. The wind lifted his collar against the back of his neck. He took a handkerchief from a back pocket of his pants and wiped the sweat from his eyes, then mopped his face and neck, sighing.

"Just in time," he said. "This wind feels like it's meaning to stay around awhile."

"A sirocco," Daniels said, coming up to them. "One of these starts to blow and a man might as well hang it up, less'n he wants to be blown down to Durango."

He looked at Tannin and a smile broke the sandy mask of his face. "Reckon your wife is up at the house along with Mrs. Parks and Mary. Maybe it'd be a good idea to join them and wait for this to blow over. You, too," he added as Parks joined them, stripping off his thick leather gloves.

Parks shook his head regretfully. "Tempting," he said, "but my stock won't feed and water themselves. I'm gonna have to get back home. It'll be dark by the time I get there as it is." He looked at Tannin. "But if'n you want to stick around, Ezra, I can pull into your place and do your chores on the way past. No sense in both of us gettin' scoured by the sand. You can bring the wife and kids back to your place, and I'll come up in the morning and collect 'em if you make it back to your place. If not, then I'll figure you all are going to stay and fence some more and come on out."

Tannin hesitated for a minute, then grinned and nodded. "I think my boys would appreciate that, given they'll be able to ride back with your girls. Matthew's been mooning over your Jane for a couple of months now."

Parks laughed and shook an admonishing finger at Tannin. "All well and good. But you keep an eye on them two. I don't want your boy sneaking off to the haymow with my girl. They have a deal of courting ahead of them before they get to that point."

"Mary and I'll keep an eye on them for

you," Daniels offered.

"You're the one I should trust," Parks said to Hood. He jerked a thumb at Tannin. "This old scudder will probably turn a blind eye toward them."

"I'll watch them." Tannin laughed. "And I think Beth and Martha will have their eyes upon them as well. You coming up to the house for a bite before you take off?"

Parks shook his head. "No, I think I'll just save the trip and head on back south. You tell Beth what I'm about. She won't mind. She's been wanting to natter with Martha for a while now and I reckon Mary could use the company. *Women* company, that is," he emphasized.

"I appreciate your help today, Jim," Hood said, stretching out his hand. "I don't think we'd have gotten this far if it hadn't been for you. And it sure was nice for Beth to come along with your girls to help out. You're a lucky man. *Both* of you are," he said, nodding at Tannin. "It's been a while since I tasted cooking like that."

They laughed, and Tannin rubbed his face with his large calloused hand. He winked at Parks.

"Well, a lot of women around here can cook as well," he said poker-faced to Hood. "Matter of fact, I'll bet that Missus Haddorn would be willing to take up with you, if you feel the need for home cookin'."

Hood shook his head ruefully while the other two laughed. "I don't think I could ever get that hungry," he said. "Sorry, I know that's a terrible thing for a preacher to say —"

"The truth is always best," Parks offered. "And believe me, there's not a man in the valley who don't feel the same way. I can't think of one who hasn't come under the lash of her tongue at least once in the past — unless it's one of the stray cowboys who haven't been here long enough."

"She's got a tongue like a rattlesnake," Tannin agreed solemnly. "And she don't rattle before she strikes. But there is some good in her."

"If you scratch deep enough," Parks said. He slapped his hands together. "Well, reckon I'd better get going if I'm going to do chores at your place as well as mine. You two gonna work again in the morning?"

Hood nodded. "If this lets up by then. We need to be able to keep a sight bearing so we don't stray over onto Box M land. That would set off a few fireworks, I think."

"Without a doubt," Parks said, turning. He climbed into his wagon and picked up the reins. He spat as a quick gust of wind blew sand in his mouth. "I'll see you in the morning then. If this wind don't bury me in the meantime."

"Be careful," Tannin called as Parks slapped the reins against his horses' backs, turning the wagon around.

Parks's reply was lost in the wind. Tannin glanced at Hood and motioned toward his boys, squatting out of the wind next to his wagon.

"I suppose we might as well get up there," he said loudly against the wind. "It might be a bit easier in the canyon, too."

"Let's hope so," Hood said, untying Sheba's reins from a ring on the tail of the wagon. He pulled himself up into the saddle. "I hope those women have supper ready."

"I hope they've got at least coffee on," Tannin said, spitting as he climbed into the wagon. The boys climbed into the back and lay down, shielding themselves behind the sideboards. "Anything to cut this dust."

"If not, I think I can scare up a taste or two," Daniels said, riding up beside them. "I brought a bottle of Old Williams with me. For medicinal purposes, you understand," he added, glancing at Hood.

"Take a little wine for your stomach's sake," Hood said. "As long as it doesn't get

218

habit-forming. The devil can grab a man by the throat as quick as he can by his suspenders. Fact is, I wouldn't say no to a little sip myself after today's work."

"Then, let's travel," Daniels said, touching his heels to his horse.

17.

The wind blew itself out in the night and the next morning came up bright blue and sunny. Hood rolled out of his blankets and groaned when stiff muscles protested as he rose. He sighed and went outside the barn to the pump and washed his face, pushing his hair back with his hands. He looked down sourly at his grimy clothes and grimaced. He should have packed a change in his saddlebags, but he hadn't known that the wind was going to come up and spoil his plans to return to town.

"I imagine that some tongues are certainly going to be torching me after this," he said to Sam when the wolf appeared beside him. He scratched Sam between the ears. "But there's nothing to do but ignore it. I don't think I want to do anything else but ignore it anyway."

"Talking to yourself?" Tannin asked as he and Daniels emerged from the barn behind

Hood. Tannin yawned and scratched himself and motioned to Hood to stand away from the pump.

"Have a good sleep?" Hood asked.

Tannin shook his head. "Good enough, though I've slept better. Hay ain't a mattress."

Daniels laughed. "Well, you could have stayed up in the house with your wife."

Tannin grimaced. "Not smelling like this. 'Sides, there wasn't enough room, given Parks's wife and kids. And," he added, grinning as Matthew staggered out of the barn, "I had to keep an eye on certain young men who are looking to sow oats out of season."

"Aw, Pa!" Matthew protested, his face flushing beet-red. "You know me!"

"Uh-huh," Tannin said. "And I know what I was like at your age, too, and blame me if I'm going to let you go by way of *that* road!"

The men laughed as Matthew splashed water onto his burning face and dried it on the tail of his shirt.

"We going to fence some more, sir?" he asked Hood, changing the subject.

Hood nodded. "If I can talk you and your father into helping. I'd like to get the Bar S fenced in as soon as possible. Today and tomorrow should do it. You have to go back home?" he asked, looking at Tannin.

Tannin shook his head. "I reckon Matthew can drive the missus back so she can pick up a few things. He can do the morning stock if Parks hasn't come by. That way, we'll have the whole day to fence. You want to do the north next?"

Hood nodded. "I figure that will eliminate the Box M right off, leaving us only the Rawlinses' spread to worry about. We can pretty much take care of that tomorrow. The creek makes a dogleg east around the mesa, narrowing the distance some."

"I was you, I think I'd worry more about the Rawlinses than McQuade," Daniels said, arching his back against the press of his hands. "McQuade will think twice about sending a gunman after you — and I'm not sure many would do it anyway. Most of Mc-Quade's riders seem to have a sense of right and wrong although they are riding for the Box M brand — but I don't think the Rawlinses would hesitate putting a bullet through any one of us at the drop of a hat. Rollie's the worst, of course, but his brother's no mean shade with his pistol as well and just as mean."

Hood nodded. "True, but I'd like to at least get one of the ranchers eliminated, and right now that stacks up as McQuade. And while I'm thinking about it," he said, turning to Tannin, "you think one of your boys could ride the fence after we're done?"

Tannin gave him a swift look. "You thinking trouble?"

Hood shrugged. "I don't know. But I don't see McQuade taking this in stride without trying at least once to cut the fence."

"I don't want any gunplay," Tannin said warningly.

"Neither do I," Hood said. "I think if McQuade or his riders see someone riding the fence line, he'll think twice about doing anything. And I can't see McQuade shooting a boy either. If he does try to cross over, your boy could ride down and fetch one of us."

"Fetch me, you mean," Daniels said. Hood looked at him and he grinned tightly. "Well, it makes sense. There might be gunplay, and the boy or you can't do it. On the other hand, I may not be a Rollie Rawlins, but I can handle a Winchester all right and I've shot my share of snakes with my pistol."

"I think I'd just as soon try to reason with them first," Hood answered dryly. "A gun has no answer to it that doesn't come back and haunt the person using it."

"You sound as if you know about that," Tannin said curiously.

Hood shrugged. "Those who live by the sword die by the sword. The Good Book tells us that. Takes no great shakes to figure out what that means."

"Maybe," Tannin said thoughtfully.

Mary stepped out onto the porch and called cheerfully, "Well, are you all going to stand out there jawing or come on up for breakfast? I've got the eggs made and Beth and Martha are whipping up some griddle cakes."

"I don't need a second invitation," Daniels said, hitching his belt as he turned toward the house. "It's a foolish man who waits long after the cook calls."

But it was Matthew who beat the three men to the house and was sitting at the table, fork in hand, when the men came through the door.

The men were hard at work at the north end of the Bar S by eight. Beth decided that she and the girls could wait behind and get the noon meal ready instead of going with Martha and Matthew back to the farm.

"You tell that no-account husband of mine to stop messing around with his bees and such and bring us a change of clothes," she said to Martha. "And while we're at it, you tell him to bring a jar or two of that honey. I'm fixing on making some baking-soda biscuits and they go down real good with a dollop of honey on them."

"I'll do that," Martha promised. She sniffed. "And I'll tell him to shake a leg, too. If I know these men, they would just as soon sit up in the shade with a bottle of whatever they were nipping on out in the barn last night instead of doing a good day's work."

Tannin laughingly warned Martha and Matthew to not dawdle along the way, but to get back as soon as they could in case they had to use the wagon to go into town and bring back more fence posts.

"You can wait until we get here," Martha said firmly, giving her husband a no-nonsense look. "And, if you want, we can pick up fence posts ourselves on our way back through town. But you're going to have to wait. Do you good to not keep expecting someone to be waiting on you hand and foot as well."

Hood allowed as to how it would probably be a good idea if she did stop by and pick up some fence posts and a couple of boxes of staples.

"We have enough wire, I think," he said.

"But if we get the posts now, then we won't have to stop tomorrow and go on in. We'll save some time."

Tannin put Mark and Luke to work as he and Daniels began stretching wire. Hood rode Sheba along the fence they had strung the day before to check on it.

"Figure a reverend would peter out after one day," Tannin said, winking at Daniels after Hood made his intentions known. "Any excuse to avoid working with his hands. Surprising that he'd be following a carpenter, given how he looks to avoid simple work."

"I know what you mean," Daniels said, pulling on his leather gloves. "There are some people who just want to let others pull their weight."

"And there are some who are born to think and tell others what they need to be doing since they can't figure that for themselves," Hood said.

"Now, if we just had someone to do our thinking for us," Tannin said, grinning.

Hood laughed as he nudged Sheba with his heels and loped south along the fence line.

The fence stood as strong as when they'd finished. Outside of a few head of cattle, the Box M range was empty. He heaved a sigh of relief as he turned Sheba back, then reined in as he saw a rider galloping toward him.

He stood in the stirrups, loosening the Spencer in its sheath, then slumped back in the saddle as he recognized Matthew riding bareback.

"Reverend Hood! Reverend Hood!" Matthew yelled as he came nearer. "Mr. Parks has been shot!"

He reined in beside Sheba and hung his head, panting for a moment.

"We found him about a mile from our place," he gasped. "He was heading back here and someone shot him. Ma's got him at our place, but he looks real bad. She says he's lost a lot of blood."

Hood's face settled into a grim mask.

"All right, Matthew, you ride on up and get your father. Tell Charlie and your brothers to keep working; then you and your father go on up to the ranch house and tell Missus Parks what has happened. I'm going down to your place and see what I can do. If need be, I'll ride on over to Trent and fetch the doctor."

"Yes, sir," Matthew said, and clapped his heels against the sides of the horse.

Hood nudged Sheba with his heels. "Well, girl," he murmured, "let's see if there's

227

something we can do. Hope we're not too late."

Sheba shook her head and stretched out, running south toward Tannin's farm.

"He's in pretty bad shape," Martha said in a low voice as Hood came up onto the porch of Tannin's house. "He's been shot three times. Winchester, I'd say. Bullets look like a forty-four or forty-five. He was lucky. I think the first one hit him in the shoulder and twisted him on around. The others caught him then. If'n they'd caught him straight on, he'd been dead before he hit the ground."

Hood's face set grimly. "Do we know who did it?"

She hesitated, then nodded. "He keeps slipping in and out of consciousness. But he's mentioned Josh Slade several times. I think it was him."

"Can I see him?"

She spread her hands. "Of course. But I don't think you'll get anything from him. The next couple of days will tell."

"I could ride to Trent for a doctor," Hood said.

She shook her head. "I don't think that would do any good. By the time you got back, he'll either be dead or alive. And if he's alive, then he'll make it. Maybe the doctor might be able to get the other bullet out. I got one and one went on through him. The other one's lodged up inside him and I didn't want to go digging around after that one. Might do more damage than good."

"You sound as if you've done a bit of nursing in the past," Hood said, removing his hat as he went through the door of the house.

She followed him. "You could say that. Pa was a doctor up in Kansas. I helped him quite often until Ezra came along."

"Where in Kansas?" Hood asked, ears perking.

"Around Abilene," she said. She made a face. "There were a lot of gunshots to be worked on in that town. I thought I was done with all that until we found Jim laying alongside the road. Mark brought his wagon on back. I didn't send it on up to Mary's place as I wasn't certain it would be safe. I don't want him shot."

Hood sighed and ran his fingers through his hair. "I'll take it up in a little while. Matthew and Ezra can bring Mrs. Parks back. I think it'll be safe, but I'll send Daniels along with them. Not even Slade will come down on a group that large. At least," he muttered to himself, "I don't think he will."

She led him to a back bedroom and carefully opened the door. Hood stepped in and looked at Parks lying on the bed, propped up by pillows to keep fluid from running into his lungs. His face looked dirty white and he labored for breath. His eyes were closed, but opened when Hood stepped next to the bed. He placed his hand on Parks's forehead. His forehead felt hot.

"How you doing, Jim?" Hood asked.

Parks gave a weak smile. "Feel like I been rode hard and put up wet," he said his voice rasping like a file over old wood. "You didn't tell me that stringing fence would mean I have to dodge bullets as well."

"Who did it?" Hood asked. "Was it Josh Slade?"

"He stopped me," Parks said. "Funny thing, though. He had his gun out, but the shot seemed to come from somewhere else. Almost like . . . someone was waiting for me and Slade just happened by."

Hood chewed his lower lip thoughtfully. "You didn't see anyone else?"

"No. Just . . . a horse. A piebald. Ain't that many in this country. Most come . . . from up north."

Hood looked at Martha. "You know anyone who has a piebald?"

She frowned, thinking. "About the only one I know of is Hoffman's." She shook her head. "But that couldn't be. Hoffman's never done anything to anyone that I've heard about. Fact is, he often goes out of his way to help folks. Farmers included. No, it couldn't be him," she finished emphatically.

Parks licked his lips. "I . . . don't . . . know. Just . . . saw . . . it."

His eyes closed and the rhythm of his breathing changed. It was labored, but deep. A muscle twitched in one cheek. His lips moved, but no sound emerged.

Martha put her hand on Hood's arms, tugging gently. "I think we'd better leave him to rest," she said. "That's enough for now."

Hood nodded, lips pressed tightly together. He walked out into the main room and stood, shifting his weight from one foot to another. He turned as Martha came out of the bedroom and softly closed the door behind her.

"I'll ride on over to Trent and tell the sheriff what happened," he said. "Might as well send the doctor, too. Won't do any harm other than give him a drive."

She shrugged. "I think it'll be a waste of your time unless he figures that bullet has to come out. The sheriff won't do anything but promise to keep his eyes and ears open in case he hears something. I don't recollect the last time the sheriff made it over to Jericho or anywhere around this part of the county. He's pretty content to collect the taxes or, more likely, send a deputy out to collect taxes, and to hold down a poker game in one of the saloons. As for the doctor, well, he might come on out, but he's the only one in the area and you might or might not find him in Trent. More'n likely he'll be out somewheres south of Trent. There's a lot of homesteads and mines down that way."

"I see," Hood answered. "What can I do? I feel like I need to do something."

"Pray," Martha answered. "That's about it. And bring Missus Parks and the girls back here. She should be with her husband. Matthew and Mark can go on over to their place and handle the chores for a while. Beth and the girls can use their room while Jim is healing. Other than that, I don't know what it would be. Get word out to the other homesteaders down in this part of the valley, I expect. Sommers, Drabble, and Roberts will come on over and spell Matthew and Mark when they can. Drabble used to do bees when he was a young'un back on his father's place in Ohio. He'll probably watch the hives for Jim. And Sommers and Roberts can help bring in what crops Jim has in when the time comes. For that matter, Roberts might go on up and help you all on the Bar S. I can let you have Luke, unless Ezra wants him back here. But right now, we don't have much to do on the place other than fixin' up here and there, and Ezra can handle that all right by himself. The main thing, I think, is to get everyone resettled where they need to be."

Hood nodded. "Well, I reckon I'd better head back to the Bar S and have Ezra and Matthew bring Missus Parks and the girls on down. I'll stay up there with Mary while Daniels rides down and back. I don't think anyone will come up there, but it'll be best if a man's around. Make others think a bit before riding down on a woman. Even," he said, giving a harsh laugh, "if that man's a minister."

"You take care," Martha cautioned. "Some folk around here don't think ministers are worth the dust. They'd as lief put a bullet in you as anyone else."

Hood nodded and looked at the closed door. "I wonder why someone would shoot Jim. It just doesn't make any sense at all."

"Makes sense to them, I reckon," she said.

"Doesn't have to make sense to us."

The sun swam in a coppery sea of heat as Hood rode Sheba back up the road toward the Bar S. The horizon appeared lost in heat waves rising up from the land, and sweat trickled down his face from under his hatband and ran in rivulets down his sides from under his arms. Sam trotted just ahead of Sheba, tongue lolling out of his mouth as he panted. But he kept his head up, swiveling from side to side as if searching for something.

The road curled around a mesquite thicket and Sam suddenly halted, the hair on the back of his neck rising, teeth bared, a growl coming from deep in his throat.

Hood reined in Sheba as he reached down and slipped the Spencer from its sheath, thumbing the hammer back.

"What is it, boy?" he asked, eyes flitting from side to side. Sheba danced nervously, tossing her head.

Josh Slade rode from around the mesquite, grinning at Hood.

"Well, well," he said, stopping in front of Hood, blocking the road. "What have we got here?"

"Slade," Hood acknowledged.

Slade glanced at the Spencer in Hood's

hands. "And what you doing with that rifle, Preacher?" he drawled. "You look like you're ready to shoot someone. Thought you all believed in turning the other cheek."

Hood shrugged "Never know when a rattler will crawl in front of you. They may be God's creatures, but I'm fairly certain that God won't hold it against a man for shooting one when he has to."

"You see any rattlers around?" Slade asked. His right hand slipped from the pommel to rest on his thigh below his holster.

"Sometimes they strike from hiding," Hood answered. "Speaking of which, did you shoot Jim Parks?"

Slade smiled lazily as his hand slid up to the holstered pistol. Hood dropped the barrel of the Spencer, grounding the stock against his hip. His finger took up the slack in the trigger and squeezed. The Spencer roared and Sheba shied to the right as Slade's bullet split the air where Hood's head had been. The heavy bullet slammed into Slade, knocking him backward off his horse, a splotch of red seeming to explode from his blue shirt.

His pistol flew out of his hand as he lay, sprawled on the ground, a confused look spreading over his face.

"Damn you! You . . . you shot me!" he

exclaimed, then coughed. His eyes grew wide with fear.

Hood dismounted and walked forward to kneel beside him. He cupped his hand under Slade's head and raised it.

"I'm sorry," he said. "But you pressed it."

"Shot . . . by a preacher!" Slade tried to laugh, and choked as blood spilled from his lips. "This is . . . funny."

"Why'd you shoot Parks?" Hood asked.

"Didn't," Slade gasped. "Don't know . . . Funny . . . Thought I . . . saw Hoffman . . ."

He convulsed and blood spurted from his mouth. His legs twisted in a spasmodic jerk and the light slipped out of his eyes.

Hood lowered Slade's head back to the earth, then sat back on his heels. He shook his head. Sam came up to him and slipped his muzzle under Hood's arm, whining. Hood automatically patted him.

"Thanks, boy," he said softly. "But I sure wish it wouldn't have been necessary."

He rose and walked to Sheba, steadying her with a word, running his hand down her neck. He slipped the Spencer back in its sheath and walked slowly to Slade's horse, talking soothingly when the sorrel shied away from him. He gathered the reins and brought the horse back to Slade, and stood patiently until the sorrel stopped trembling.

Then, he bent and gathered the body and draped it over the saddle, using piggin strings to tie it onto the back of the sorrel.

He stepped up onto Sheba's back and took the sorrel's reins. Slowly, he rode away, taking the road toward Hoffman's ranch when he came to the turnoff. He would leave Slade's body there and let Hoffman take care of it while Hood continued on up to the Bar S. A black cloud seemed to settle over him as he rode, regretting the shooting and thinking about what his congregation would have to say about their minister killing a man. The past seemed to gather around Hood, ghosts from his days as sheriff of Walker in Kansas drifting around him as he rode, and his hand went automatically to his side where the Schofield once rested.

18.

Three weeks later, Hood was working on the fence between the Rawlinses' ranch and the Bar S when he saw the cloud of dust and the first of the herd Hoffman and his men were driving toward Mary's ranch. He rose thankfully from stapling wire and motioned with his hammer.

"I'd say we can take a break now," he said to Matthew, who was holding the wire taut against the post for Hood.

Matthew cautiously relaxed his hold, making certain that the wire didn't whip back against them, then wiped the sweat off his face. Daniels saw the herd approaching, and mounted his horse and rode back from digging holes for the fence down the line. He reined in beside Hood and said, "It looks like Hoffman is good for his word. I'd say that he's brought more than what you bargained for. Right neighborly."

Hood nodded, deciding to keep his suspicions to himself for now, and walked to Sheba, mounting. He swung her around.

"Why don't you gather the tools?" he said to Matthew. "I think we're done down here for the day. By the time we get the cattle settled and Hoffman back on his way, it'll be coming on evening. We can finish tomorrow." He smiled. "I reckon your father will be grateful for that. He's probably got a lot of work for you to do on your own place."

Matthew made a face. "I suppose so," he said. "But I like it here. And he's still got Mark and Luke to help out. Frankly, I'd just as soon work up here."

Daniels laughed and reached down to tousle Matthew's hair. "Think you'd rather work cattle than walk behind a plow, huh?"

Matthew jerked his head away and mopped the sweat from his face with the sleeve of his shirt.

"I don't think I'm cut out for farming," he said seriously. "I'd like to see a bit of the world before settling down." The men smiled at him. "I'm going on eighteen, you know," he added defensively.

"That don't make you Methuselah," Daniels said. "And there's more to belonging on a farm than riding the grub line. That can get pretty lonely at times, not knowing where your next meal is coming from.

Besides, I think the day of the cowboy is coming to an end."

"I keep meaning to ask Miss Riley if she can use an extra hand on her ranch," Matthew said, eying the coming cattle. "You wouldn't object, would you?"

"No," Daniels said. "I wouldn't object. And there should be enough work for another set of hands. We can't be expecting the reverend to come out every day or so to help out. He's got his own work to do."

Hood said, "It does give me a break, though. My job is sort of easing out."

"Yeah," Daniels said drily, "I expect it is. I hear that your congregation is thinning out some."

There had been objections lately from many of the people who had first greeted Hood enthusiastically when he came to Jericho, and over the past few weeks, fewer and fewer were coming into town for Sunday services since Hood had refused to stop visiting the Bar S. He could, he reflected sourly now, see Mrs. Haddorn's hand in some of the complaints sounded against him despite Tannin's stout support.

"Yes, it is," Hood said. "But I can't help what others think or want to believe. I'll be glad when Parks is back on his feet. I miss him and his family."

"You've been out enough to see him," Daniels said, gathering the reins. "They can't fault you for that. And you made the ride down to the Sorensons' place when you learned their baby came down with the croup. There are some who allow you are doing what you should be doing. They'll come back soon once all this levels out. And," he added on reflection, "there hasn't been much from the Rawlinses or McQuade lately."

"That does worry me some," Hood said, touching Sheba with his heels. "Neither seems the type to let this slide on by without doing something."

"There's that," Daniels said, nudging his horse.

Together, they rode down to meet Hoffman.

"About gave you up for lost," Hood said as they came up on the rancher.

Hoffman laughed. "Well, it does take time. I told you that. But we sorted out some yearlings for you. Added a few, too, as I said I would. Fact is, I probably will have to take on a few extra men to make the drive to market, what with my stock and that which I'm going to pick up here."

Hood nodded as he looked the cattle over speculatively. The yearlings appeared sound, many of them without brands.

"All steers?" he asked. "Or did you bring any seed animals along?"

"There's a few," Hoffman said, pointing. "I figured you might like to work some new blood into your stock. Wouldn't mind doing that myself. You got any you'd like to let go?"

"We included a couple," Hood said. "I see you got some Texas stock in there as well." He pointed to a couple of longhorns trailing behind the herd.

"There's some," Hoffman admitted. "Most ranchers have a few left over from when they came in from Texas way. But they're starting to breed out. And that's a good thing. Longhorn meat can be a bit tough. Longhorns don't fatten up the same way as other breeds, and buyers are starting to get picky. I hear the big trail drives are becoming fewer and fewer up Kansas way."

"I hear that, too," Hood said. "But I think they'll still last for a few years. At least until the railroad is completed. I wouldn't say that everything is done yet."

"No, but it's coming," Hoffman said. "A man is smart to prepare for the future."

They rode down to the Bar S pasture where Hood and Daniels had gathered the fatted stock for trade. Hoffman looked them over approvingly.

"I think I'm getting the better of this," he said, shaking his head. "Maybe I should bring a few head more up."

"A deal is a deal," Hood said, smiling at the rancher. "Of course, you want to donate a few more, I don't think Miss Riley would argue too much. You still have to get these to market, though."

"I know." Hoffman laughed. "I'm not counting dollars until they are in my hand." His face sobered. "I thought I saw Rollie Rawlins and his brother riding up into the brakes, heading up this way. Thought you'd like to know."

"Good news to have," Daniels said, his face tightening. Unconsciously, he touched the pistol on his hip. "I've been expecting them before this. The Rawlinses are probably taking the fence worse than McQuade. Although," he added, "I don't think McQuade is done with this yet. I still think he'll make a move against us before too long. He's probably just waiting until we're finished and not riding the line so regularly."

Hood nodded. "You're probably right. I think I'll ride over and sound him out. Maybe if I let him yell enough at me, he'll think again about whatever he might be planning."

"Better you than me," Daniels said.

"Now that you mention it," Hoffman said, "I heard in town that McQuade sent someone to bring in a new man. Someone from Mogollon called Will Hardesty. You know of him?"

"I've heard of him," Daniels said, breaking in. He looked bleakly at Hood. "He's a gunman. Killed a man down Durango way. I understand he sells his gun to the highest bidder and don't care a lick who buys it."

Hood pressed his lips together, nodding. Hardesty again. *Well, you knew it would come sooner or later. You've had a spell without having to deal with the Johnsons or Hardestys. Blood still runs long back in the Tennessee hills.*

Unbidden, the memory of his last run-in with the Johnsons, when he was still Tom Cade, the sheriff of Walker, Kansas, came to mind.

"Hello, Toad. Pea," Tom said casually. "What brings you to Walker?"

"Well, if it ain't young Cade," Toadknock said, pushing himself away from the two women. He stood and pulled his coveralls up, slipping the suspenders over his shoulders. He smiled, revealing mossy teeth beneath his black and scraggly beard "You remember

Eula, I 'spect."

"I remember," Tom said quickly. He nodded at the Johnsons' guns. "You boys have a problem, though. Guns have to be checked at the sheriff's office."

"And I see yer wearin' the star," Peapod said, trying to squirm out from under the fat woman.

"I am," Tom said quietly. "Now, you Johnsons take your guns up and check them with the jailer. Or else ride on out of Walker. Choice is yours."

Toadknock laughed. "Damned if I'll run from a preacher's kid. You know your old man's dead, I 'spect."

A cold chill ran through Tom.

"No," he said. "I didn't. How'd it happen?"

"He got in the way of a bullet," Peapod said, staggering to his feet. "Toad was shootin' at a tinker when the preacher tried to stop him. But the bullet stopped the preacher. I 'spect your brother's written you a letter that you ain't got. But now, there's no reason for you to have to read it, is there?"

"I see," Tom said slowly. "So, what brings you boys to Walker?"

They exchanged glances, then Peapod started to slip over toward their guns.

"Nope," Tom said, tapping his fingernail against the Schofield's handle. "You get much closer, I'm going to have to figure that you're being a bit unfriendly."

Toadknock wiped his hands down the sides of his coveralls and nodded at Peapod.

"Well," Peapod said, "reckon you know why we're here."

"No, I don't," Tom said. He watched them carefully. Peapod caught his concentration and pulled up short.

"Matter of Johnson honor," Peapod said. Suddenly, he turned red in the face and shook a dirty finger at Tom. "You plowed a little corn with Cousin Eula, didn't you? And then you got her with child and ran out on her."

"That's a lie," Tom said calmly.

"You calling our cousin a liar?" Toadknock asked, his voice low and dangerous. "Seems like you got all the say, what with your pistol there and our'n over there."

"I wasn't the first one with Eula," Tom said calmly. "And it doesn't take much of a farmer to figure out when a heifer's due after she's been with a bull. With Eula and me, it just didn't add up. And I think you know that."

"Don't make no matter what we think. Or what happened. You didn't do right with Eula and that ain't something that no Johnson's gonna fergit," Peapod said angrily.

"What happened between Eula and myself is our business," Tom said. "That's in the past and should remain in the past. You bringing such things here doesn't change that one bit."

"It damn will change," Toadknock said.

"You two have worn out your welcome," Tom said. "Get dressed and ride on back to Tennessee. There's nothing here for you."

"Free country," Peapod said.

"Not that free," Tom answered. "Get dressed and leave town. You've been warned. I see you on the streets of Walker, I'll arrest you. And tell Eula and her father not to send any more of their kin around. This is senseless."

"A preacher's kid," Toadknock sneered.

"I said what I had to. Now" — he gestured at their clothes — "get your things together and leave."

He drew the tattered curtains together and backed away, keeping his eyes on the curtains. His intuition was right; he was halfway across the room when the curtains swept aside and the Johnsons stormed out, guns in hand. He hadn't expected that, and cursed himself as he pulled the Schofield from its holster, thumbing the hammer as he brought it up. Peapod shot first, the bullet taking Tom in the left shoulder and spinning him around, saving his life as Toadknock fired where he had been. Tom crashed into a table and rolled, coming to his knee. He fired, hitting Peapod in the middle. Peapod folded and fell to the floor. Toadknock fired again and the bullet slammed high into Tom's chest, knocking him backward. Tom fired again, and Toadknock's head jerked back as if poleaxed. With an effort, Peapod pushed himself up and fired and missed, but Tom steadied his pistol and the next bullet took Peapod in the throat. Then, he fired again, hitting Peapod in the chest.

The room was a dim haze of black powder smoke. Tom tried to rise, but fell back on his side as a small crowd burst through the door. Then, he heard Fred Wilson's shotgun and a warning for all to get back. Again, he tried to rise. The room spun and went dark and he felt himself falling forward into the darkness.

Aloud, he said, "Maybe McQuade just needed another hand to replace you, Charlie."

"I'm not a gunman," Daniels said, flushing. "He hire someone for me, it'd be a cowboy. Maybe one who has a hot temper and don't mind a little hoorawing on Saturday night, but still a cowboy. Hardesty don't sound like no cowboy to me. I'll bet he can't even use a rope."

"No sense in worrying about it now," Hood said easily. "Time enough for that later. Right now, we've got some cattle to trade. You going back tonight?" he asked, turning back to Hoffman.

The rancher nodded. "Yep. Ranch don't run by itself and I'd like to get the cattle settled in their new ranch before driving them out. I don't know if it makes a damned bit of difference to the cow, but I think it goes easier if they're not mixing in with strange cattle on a drive." He smiled. " 'Course I'm probably giving cattle more brains than they got, but when I was younger, I went up the trail with Goodnight and we worked our tails off trying to keep the cattle bunched. Since then, I've taken a few others of my own and a couple for a few homesteaders to market, and found that I have a lot less trouble if they get a chance to settle in amongst themselves before driving."

Daniels laughed and shook his head. "Never thought I'd hear a rancher give a steer credit for anything. They gotta be the dumbest animals around."

"No," Hood said ruefully. "I think that's reserved for man."

Together, they rode into the pasture and began pushing the cattle to the east fence to gather them before Hoffman's herd came into the pasture.

19.

Moths battered the glass surrounding the kerosene lamp on the small table in Hood's room. He sat thankfully in a chair, listening to tired crickets sing, enjoying a moment's relaxation. He glanced at the table, where his sermon for Sunday lay finished, and smiled in relief. Preparing a weekly talk was proving more difficult than he'd thought when he had decided to follow in his father's footsteps and become a preacher. But, he reflected, he was happier than he had been as sheriff of Walker in what he had now come to view as his other life.

Of course, he thought ruefully, that life was generally simpler, too — if you didn't mind being shot at and always living in expectation of a bullet from the dark. But the people he worked with now were generally nicer. Although there were some who could cross over into the other life easily enough. At least, they seemed to have the temperament for it.

He looked down at Sam, lying on the hooked rug. Sam sensed his attention and raised his head, a hopeful look in his eyes. "I guess people are really not much different, are they, boy? It's only that some are a bit more pretentious than others, hiding their prejudices behind their religion. I never saw that back in Tennessee, and Pa never mentioned it when he did his visiting around the country. I guess it was something that he hoped I would miss."

Sam whined uncertainly, cocking his head to one side. Hood's stomach rumbled. He laughed.

"I guess I know what's on your mind, Sam. I plumb forgot to eat supper. And I'll bet Mother has a bone for you, too."

Sam climbed to his feet and went to the door, tail wagging hopefully.

Hood climbed to his feet, collected his hat, and blew out the lamp.

"All right, let's go get something to eat."

Together, they went down the stairs, Sam staying close to Hood's side. The night clerk raised his head and frowned when he saw Sam next to Hood. Although Halsey Barth had allowed Hood to keep Sam in his room, there were some who still resented it.

Hood smiled as he remembered the look

on the drummer's face when he first saw Sam the day after he'd stepped down from the stage and taken a room in the hotel. Pure panic and a blustering demand that the hotel manager get rid of "that animal before he tears someone's throat out."

Too many penny dreadfuls, Hood thought. *That's another thing that is changing out here. We are getting more and more stories written about the West and the frontier. And from that people form their ideas about what life is like, and their expectations crowd their common sense.*

He thought about the time a writer had come to Walker, hoping to see the infamous Tom Cade in action, and was disappointed when he learned that Tom spent most of the time walking the streets, his mere presence keeping order in the town. Tom hadn't bothered telling the writer — Colonel Nichols, wasn't it? — that his presence was enough only after a period of difficulty when he'd had to use the Schofield to enforce his will on restless cowboys and young would-be gunmen who were after a reputation on a fast track that led only to the cemetery if they were unlucky enough. But Tom had read enough of the stories by Ned Buntline to figure out the trouble that could be caused by exaggeration of the truth. Bill

Hickok was a fine example of that, being constantly hounded by writers who wanted more and more killings to add fodder to their stories. Of course, there were always some like Bill Cody who relished the stories and used them to further their careers on the stage. Most of those who constantly lived with their pistol — those like Dave Mather, King Fisher, Ben Thompson, and Bill Longley — avoided writers like the plague. Some even dropped out of sight when stories began to be written about them.

Hood and Sam stepped out on the porch and walked down the street toward Mother's Place. The air smelled like dust and a full moon was rising. Hood glanced at it: bloodred, a hunter's moon. He sighed. Although he wasn't superstitious, enough had happened in the past for him to be at least wary of the possibilities that such omens brought with them when they occurred.

Mother's was crowded when they walked in, but Hood saw his usual table was unoccupied and made his way toward it. There were some murmured hellos as he passed other tables, and he stopped and exchanged pleasantries with a few customers. Some, who had come to church a few times before his association with Mary Riley became common knowledge, ignored him, although he made a point of speaking to them anyway.

He settled behind the table, his back to the wall, Sam dropping by his foot. Mother beamed when she saw him and waddled to his corner, carrying a mug and a pot of coffee. She set the mug in front of him and filled it with coffee.

"Good to see you, Amos," she said, her eyes twinkling merrily. "Been a spell. How's Parks doing?"

"Fine, Mother," Hood said, smiling at her. "He's making progress every day. I expect him up and about in due time, although he'll have to take it easy. Ezra's boy Mark goes over to his place to help with the chores, and Ezra and a couple others got his fields turned under for spring planting. It pays to be a good neighbor, it seems."

"Always," Mother said, glancing around to see who had heard them. She lowered her voice as she jerked her head toward the far wall.

"You see that ranny sitting against the wall? The one with the gray shirt and black scarf?"

Hood glanced toward the wall and saw a man staring at him. Hood nodded. "Yes.

What about him?"

"He's been asking a lot of questions about you. And he wears a gun like he knows how to use it. Low, you know?"

Hood smiled, not bothering to tell her that those men who wore their guns level with their palms usually didn't amount to much. It was the mark of one who wanted to be more than he was.

"I understand," he said softly. He looked again at the man. His black hair had been carefully combed back from a high forehead, but that only enhanced his face, pinched like a rat's. His lips curled back when he saw Hood looking at him. A canine tooth was snaggled and prominent.

"Well," Hood said, "I'm here if he wants to talk about something."

"That kind don't talk about nothing worth hearing," Mother said stoutly. "I've got fresh meat. How about a steak and some fried potatoes?"

"You got apple pie?" Hood asked. "It's been a while since I've had something sweet."

Mother grinned at him. "You sure about that? Missus Haddorn thinks otherwise."

He colored and rubbed the side of his nose with a forefinger.

"You do have a way of getting right to

the point," he said. "And don't you go listening to Missus Haddorn. She likes to talk about the bees when there aren't any buzzing."

Mother laughed. "You pinned that one right." She glanced down at Sam looking hopefully up at her. She reached down and scratched him behind the ears. "And I haven't forgotten you either. I've been keeping some bones back just waiting on you to come in."

She straightened, glanced at the man against the wall, then nodded at Hood. "I know nothing will probably come of it, but you take care anyway." She hesitated, then added, "You know, you look an awful lot like a Tom Cade from Kansas way. I have a sister up there who likes to keep tabs on the stories."

Hood's face tightened. He reached for his coffee, sipping. "A lot of men look alike. I expect there are some unfortunate enough to look like me. Of course, I'm not the type who would wish that on anyone."

"Uh-huh," Mother grunted. "But there are some around who may think the same as I think. You know about Tom Cade, I expect."

Hood avoided her eyes and nodded. "Yes, I know about him. But I don't think he's probably at all like those stories going around. People have a habit of talking out of turn, and everything gets so colored that no one can tell the truth from the stories. Look at Hickok. If he'd killed all those men that they say he did, Abilene and Hayes would be ghost towns."

"Yeah, but there's gotta be something there to begin with," Mother said, turning to go. "I'll get your steak and potatoes on right away. And bring a bone for Sam."

Hood thanked her as she left, and leaned back in his chair, considering the man across the room. He couldn't remember having seen the man before, but that meant nothing out here where men moved around whenever they got the feeling to see new country.

The man suddenly rose, gathered his hat, and wove his way through the tables to the door. He paused, settling his hat on his head, then gave Hood a sneer and touched his fingers to the brim of his hat before opening the door and leaving. Hood glanced quickly around the room and saw some cowboys looking strangely at him. A chill of premonition swept over him, and he shuddered as he felt ghosts suddenly crowding him, and he recognized the ghosts as those who once fell from his Schofield. The pistol felt heavy upon his thigh, although he knew it wasn't there.

The night had fallen full when Hood left Mother's, Sam carrying his bone by Hood's side. Hood paused for a moment, his eyes sweeping the street between Mother's and his hotel. A couple of cowboys lolled outside The Cattleman's, and Halsey Barth stood, leaning against the side of the saloon, sipping from a glass he held. For a moment, Hood thought he caught movement in the shadows of the alley beside the saloon, but after a moment, the shadows stilled and he laughed ruefully to himself.

"Flinching at shadows, Sam," he said. "Mother has me seeing things where there's nothing."

Nevertheless, he moved automatically to the street and strolled toward his hotel. Halfway there, a shadow slipped from between two buildings and stood in front of him. Simultaneously, Hood recognized the man from Mother's and saw the moonlight glinting off a pistol in his hand.

"Reckon you're not as careful as some make you out," the man said. He raised the pistol slightly as Hood stood helpless. Then, a gray blur whipped past him and Sam launched himself at the figure, his paws striking the man full on the chest. The man staggered and Hood was on him, one hand clamping hard on the man's wrist that held the pistol while the other hand folded into a fist and struck like a hammer on the man's jaw.

The man slumped to the ground, the pistol falling from his hand. In a second, Sam stood half on the man's chest, lips curled back in a snarl, saliva dripping from his mouth a scant few inches from the man's throat.

"Sweet God," the man said hoarsely. "Get him off me! Get him off!"

Hood reached down and collected the man's pistol — a Navy Colt converted to cartridges — and slipped it into his waistband.

"Easy, Sam," Hood said. He patted Sam on his head, shoving the wolf away from the man.

Sam moved reluctantly, deep growls rumbling from his throat, his eyes bright yellow in the moonlight.

Hood reached down and pulled the man to his feet. The man cringed and tried to back away from Sam, but Hood held him fast.

"Who are you?" he asked quietly.

"Billy Talbot," the man gasped. He gulped.

His eyes rolled wildly, trying to keep Sam in sight.

"Why did you lay for me?"

"Someone sent me . . . money," Talbot gasped. "Please! Keep him away!"

"Who?"

The man didn't answer, and Hood shook him until the man's teeth clicked together.

"I don't know!" he cried wildly. "Just a letter and the money! A hundred dollars! Easy money!"

"Not good enough," Hood said grimly. "Now, who . . ."

A shot rang out, and Hood felt the bullet slap into the man. He sagged in Hood's grip, his face registering the shock.

"You . . . shot . . . me!" Talbot said. Blood spurted from his mouth. His hands clawed at Hood's wrist "Damn . . ."

"No." Hood said. "It wasn't me. Who hired you?"

Talbot tried to speak, but coughed and bright blood rolled out of his mouth. His eyes rolled back in his head and he became a deadweight. Hood lowered him to the ground and crouched, eyes swinging back and forth, looking for the shooter. A bullet slapped the side of the building next to him, and he dived behind a barrel standing in the mouth of the alley. Sam ran across the street, but Hood called him back and the wolf spun as another bullet struck the ground where he had been a moment before. Sam raced back to Hood and slipped behind him in the alley.

"Still, Sam!" Hood ordered, and the wolf whined as he crowded in behind Hood.

Cautiously, Hood raised his head and slowly scanned the buildings across the street. He waited for a minute, then stood, ready to drop back behind the barrel at the first flicker of flame from a gun. But no shot came and he moved carefully out into the street.

The street was empty, the cowboys outside The Cattleman's having ducked inside the saloon at the gunfire. But Halsey Barth still leaned carelessly against the side of the saloon. He saw Hood staring at him, and raised his glass in a mocking salute before sipping. Hood warily crossed the street and stepped up on the boardwalk in front of him.

"You were lucky," Barth said calmly.

"I don't suppose you saw who shot at us," Hood said.

"No, I didn't," Barth answered. He nodded at the crumpled figure in the street. "He dead?"

"Yes," Hood answered curtly.

Barth shook his head and gave Hood a slight smile. "I'd say that you were dangerous to be around, Preacher. Parks gets shot, and now that stranger killed."

"Curious, though, wouldn't you say?" Hood asked. He felt the old recklessness surging through him, wanting to lash out but restraining himself with difficulty.

Barth raised his eyebrows. "Curious? What's curious?"

"You seem to be around when trouble comes my way in Jericho," Hood said.

"Oh? I can't say that I've noticed," Barth said. He finished his drink and held the glass loosely in two fingers in front of him. "I'm just having a drink and enjoying the night." He gestured at Sam. "I'd say he was pretty good as a guardian angel. Even if he's only half-grown. He hit that man hard enough to give you a little edge. Wouldn't think that he was big enough to make that much difference."

"You might be surprised at what Sam can do," Hood said.

"Could be," Barth said calmly. He pushed himself away from the saloon and turned toward the saloon doors. "Then again, now I know."

"Halsey," Hood said slowly, "I'll take it pretty personal if it happens again."

Barth stopped and stared at Hood, eyes narrowing. A tiny smile played across his lips. "You accusing me, Preacher?"

"No. I figure that you'll get the word out, though. You will do that, won't you, Barth?" Hood said.

Barth laughed softly and stepped through the doors into the saloon without speaking. The doors swung to behind him and Hood bent to ruffle Sam's fur.

"I owe you," he said.

Sam whined and trotted off the boardwalk, crossing to where he'd dropped his bone before launching himself at the gunman. Slowly, Hood followed him and stood in front of Talbot, staring down at the crumpled figure. He sensed others gathering around him and looked up.

"I reckon you better take him to the undertaker," Hood said.

"Ain't got one," one man — Jarvis, Hood remembered — said. "The blacksmith usually hammers together a coffin, though."

"Then, take him down to Bert's shop. And notify the sheriff."

Jarvis shrugged. "Ain't no reason to do that. We usually just plant him and hold his belongings until the sheriff comes through. Whenever he does that," he added. "Ain't seen him in a coon's age."

Hood shook his head. "I see," he sighed. "Then, tell Bert I'll read over this man in the afternoon. His name was Billy Talbot. I don't know anything more about him. Maybe Bert can find something in his pockets. If he does, tell him to let me know and I'll try to contact his next of kin."

Jarvis nodded and turned toward the man standing next to him. "Give me a hand."

Silently, the man bent and took Talbot by his ankles while Jarvis slipped his hands under Talbot's arms, lifting. They trudged down the street with the body swinging awkwardly between them.

Hood looked around at the others, recognizing a few only as being regulars in The Cattleman's.

"Any of you see anything?" he asked.

Silently, they shook their heads.

"What happened?" Peterson asked breathlessly, coming up to Hood. His breath smelled like whiskey.

"That man waited for the preacher with a drawn gun," someone answered.

Peterson's eyes narrowed as they settled on Hood. "You shoot him?" he asked.

Hood shook his head. "Somebody did. But I don't know who."

Peterson frowned. "You know why?"

"No, but I have an idea or two," Hood

answered. He looked down at Sam. "Come on. Let's go home."

Together, Hood and Sam walked down to the hotel and entered, leaving the others on the street to exchange their own ideas about what had happened.

20.

Nightmares pulsed through Hood's sleep. He tossed and turned, sweating through the sheets. He awakened with the first purple and red streaks appearing in the sky and swung his feet to the floor, gripping the side of the bed, his head thudding ponderously. Sam whined and scraped his nails across the floor, waiting to see if Hood would wave him over. Hood grinned bleakly at him.

"You have a good night, Sam?" he asked.

The wolf ducked his head down on his paws, then back up, ears perked alertly.

"Hope so." Hood sighed. "I kept seeing ghost riders."

He rose, stretching the night knots from his frame, and moved over to the washstand. He stared into the small mirror hanging over the basin. His eyes looked bruised with heavy lines hanging beneath them; his face was set in a hard mask. It was the face he had seen hundreds of times while Tom

Cade, Sheriff, in Walker, Kansas. He splashed water from the ewer into the basin and scrubbed his face briskly. Then, he took his shaving cup and brush and slowly built a thick lather, spreading it over his cheeks and throat. He stropped the ivory-handled razor and shaved carefully. He dressed carefully and looked again into the mirror. Better, he thought. But still not someone who looks as if he should be in a pulpit.

He shook his head, called Sam, and left. Sam looked at him questioningly as he did not turn toward Mother's for breakfast, but instead went the opposite direction and made his way down the street to the blacksmith's shop.

Bert was hammering out a wagon rim when Hood stopped at the front of the forge. Bert nodded, lifted the rim from his anvil, and carefully draped it across the hearth of the forge, one quarter lying in the hot coals. He wiped his hands on his leather apron and said, " 'Morning, Reverend. Hope you slept easily."

"Wish I would've," Hood said ruefully, shaking Bert's proffered hand. "But last night upset me some."

"Would've upset me too if someone shot at me," Bert said. He rubbed his hand over the stiff bristles of his hair. "Beats me why anyone would be shooting at you. Most scallywags in this town may get a bullet or two winged their way from time to time, but a preacher? Well" — he jabbed a thick forefinger toward Hood — "it ain't like I didn't warn you. Some don't cotton to preachers comin' around here."

"Like who?" Hood ventured.

Bert glanced around hurriedly, then nodded toward The Cattleman's across the street.

"It's kept pretty quiet around here, but I figure you ought to know if'n you gonna start poking your nose into other folks' business. Not," he added hastily, "that I'm saying you shouldn't, you understand. Reckon that just goes along with being a preacher and all, but some things are better left alone. The preacher before you, well, he did what he thought a preacher should do and they found his body up by the red mesa. Shot full of holes, he was. Sheriff came to town to try and find out who done it, but he ended up in boot hill, too. Sheriff we got now, well, he weren't elected. The town council over at the county seat just appointed him until the next election rolls around. He saw the writin' on the wall and keeps hisself pretty much occupied in the other end of the county. Best for him, I 'spect. At least, he'll keep on breathin' and not sleepin' permanent-wise. Folks around here have taken to you. They'd hate to see somethin' happen to you. I would, too."

"I thought the last preacher just left and the one before him was killed," Hood said.

Bert looked at him curiously. "Now why would you think that? No, 'twas the other way around."

Hood studied the ground between his boots for a moment. What had the preacher been doing up at the red mesa? Had he stumbled onto the same thing that Hood had in the little canyon north? If he got caught, that would explain what happened. Of course, he could have simply been making calls on Mary Riley, and McQuade or some of his riders may have taken exception to it. Or the Rawlins brothers. Both wanted the water on the Bar S. He'd heard about water wars happening elsewhere when a drought was on, but somehow, Hood didn't think that was the answer. Water was needed — no doubt about that — and in such times, water could be as precious as gold for a rancher who saw his cattle beginning to wither away and knew his livelihood was withering away as well. Either finding the mine or visiting Mary could have resulted in the preacher's death if he wasn't careful. So, which was it: a death of convenience or greed?

"I appreciate that, Bert," Hood said. "But if you know something, then you'd better tell me so I can take care of going the other way. Don't you think?"

The blacksmith turned back to his forge, staring into the hot red coals. Tiny orange flames flickered above the coals and the heat rolled out of the fire pit, joining with the promised heat of the day.

"All right," Bert mumbled, "but it get out that I talked to you about this, then my life wouldn't be worth the wind to blow my dust away." He heaved a great sigh, made a show of picking up his hammer and tongs, and began banging on a strip of iron he'd been working on before Hood came to the shop. He punctuated his words with blows of the hammer.

"Preacher's name was Sheldon Black. He was a good man. Heart of gold. He made a circuit of everyone at least once a week. Even helped Hoffman bring in some hay once when we had our last rain and everything grew like weeds. Something about him made him seem a saint around here. Church on Sunday had standing room. One day he rode out early just 'fore sunrise to make his rounds. I was working at the time. Barth rode out an hour later. Missus Haddorn was pruning her bushes and saw him too. Next day, they found the preacher shot full of holes."

"Then, he didn't leave on his own?"

"Who told you that?" Bert asked, pausing in his hammering.

"Barth."

Bert shook his head. "Nope. A drifter found him in a wash. After shooting him, his killer tried to tumble some rocks on him to hide the body. Coyotes managed to drag him out."

Hood chewed his lower lip, thinking. "Barth told me he doesn't ride. Doesn't like it."

"He tell you that?" Bert asked. Hood nodded. Bert gave a short laugh, then pointed toward the back. "That sorrel back there is his. He won it in a poker game. He rides. Not often, but he rides. The Cattleman keeps him busy enough that he don't get much chance of riding out. When he comes back, that sorrel is restless like it wanted to be out more. Sometimes, I walk him around to keep him from becoming stall-bound."

"You think Barth killed him?"

Bert hesitated, then gave a curt nod and turned back to hammering on the iron. "That's what I think. And what others think, thanks to Missus Haddorn's flapping lip. That was before someone apparently told her to mind her own business. Didn't see much of her for a while after that. 'Course, no one says it outright. Ain't smart to talk too much about Barth. He killed a man once when the fellow thought he caught Barth cheating when Barth first came to town. Probably was. He's good with them cards. But no one will say so. They figure pretending to know nothing's the best way to keep breathing. No sense taking chances when all they got is figuring. He brought that sorrel in all lathered like he'd been out on a long ride," he added.

"Thanks," Hood said quietly.

Bert shrugged. "Like you said. Best to know something about rattlesnakes before you step into a den."

Hood walked back to Sheba's stall and stood for a moment, murmuring to her before saddling and riding out with Sam on her heels. Sheba seemed to sense his mood, and kept the steady pace Hood had chosen instead of straining at the bit to run a little.

"So," Hood said to himself. "Barth lied about not riding. Why? This is the country for a man to be riding. Nothing unusual in that. Why pretend otherwise? And why would Barth care one way or the other if folks knew he was riding?"

He shook his head.

"Makes sense, I suppose, if someone looks at it the way Bert does. But it's only speculation. Nothing there for anyone to take to the judge. Barth's no cattleman. He doesn't care about water one way or the other. And if Bert's right, and I expect he is, Barth doesn't ride often enough to have found the silver. And," he added ruefully, "Bert probably remembered such things only after Missus Haddorn started talking. She does like to see the dark side of folks instead of their good."

He lifted Sheba into a trot as he neared the Bar S turnoff and sat back in the saddle, rocking easily to Sheba's gait, but his eyes missed nothing, including a rattlesnake coiled beneath a mesquite bush as he rode. Better to ride on the side of caution rather than regret not taking care to avoid any surprises.

He rode easily up the green canyon to the Bar S. Daniels and Mary were standing on the porch, coffee cups in hand, as he reined in at the house.

"We weren't expecting you today," Mary said cheerfully. "But there's still coffee if you want some." She glanced up at Charlie and smiled teasingly. "And Charlie left a couple of biscuits if you've a mind. Fresh honey, too. Beth sent a couple of jars over, gleaned from Parks's hives."

"I'll take you up on that," he said, swinging down. He led Sheba over to the cottonwood and tied her in the shade. "Coffee'd be good, and I must admit to having a sweet tooth."

"Be just a minute," she said, walking into the house.

Hood shook hands with Daniels and tipped his hat back.

"Felt like getting out of town. There was some trouble in there last night," Hood said.

The smile slipped from Daniels's face. "What happened?"

"Someone tried to kill me," Hood said. In quick words, he told Daniels what happened. When he finished, Daniels sighed and took a sip from his coffee.

"But you don't know who," he said.

"No. I can't figure out why. Unless it's because someone doesn't like what we're doing out here. You'd better watch yourself when you ride out."

"I will," Daniels said grimly.

Hood hesitated for a moment, then asked, "You know anything about that preacher's murder?"

"You found out about that, huh?" Daniels

said. "Well, reckoned you would sooner or later."

"McQuade involved?"

Daniels shook his head. "No, I don't think so. McQuade's a hard man and given to temper fits when things don't go his way. But he wouldn't harm a preacher. He might some other folk, but not that."

"He sent you and Slade to get the Bar S," Hood reminded. "And later, Slade tried to dry-gulch me."

"That was after McQuade let him go," Daniels said. "McQuade ain't above trying to force others to do what he wants. But gunplay?" He frowned. "Nope, can't see him doing that."

"He's sent for a gunman," Hood said. "Remember?"

Daniels scratched his head. "And that's got me puzzling. I worked for him a little over two years and never knew him to do anything like that. Don't make sense."

"Any man can do the unexpected if he figures he's been pushed far enough. And we've been pushing him," Hood said.

He broke off as Mary came out the door, carrying a cup of coffee and a plate with biscuits and honey. She handed them to Hood and nodded toward a chair on the porch.

"Put some of this in your stomach," she said cheerfully. "I can fry up some bacon and eggs, too, if you want something more."

"These will do just fine," Hood said, sitting.

He took a sip of coffee, nodded, and set the cup on the floor beside him. He ate the biscuits with relish.

"I thought we'd take a ride around, checking things out," he said. "Best if we ride the wire. Men see us taking care might keep them from doing something we'd regret later."

"Or *they'd* regret," Daniels said. "I'll go saddle up."

He finished his cup and handed it to Mary.

"Maybe it'd be a good idea if you stick around the home place," he said.

She frowned. "Why? I've ridden out with you before."

"It's been quiet for too long," Daniels said. Hood raised his eyebrows at Daniels's words. "I don't think it'd be a good idea to let our guard down right now. We got a good start at rebuilding the place and it'd be a shame to have to start all over again."

She nodded slowly, grudgingly. "All right. I'll busy myself around here."

"That'll do," Daniels said. He hitched his belt and stepped off the porch, heading toward the corral. She glanced at Hood.

"Something going on that I should know about?"

"Just being careful," Hood said, finishing the biscuits. He handed the plate to Mary and finished his coffee. "Besides, there isn't much left to do. The cattle should be settled by now and as long as the wire's all right, I'd say we've got a breather before anything else breaks. I don't think anyone will try to take the cattle until they've fattened up a bit. Someone who rustles cattle doesn't want to hold them in the country for long in case a cowboy spots them and starts asking questions. "They'd take them and drive them away to market as fast as they can."

"The Rawlinses?" she asked. "You think it might be the Rawlinses?"

"Probably," Hood answered, rising and handing her the cup and plate. "I wouldn't put it past them anyway. They rode for the Hash Knife outfit for a while, and surely know the ins and outs of the trade. And they strike me as the cautious type who wouldn't want to take a chance on upsetting the balance they've got here now."

"You be careful," she said in warning. "You made Rollie look bad and he won't forget that."

"We'll be careful," Hood said, setting his

hat over his forehead and stepping off the porch. He turned and grinned at her. "And, if you've a mind to, you could have dinner waiting when we get back. You're a good cook."

"Thanks," she said, coloring.

They rode back down the canyon toward the lower pastures. Daniels waited until they were out of hearing then gave Hood a curious look.

"You know, at times you don't sound like a preacher," he ventured. "You sound like you've ridden the trail for a while."

"A preacher's got to go where he's needed," Hood said. "The only way to do that is to spend time moving from one town to the other. A man learns to do for himself if he's traveling. No one to do it for him."

"Uh-huh," Daniels said skeptically, but he refrained from voicing his doubts as they emerged from the canyon and onto the lower ground. He turned his horse toward the south, but Hood stopped him.

"I thought we were going to ride the wire," Daniels said, resting his hands on the pommel of his saddle.

"I want to show you something first," Hood said. "Just in case something unexpected happens. We can check the fence from the north down as easily as from the south up."

Daniels sighed. "You're just full of surprises. I'm getting so I don't know what to expect from you one day to the next."

"Always good to keep another man guessing," Hood said, turning Sheba's head toward the north.

They rode in silence, keeping to the trail that wound close to the red mesa. Daniels glanced at him from time to time as if he wanted to ask where they were going, but kept his questions to himself as they kept riding north.

At last, Hood reined in and nodded toward the narrow cleft in the mesa wall.

"We'll go in there," he said.

"No cow would work his way through there," Daniels said, eyeing the opening critically. "Leastways, it don't look like any would. Cattle would stay on the grass rather than go climbing up where none grows."

"Cattle would," Hood said, turning Sheba into the cleft.

Daniels shrugged and followed him, letting his horse pick its way over the rocks.

They emerged into the amphitheater-shaped canyon and Daniels looked around, surprise etching his face as he saw the abandoned cliff dwelling across from them. Then he shook his head as he considered the boulder-strewn ground in front of them.

"Like I said, this ain't no place for cattle. A steer managed to work his way in here would just turn around and leave."

"A steer would," Hood said, riding forward.

He led Daniels across the floor of the canyon to the mine. He reined in and waited for Daniels to come up beside him. Daniels frowned as he studied the opening.

"There's silver here," Hood said quietly. "I took a sample down to the assayer in Trent. It's rich. But the interesting thing is someone had brought a sample to him earlier. He recognized the ore and didn't even have to run the sample I gave him."

Daniels stared at the opening for a long moment before turning slowly to look at Hood.

"You tell Mary?" he asked. "She could use the money."

Hood nodded "Yes. But she's keeping it pretty quiet for now. I agree. I think it would be better to try and find out who the man is that took that ore down to Trent. It might answer a lot of questions if we know that before letting others know that silver can be found up here. Soon as we do that, prospectors will be running all over the mesa and they won't care whose land they cross. Mary will need more hands than you to keep them out and away from here. We'd just be adding to the troubles we already have."

"I reckon that makes sense," Daniels said. "But why did you bring me up here?"

"I have to trust someone. Most folks think you're just a hired hand. I don't think they would expect you to be privy to the doings of everything on the ranch. If something happens to me, then you'd be able to pass the location of the silver on to Mary. But," he emphasized, "I don't want others to know about the silver until this is settled. It won't be long. I think things are coming to a head right now. All I'm asking is that you be patient."

Daniels scratched his head, considering. At last, he sighed and said, "Seems like you're taking a lot of unnecessary precautions. But I reckon I'll follow along with you. For now."

"Fair enough," Hood said. "One other thing. Someone else knows about this. I'm not certain who that is, but you watch yourself around here. Whoever it is knows I know what is happening, and might take it in his mind to shoot first on the offchance that you might know what's in here."

Daniels moved uneasily in the saddle. "I'll watch. I'm no gunman, but I'm pretty fair with a rifle."

"Better safe than sorry," Hood said, gathering his reins.

21.

The man nestled between two boulders at the top of the mesa raised his rifle and took careful aim at Daniels and Hood as they turned their horses to ride out of the small canyon. Then he lowered the rifle and frowned. He had no doubt that he could make the shot. Still, there was a risk that he'd only hit one before the other found cover.

He glanced at the faint trail made by long-forgotten Indians, snaking its way down from the mesa top. By the time he worked his way down the steep mesa wall, Hood and Daniels would be gone. Worse, he reflected, he would be exposed to return gunfire once he was on the trail.

He sighed and inched back from his hiding place. He knew one of the riders was that preacher fellow, but the other he couldn't tell from this distance. No, he thought, better to let them go for now. He was patient and time would slip around to his advantage. There was too much at stake to take chances now. He grinned to himself as he walked to his horse and slipped his rifle into the saddle sheath. Whistling softly, he mounted his horse and rode away.

Hood lifted Sheba into a canter as he rode back toward Jericho. He'd bade good-bye to Daniels after they had made a circuit of the fence, and told the cowboy to give his apologies to Mary and that he had to get back to town to finish preparing his sermon for Sunday. It was only a tiny lie, he thought. But he needed time to think about his next move. He was certain that Halsey Barth was one of those trying to force Mary off the Bar S, but there had to be someone else as well. Too much had happened for one man. There had to be at least one more — probably McQuade. But he had a hunch that there was another who remained in the shadows. Someone not as obvious as Mc-Quade.

He chewed his lower lip thoughtfully as he rode. McQuade was all bluster and hotheaded. Despite what Daniels said about him, however, there was something about the man that didn't fit with Daniels's impression of him. Beneath McQuade's bluster was a hair-trigger temper and a mean streak that ran a mile wide. He was, Hood thought, a bully used to enforcing his will on others, and Hood was certain that McQuade would work his will any way he could. Even, Hood thought sourly, if it meant bringing in a hired gun.

A rabbit ran in front of Sheba and Sam ran after it. Hood grinned, enjoying the sight of his wolf pet in pursuit. For a moment, Hood's attention slipped, and he felt the slap of a bullet and grabbed the saddle horn to keep from falling. Sheba felt his weight shift and stepped aside, saving him from another bullet that whined past his head.

He clapped his heels against her sides and leaned over her neck as she burst into a gallop. He weaved in the saddle, trying desperately to hang on. Another bullet kicked up dust and he turned Sheba into a dry wash. He snugged the reins around the saddle horn, giving her her head, and hung on with both hands as she ran down the wash, twisting and turning, making her way back toward the mesa. His head began to swim and black spots appeared in front of his eyes. Desperately, he tightened his grip. She came to where the wash turned south along the mesa. The mesa wall reached high above them. Heaps of talus had scattered along the floor of the wash along with scattered fragments of rocks eroded from sandstone.

Hood's breath came in ragged gasps as Sheba slowed, then settled into a walk, picking her way carefully among the stones. He raised his head and dimly made out a faint narrow trail leading into the mesa. He turned Sheba into it, and reached into his saddlebags for piggin strings and tied his hands to the saddle horn. Then, he fainted.

Twice, he came awake when Sheba paused, only to pass out again as pain wracked through him when she began to move again, working her way deeper and deeper into the mesa.

Finally, he felt Sheba stop and her head drop down to pull at a clump of grass. He lifted his head and saw they were in a small canyon that couldn't have been more than fifty yards wide. Halfway up the side of the canyon was a small abandoned cliff dwelling. A tiny spring bubbled through pines. He saw signs of deer, but no hoof prints.

Fumbling at the piggin strings with swollen fingers, he finally slipped free and fell to the ground. He lay still, looking at the sky, surprised to see lavender streaks across it as the sun neared the horizon. Sam crept to his side and laid his head upon his leg, whining anxiously.

"Good boy," Hood said hoarsely. "Good boy."

Moving slowly, he crawled to the stream and sipped water. The coolness spread through him. He panted heavily for a moment, then pulled himself to the trunk of a pine and eased his shirt away. The bullet had taken him low on the left side. He probed gently with his fingers, finding the exit wound at the back.

He took a handkerchief from his pocket and rinsed it in the stream, then gently wiped the blood away. He saw a small prickly pear cactus and broke off a leaf. He slipped a jackknife from his pocket and cut the spines off, then slit the leaf lengthwise in half. An old Indian remedy for wounds, he recalled. He tore strips off the tail of his shirt and bound the pulp over the holes made by the bullet.

He had no idea where he was or if anyone was following him. But there was nothing he could do about that. Right now, he needed to survive.

A small distance from where he lay grew a clump of squaw cabbage. He crawled to it and broke off leaves, chewing them slowly and washing them down with sips from the stream. Then, he crawled under the low-hanging branches of a pine and fell asleep on a mat of soft pine needles.

When he awoke, stars were shining and the crescent moon was moving slowly across the sky above the canyon. He gritted his teeth and crawled to Sheba. He fumbled at the cinch, undoing it, then pulled the saddle off, letting it fall to the ground beside him. Sheba lowered her head to nuzzle him and he slipped the bridle off.

"I'm all right, girl," he whispered.

Nearby, Sam whined, and he turned to look at the wolf.

"Good to see you, too, boy," he said. His voice sounded like a raspy file.

He must have fainted again for the next thing he knew, the sun was high in the sky. He turned his head and saw Sam lying close to him, a dead rabbit beside them.

"You know, don't you?" he whispered.

Sam whined and Hood pulled the rabbit to him, taking the jackknife from his pocket. Laboriously, he skinned and cleaned the rabbit, then crawled to his saddlebags and dragged them back into the shade of a pine. He pulled dried sticks to him, and took matches from his saddlebags and built a small fire. He spitted the rabbit on a stick and concentrated on holding it over the flames, making himself wait patiently until it was cooked. He ate it slowly, sharing with Sam. When he had finished, he felt strength returning to him, but knew it would be a while before he would be able to saddle Sheba and ride out of the small canyon.

He reached out and ruffled Sam's fur.

"You're going to have to find food for both of us," he whispered. "Sure hope you understand."

Sam moved close to him, stretching out along Hood's leg. Hood smiled faintly, then leaned back and slept.

Slowly, a week drifted by as Hood waited to heal. He kept bathing his wound in the cold water of the stream, but still felt feverish. Streaks of red ran down from the wound, and he knew the wound had become infected. He drank a tea he made from a clump of amolillo, boiling it in a crude pot he made from birch bark he peeled from a tree. He knew that the water would keep the fire from burning the pot, but he had to handle it carefully to keep it from falling apart.

He managed to shoot a deer with the Spencer on the third day, and had laboriously butchered the deer before suddenly realizing that he should not have shot as the sound of the gunshot would echo through the canyon and lead someone to him. For two days, he waited in wary anticipation, sleeping lightly with the Spencer at hand while he jerked some of the meat over his fire.

But no one appeared and he relaxed, and on the fourth day, began to explore the canyon. The pain left his wound and his strength began to come back. He made snares to catch rabbits. He used an old broken pot made by the unknown Indians, which he discovered at the base of the cliff, to cook a stew that he supplemented with wild onions, squaw cabbage, breadroot and sego lily bulbs. He found many arrowheads of a strange design with long, tapering points.

On the seventh day, he rested, gathering his strength before leaving on the eighth. He thought about his congregation and how some would worry about what happened to him. And Mary. And Daniels. Within him, a slow, smoldering anger began as he tried to figure out who had shot him. McQuade? Rawlins? Had the Hardesty gunman arrived and taken matters into his hands immediately? No, he thought, he could probably eliminate Hardesty. The Hardestys he had encountered in the past came straight for him face-to-face. Of course, maybe one of the Johnsons from Tennessee had managed to track him down, although, he had to admit, that was a vague possibility. Not many people had made the connection between Hood and Tom Cade yet. And then, there was Halsey Barth.

Barth. He thought much about Barth as he lay on his saddle blanket, watching the birds in the pines and listening to the small stream bubble near at hand. Bees hovered lazily here and there nearby, and squirrels moved timidly along the branches of the pines. But it was Barth that occupied his thoughts most of the time. The man was becoming more and more of an enigma to him, slipping in and out of his reveries like a malignant shadow.

On the morning of the eighth day, he rose. Sam whined and sidled close to Hood's side. Hood reached down and patted him.

"You've been good, Sam," he said. "But now it's time to return. I think," he added wryly.

He glanced ruefully at his torn and dirty shirt, the bloodstains almost black by now, then picked up his saddle, panting from the effort, and walked toward Sheba. For once, she stood patiently while he approached. He managed to get the saddle up on her on the second effort, but had to stop, leaning against her side, panting heavily. Perspiration covered him and he felt his wound ache from the effort. Laboriously, he tightened the cinch, and slipped the bridle over her head, and pulled himself up into the saddle. His head swam from the effort, and he clutched the pommel until the feeling passed.

"This might take more than I thought," he muttered as he nudged Sheba's sides with his heels.

He rode carefully down the small canyon. He found the niche where Sheba had climbed over stone, and knew that few could have tracked him into the refuge where he had spent the past week. The canyon narrowed here and the stream disappeared. On both sides, the walls lifted sheer along the trail leading into the canyon, rock sheltering the trail in places so it seemed at times he was riding in twilight. He emerged from the opening and studied the country carefully before riding down to the flatland. At the foot of the mesa, he found where horses had followed him before coming to the gravel pan and turning back. He followed their trail as the best way to find his way out of the maze.

He came to where he'd been shot, and turned Sheba up and away from the trail, looking for where the shooter had been. His vision blurred, but he clung stubbornly to his task. At last, he found where the shooter had waited. He stayed in the saddle as he studied the ground. The man had dismounted and waited near a thicket of manzinita bushes. A large man, Hood thought, wearing low-heeled boots. But that was all he could find and he turned Sheba back, riding down to the trail.

Perspiration soaked into his shirt as he rode, holding Sheba to a walk as he was unsure if he would be able to stand the jar of her canter. Heat waves rolled from the ground and shimmered in the distance. Overhead, a buzzard circled lazily. A ground squirrel dashed across his path and disappeared beneath a mesquite bush, but this time Sam didn't give chase, trotting easily by Sheba's side, casting wary looks up at Hood as he reeled occasionally in the saddle.

Twice, he reined in Sheba under the shade of a desert willow and sat panting in the saddle, knowing instinctively that he would not be able to remount if he stepped down. His throat burned from the heat and he licked his lips to ease their dryness. His hands shook on the reins.

He passed the turnoff to Tannin's farm

and then the turnoff to Hoffman's spread, each time tempted to turn up the road as his wound began to throb. But he stayed stubbornly on the trail, willing himself to remain in the saddle. He began to estimate distance, and counted off the miles as Sheba covered them, reminding himself grimly that soon the trial would be over and he would be able to stop and rest.

He came back to the trail he knew, and followed it along to the Bar S and turned up onto it, following it along until he came to the canyon. He rode easily, more relaxed than before, making his way up to the home place, praying that Mary and Daniels would be there and not out tending stock or riding fence.

He blinked the perspiration out of his eyes as he neared the ranch house. Blearily, he saw Daniels and Mary standing on the porch, regarding him as he rode up. Then, they were down from the porch and running toward him.

"I . . ." he managed before a blackness washed over him and he fell gratefully into it, unaware of Daniels catching him as he slipped from the saddle.

Fevered images blurred and danced. His father appeared, looking sadly at him, then shadowy figures from his youth: Eula May and her nubile body, men who had tried to gun him down when he was Tom Cade in Walker, the Johnsons, the Hardestys, his dead fiancée, Amy, the congregation before him his first time in the pulpit, and others he couldn't recognize but who made a tendril of fear lace through him.

He awoke in the cool dark of a room, uncertain of where he was for a moment. A dull ache throbbed in his shoulder. Then he became conscious of the soft bed under him and turned his head, studying the room. Calico curtains hung from the sole window. A wardrobe snugged against the wall at the foot of his bed. A cane-backed rocker stood on a braided rug beside the bed next to a small table with a pitcher and basin on top. A cloth was folded neatly over the lip of the basin. His Spencer leaned in a corner of the room, and his eyes rested on it for a moment as memory came slowly to him.

The door opened and Mary came in, holding a glass of water. Worry lines were etched between her eyes and in tight circles around her mouth. She saw he was awake and smiled, the lines easing slightly.

"You're awake," she said. She came to the side of the bed and raised his head so he could sip from the glass. The water seeped into the dry tissues, easing his parched throat. When she took the glass away, a faint taste of medicine remained in his mouth along with a touch of whiskey. He looked at her admonishingly.

"Don't say anything," she said severely. "It wasn't much and you can't tell me you haven't had a little whiskey now and then. I put an egg in it."

"Thanks. I guess a little now and then won't hurt," he croaked. He swallowed painfully and tried to smile at her, but the effort was more than he could manage.

"How long?" he asked.

"Two days," she said, placing a cool hand on his forehead. She frowned. "You still have a fever, but not as bad as it was when you came here. Your wound was infected. We had to open it again and drain it. You were lucky. I'd say you weren't far from gangrene."

He sighed and rested his head back against the pillow. "The church . . ." he began.

"People think you left without telling anyone. Some folks are mighty disappointed. Tannin rode over twice to see if we'd heard anything about you."

"I better get back to town," he said.

She pushed gently on his good shoulder before he could attempt to rise.

"If you wanted to go to town, you'd have gone instead of riding up here," she said. "You must've come up here for a reason instead. Best stay here until you think things out."

"I don't want to worry folks," he said.

"Too late for that," she said dryly. "Charlie rode in and collected your things and brought them out here."

She hesitated, glancing at his saddlebags resting in the corner beside the Spencer.

"We opened them, thinking we might get an idea of where you might've gone. We found your pistol," she said. "Want to tell me why a preacher would carry around something like that?"

"No," he said bluntly. He looked at the glass in her hand, and she raised his head to help him drink deeply this time. He sighed as he lay back against the pillow.

"Charlie also told me you showed him what you found," she said.

"The silver?" She nodded. He sighed. "I thought it best if another person knew as well."

She placed the glass on the small table next to the basin and rose to sit in the rocker. She composed herself before speaking.

"Why didn't you tell me where it was?"

she asked. She looked away from him, and he could see the brightness of tears in her eyes but didn't know if they were from anger or concern.

"I don't know," he said. "I guess there just wasn't time."

"I wish you would have told me where it was," she said.

"I'm sorry. But sometimes people let things slip whether they want to or not. It wouldn't take much before you had prospectors swarming all over your land. And" — he paused deliberately — "you said you wanted to get the Bar S going before you opened the mine. You were right in that. There's a certain contentment that a person gets from having a simple life. You begin taking silver out of that canyon and your whole life's going to change. You're building a new life here now. You want to go back to the old way again after fighting to get yourself out of it?"

A thoughtful look came into her eyes. She folded her hands and leaned back in the rocker.

"I think I understand," she said softly.

"Right now it's more important to get the Bar S up and running full. The silver will always be there if you need it."

She nodded. "What now?"

He took a deep breath. "Things are beginning to come to a head. Sometimes you have to shake the tree to see what the hounds chased up it."

"You might not like what comes out of that tree."

A slight grin crossed his face.

"It's time. Time to cry 'havoc' and let slip the dogs of war. A man can't always step aside when folks are trying to push others out of the way of their march. It may take a while sometimes, but God eventually brings every work into judgment with every secret thing, whether it's good or bad. He brings every work into justice sooner or later. I figure later's come."

"You're talking about McQuade and the Rawlinses," she said.

"And someone else," he said slowly. "I have a feeling that they're just the doers and the shakers. There's someone else behind all this."

He heard boots striking the hardwood floor and then Charlie Daniels walked in, his broad face breaking into a smile when he saw Hood awake.

" 'Bout time you rejoined us," he said. "You had us worried."

"It was questionable for a while there," Hood said.

"Yeah. That it was," he said. He took off his hat and wiped his sleeve across his face. "You gave us quite a worry."

"Oh ye of little faith," Hood answered.

"Maybe. But I don't think I want to be trusting God to turn aside bullets. You know who shot you?"

Hood shook his head. "No. But whoever it was wears low-heeled boots."

A thoughtful look slipped over Daniels's face. "Then he shouldn't be too hard to find. Not many wear them around here. A cowboy wears heeled boots to keep his foot from slipping through the stirrups. Nobody wants to chance being dragged by his horse."

"You hear anything in town?"

Daniels shook his head. "A lot of upset folks who think you just up and took off without saying anything. Tannin and Parks keep saying that something must've happened to you 'cause you wouldn't do that. But that don't set with others. McQuade tried to take advantage of you being gone and cut the wire to move some cattle on Bar S land. But I pushed them back and repaired the wire. I made certain that he knows the next time I'll shoot the cattle," he added grimly. "So far, the wire's held."

"That's to be expected," Hood said.

"About McQuade, I mean. He's the type who makes his own invitation. Anyone know I'm here?"

"Nope. I put your horse up in the barn and your wolf has been staying close by. We ain't had visitors up here. 'Cept for Tannin and Parks, who came by to see if we had heard anything about you. They're gloomier than an owl's song. But I don't think we should run and tell them that you're back," he said in caution. "You ain't well enough to fight off a fly. Although," he added, casting a swift glance at Hood's saddlebags, "I reckon you've swatted a few flies in your time."

Hood's lips tightened. "Even David had to use a sling or sword now and then. Some folks just can't be set right with words. But you're right about one thing. I know I need to rest up for a while." He looked at Mary. "That is, if I'm not putting you out."

"That's the first stupid thing you've said since I've known you," she said, a spot of color appearing in each cheek. "You just try and get out of that bed before it's time and I'll . . . I'll brain you with a frying pan."

"And I've seen her swing it," Daniels said. "You don't want to be on the receiving end. Best you just lay up for a while. You've been gone long enough that a bit more ain't gonna make one damn difference."

"You've convinced me," Hood said, relaxing. "Right now, though, I don't think you'd need a frying pan. You could knock me over with a feather."

"Feather or frying pan. Just you take care and remember that I'll do it," Mary said firmly, rising. "Now, you take your own advice and rest awhile. I'll bring you something to eat later."

Gratefully, Hood sighed and closed his eyes. He didn't hear Mary and Charlie walk softly from the room as he slid into slumber. This time, without the shadows.

22.

Days passed slowly as Hood gave himself over to Mary's ministrations, resting and thinking about what had happened. From time to time, he felt a nudging of guilt about staying away from town and his church, and thought about sending word to Tannin and Parks that he was all right, but he remembered that to do so would take Daniels away from the ranch, leaving Mary alone to face anyone who decided to ride up the canyon to the ranch house. Best, he reflected, to think on what had happened and be wise.

But eventually, as time passed, he began to become restless, and found himself up and away from bed despite Mary's threats with a frying pan. He walked with Sam beneath the pines along the stream — short distances at first, but gradually increasing the distance as time passed and he grew stronger. He did odd jobs around the ranch yard, repairing the corral, currying Sheba, cutting the long grass down on the home pasture with a scythe he found hanging in the tack room.

Twice, he took the Schofield from his saddlebag, only to wipe it down and replace it. But he felt the pull of the pistol working on him, and finally buckled the holster around his waist and began working with it, surprised at the memory in his hands and muscles as he drew the Schofield faster and faster with time. But he was careful that Daniels and Mary didn't observe him working with the pistol, practicing mainly at night when the house fell silent and owls hooted in the trees.

He used the rest of the time for thinking about what had happened. At times, frustration filled him and he lapsed into long and moody silences that resulted in Mary hovering anxiously around him. But the thread he was seeking kept slipping away from him. McQuade, the Rawlinses, but who else? And who was the man with the low-heeled boots? Somewhere he felt he had seen something that should bring everything together, but where? What? But the thought remained tantalizingly out of reach, there but not there when he grasped for it.

"It'll come," Mary said when in frustration he told her.

"Yes," he answered. "But will I remember in time?"

Time was his enemy now, he knew, as events were beginning to percolate faster and faster and he instinctively felt the end coming, with a deep dread that both excited and repulsed him, knowing as well the thrill of what he had been before putting away the Schofield.

Yes, it is the pistol. But why can't I get rid of it? Throw it away or sell it and use the money for good? You know why. Yes, you know why. Because giving it away would be giving away a part of yourself, and you are afraid that the emptiness of being only a part of yourself would haunt you and you would become bitter and resentful of your own life. But don't you resent what you were and are now? Yes. So what do you do? How do you resolve what you were and what you will become? For you will become what you were. It's as certain as the turning of the earth.

The morning came when he knew he no longer could delay his return to Jericho, and over Mary's and Daniels's protests, he saddled Sheba and left the sanctuary of the Bar S, his saddlebags securely tied behind his saddle, the Schofield wrapped in its

305

protective cloth at the bottom of one saddle-bag.

Perspiration collected under his hat and trickled down his face as he neared town. Heat waves danced already, although it was not yet noon, and the sky was a cobalt blue that hurt the eyes from staring at it. The sun burned like a smith's forge, the heat making all living things sluggish. Yet, Mrs. Haddorn was out in her sunbonnet and long-sleeved calico dress, working in her flower bed, a bucket half-filled with water beside her. She stared open-mouthed at him as he neared her fence; then her mouth tightened and set in a disapproving line.

"Good morning, Missus Haddorn," he said, reining in near her fence. He remained in the saddles as her eyes roved over his tattered clothing.

"You look the worse for wear," she said acidly.

He gave her a small smile. "I feel the worse for wear. The heat doesn't make it any easier."

"Mind telling me where you been?" The question was a demand, not a pleasantry.

"Yes, I would," he answered easily.

"Out with that Riley woman, I imagine," she said distastefully. "And for a couple weeks, too, while your people go wondering if you're here or in heaven. Or elsewhere," she added pointedly.

"I reckon that's nobody else's business," he said.

Her face hardened. "If you weren't the pastor, that'd probably be true. But you are the pastor so it's everybody's business. We got a right to know what you're up to. You have responsibilities to others and they got a right to know what to expect from you."

Irritation swept through him. He thumbed his hat back and wiped his forehead on his sleeve, studying her for a moment before answering.

"No," he said quietly, "you don't have that right any more than I have the right to know what you're up to, although others are quick to tell me about you poking into their ways."

Her face flamed as red as the sun. She opened her mouth, but he rode on over her words.

"You hold to strict ways, Missus Haddorn, but your strict ways are messing around in others' business to find out the dirt about them. You take great pleasure in that, picking up on the smallest problem and building it into a sin to satisfy your own miserable little self. You've ruined the reputations of some and made others feel as if they weren't worth the time it'd take to bury them. You claim to be a Christian and that you stick closely by the Good Book, but you don't practice what you preach. The Bible has a lesson in it that you apparently overlooked or else ignored. You are like a whited sepulchre that appears beautiful outward, but within you are full of dead men's bones and all uncleanness. I direct you to the source, Missus Haddorn: Matthew, chapter twenty-three, verse twenty-seven. You are going to die a very lonely woman unless you change your ways. But," he reflected, "you've had plenty of time for contemplation, so I reckon you're as set in your ways as the wild goose that flies north and south according to the seasons."

He tugged his hat brim back down. "Good day, Missus Haddorn. By the way" — he pointed at her flower garden — "your lilies are wilting. I'd say they need good water."

He reined Sheba around and nudged her with his heels, ignoring Mrs. Haddorn as her mouth began to flap indignantly like a fresh-caught catfish.

He rode to the blacksmith's shop and dismounted as Bert glanced up, startled at seeing Hood. Bert grinned and put aside the glowing bar he was working, wiped his hands, and came out to greet him.

"Thought you were gone for good, Parson," Bert said, shaking hands. "Some been saying that you got fed up with Jericho and its doings and took off for greener pastures."

"Good to see you, Bert," Hood replied. "No, I just had a little problem that demanded my full attention for a while. Sorry if I worried you."

Bert beamed and shook his head. "That's all right. It's good to see you. I was wondering if you had fallen the way of our previous pastor. No one seemed to have any idea about what had happened to you. Everything okay?"

"About as right as it can be," Hood answered. He glanced around the street and lowered his voice. "Any news?"

Bert's eyes flickered involuntarily over the street before he spoke.

"There's a couple of new men in town been asking for you. People told them you were gone, but they're still here. Hang out over at The Cattleman's. I don't like the look of them. Hardcase cusses. Carry their pistols like they're used to using them. One calls himself Will Hardesty. The other Ben Johnson. He keeps a Henry rifle close at hand as well. Came separately but stay together now." He cleared his throat and wiped the back of his hand over his mouth before continuing. "Barth's been pretty friendly with them."

Hood nodded thoughtfully. "When did they come in?"

Bert furrowed his brow, thinking. "Let's see. Johnson was first. The day you last rode out, I think. Hardesty a few days later. Yeah, I remember now. Johnson came in to put up his horse and asked about you. Statler was with me about me hammering out a boot scraper for him, and he told them that you rode on out toward the mesa. Johnson changed his mind and rode out that way, too. Came back near sundown to put up his horse. The bay gelding back there's his. The sorrel with the white stocking's Hardesty's.

"Funny thing, though," Bert said, frowning. "They said they knew you and you were expecting them. I didn't believe them, but I learned long ago to mind my own business and let people mind theirs. Can't help what others say and I hear, though." He touched his nose with his index finger and winked. "I hear anything else, I'll let you know. Like I said, I don't like the looks of those hard cases."

"I appreciate that, Bert," Hood said gratefully. "Forewarned is forearmed."

"One thing else," Bert said. "One of them

— Hardesty, I think — said something about a Tom Cade. That mean anything to you?"

Hood was silent for a moment, then nodded. "Yes. A while back. He's retired now. I hope."

Bert's face mirrored his confusion at Hood's reply. "Probably means nothing, but it got me to wondering what he meant. Thought you might know."

"Thanks again, Bert," Hood said. "Every little bit helps. You never know when something's going to be important. I'll remember."

He shook hands with the blacksmith and walked down the street to the hotel, Sam trotting at his heels. The heat hammering on his head gave him a slight headache.

Inside, the hotel felt stuffy and hot, hotter than outside despite the high ceiling of the lobby. Statler looked up when he heard Hood enter, his thin lips pursing like someone had slipped him a shot of vinegar.

"Thought you'd pulled out," he said, glancing down at Sam.

"People tell me that," Hood answered. "I'd like my room back."

Statler started to turn to the pigeonholes behind him where the keys were kept, then caught himself and faced Hood.

311

"Sorry. All filled," he said, drawing himself up.

Hood's eyes flickered to the pigeonholes, then back to Statler. "I see a lot of keys in their slots."

"Can't help that. We're all filled," Statler said. "Guess you shouldn't have given up your room. Leastways, that's what the cowboy said who came to collect your belongings."

Irritation crept into Hood. He reached for the register, swung it around, and took the pen from its holder.

"Then, I'd say you can make room for me. In my old room," he added. "It was beginning to feel like home to me."

"I told you —"

"I know what you said," Hood replied, staring into Statler's eyes. "And I think you're lying. That may not be the Christian thing to say, but there comes a time when a fellow needs to say what he's thinking. Now I'm going down to Mother's for a cup of coffee and a bite to eat. When I come back, I expect my room to be made ready. Understand?"

"Mr. Barth —"

"Mr. Barth isn't here. You are." Hood signed his name and replaced the pen. He rested both hands on top of the desk and stared at Statler. "And frankly, I really am not in the mood to care what Mr. Barth may say one way or the other. I know you're going running to him the minute I'm out the door, and you can tell him what I said. He has a problem with that, he can come and see me and we'll sort it out. But," he said emphatically, "in the meantime, you get my room ready."

Statler's face looked as if he were working on an attack of apoplexy, but he swallowed with great difficulty, his protruding Adam's apple bobbing up and down like a fishing cork.

"Understand?" Hood asked softly, an edge to his voice.

Statler's eyes fell to the register in front of him. "Yes," he mumbled.

"Good," Hood said. He turned. "Come on, Sam. Maybe Mother will have a bone for you."

Sam whined and lapped his muzzle as he followed Hood outside. Together, they walked down the street, empty except for a stray dog lying in the shade next to the general store. Still, Hood felt as if eyes were following him although he could not see anyone. He felt his neck hairs rise and looked carefully to each side, but could not find the reason for his apprehension.

"Someone's walking on my grave," he muttered to himself. The thought was not comforting.

He opened the door and entered the café. The tiny bell above the door jingled. The café was empty. Mother came out, wiping her hands on her apron. Her eyes lit up with pleasure when she saw Hood.

"Well!" she exclaimed. "I'd given you up for lost." She glanced down at Sam. "And you came just in time for a soup bone I was going to toss after saving it for you."

Sam gave a short bark and she laughed.

"I guess he knows where his bread's buttered," she said, beaming. She gave Hood a shrewd look. "You look kind of peaked. You all right?"

"Now," Hood said, returning her smile. "But things have been a bit rough."

"Uh-huh," she said dryly, glancing at his clothes. "I can see that."

"Got a steak back there?"

"Yep. And a new Chinaman to cook it. Although," she added, "I've got to keep an eye on him or he'll burn it black." She shook her head "Chicken and dumplings he can make, but beefsteak gives him a turn or two. I just took an apple pie out of the oven, too. I made it. Don't trust him to do the pies." She sniffed. "I got sourdough biscuits, too.

Put the batter up last night and baked this morning. My starter goes back about twenty years with me, and longer from my ex-husband. He was a miner and had it long before he knew me, and he got it from his father," she said proudly. "But I don't let others have a sample. No, sir. I put in eight years with that cuss and earned every bit of it before I booted him out for his night hoo-rawing. Anyone wants it is going to have to marry me to get it, and I ain't found a man I'd give a spit for. No offense."

"None taken." Hood laughed. "But if you find one, I'd be pleased to do the honors."

"And I'd take you up on that," she said. She nodded toward his usual table. "Take a seat and I'll bring coffee after I get the steak started. And your bone," she added to Sam.

She bustled out to the kitchen. Hood made his way to the table and sat with relief, his back to the wall. Sam plopped down at his side, head up in anticipation of Mother's return with the promised bone.

Hood sighed and removed his hat, placing it on the chair next to him. He rubbed his temples, trying to remove the headache. A Hardesty and a Johnson, he thought rue-fully. Well, it probably would have happened sooner or later. But what would he do now? He shook his head, feeling low about how others would size him up after they learned that Tom Cade and Amos Hood were one and the same.

A man's past always haunts him, he reflected. *You are what you are and there's nothing you can do about that. You can change what you do, but you will always be what you were and are.*

Mother came out of the kitchen, bearing a steaming cup of coffee and a large bone heavy with strings of meat.

"Here you go," she said, placing the coffee in front of Hood. "And here you are," she added, bending to offer the bone to Sam. He took it gently from her hand and propped it between his paws before gnawing at it.

She paused, eying Hood critically for a moment. "I suppose you've heard that a couple of men are in town looking for you."

"Bert told me," Hood said, cautiously sipping his coffee.

"Word has it that it was Barth that brought them in," she said. "Leastways, that's what's coming to me. What's between you and Barth?"

Hood shook his head. "I don't know. We just seem to rub each other the wrong way."

"Be careful with that one," she said. "He's

killed a couple of men in the past. Most folks walk careful around him."

"You know where he came from?"

She shook her head. "Over in Texas, I think. El Paso maybe. But then I heard he came from back East, too. So take your pick. One place is as good as another as far as a man's past. You leave a place, you leave it behind you and move on to greener pastures."

"The past is always with a man," Hood said. "Whatever he left, he brought it with him."

"You might try Ed Hoffman. He and Barth were pretty friendly when Barth first came here. Then they had a falling-out. But he might know something."

"What was between them? I mean, what caused the problem?"

"Cards, I suppose. I hear Hoffman caught Barth slipping seconds and called him on it. Strange, though," she mused. "Barth didn't do anything about Hoffman. Another man a year or so back claimed Barth was cheating and Barth killed him. Shot him over the table when the fool made a mistake of trying to pull on him while sitting. Guess he didn't know about Barth's shoulder holster. Keeps a small pistol under his left arm. Thought you might want to know that.

Or know someone who might need to know."

She gave him a meaningful look and Hood tried to laugh, but the sound was hollow and meaningless.

"If I was a guessing person — and what person ain't — I'd say that this all spins around the Bar S. Though I can't for the life of me wonder what Barth would want with the Bar S, unless he means to hold the water rights and lease them out. But Barth ain't a country boy. He's a town man and I don't think he's ever been anything else but a town man. That don't mean he's soft, you understand. Just that he's a different bent than others."

"Strange that he'd settle in Jericho, though," Hood mused. "Man like that wants more around him than this place has to offer."

"Most everybody here came for one reason or the other," Mother said. "You scratch a person hard enough and you'll find that there's some reason or the other that they came to Jericho."

"That include you?" Hood asked.

She put her hands on her hips and gave him a bemused look. "I ain't no different than other people. Jericho may not be the end of the world, but it's right close by.

Ain't many other places a person could go when he's run out of places, and that's all I'm going to say about that. A person's past is his own business here in Jericho. You don't empty a chamber pot out your front door."

"I understand," Hood said. "But there are still good folks here."

"Didn't say there weren't. Most came for a good reason that they'd just as soon leave behind them. Even those farmers you ride down to see. You ever wonder why they settled here instead of moving on to California or up to Oregon? Land's better up there and they don't have a problem with water. The red mesa country's poor land for farming unless you got water and don't mind breaking your back for little return. Oh, damn! That Chinaman's burning the steak!"

Tendrils of gray smoke drifted out the kitchen door. She hurried to the kitchen, a thundercloud settling over her face.

Hood raised his cup of coffee, and paused as the door opened and a man walked in carrying a Henry rifle. His clothes were worn, his hat heavily sweat-stained. He was unshaven, and his nose had a heavy lump in the middle as if it had been broken several times. A large red bandanna was tied loosely around his neck. His ice-blue eyes settled on Hood and a smile flickered along his lips and disappeared.

Sam stopped chewing on the bone and growled softly beside Hood.

"Easy, Sam," Hood said quietly, but the wolf's hackles stayed raised as he fixed yellow eyes on the man standing by the door.

"That wolf seems mighty unfriendly," the man said.

Hood recognized the twang in the man's voice.

"I wouldn't give him any mind," Hood said. "He's just particular about some folks, but his bark is worse than his bite."

"Never saw a wolf that I'd want to let have a bite," the man said. He hefted his rifle slightly. "Fact is, I shoot every damn one I see."

"I wouldn't do that," Hood said softly, placing his cup carefully on the table and leaning back.

"You wouldn't?"

"And I don't think you want to do that either," Hood said.

"You're that preacher fellow I been hearing about, ain't you?"

Hood shrugged. "I'm a preacher. I don't know if I'm the one you been hearing about, though."

"How many preachers they be in this hole?"

"One's enough, I think," Hood said. "Of course, it all depends upon the one who needs the ministering whether I'm the right one for him or not."

"I'll bet your pappy was a preacher too," the man said.

"You're right. He was."

"I knew a preacher back in Tennessee. He had a boy who turned out to be a real bastard."

"That so? Well, I reckon you'd recognize someone like that, given all your experience and such."

A flush the color of raw liver slowly crept in the man's face.

"What y'all mean by that?" he said.

"That? Oh, nothing. Just that it takes a man of experience to recognize the same in others," Hood replied coolly.

"I'm Ben Johnson," the man said.

"I know," Hood said.

"How d'yuh know that? Maybe you that boy I was talking about?"

Hood smiled. "Jericho's a small place. Any stranger is known for what he is. You carry that Henry around" — Hood nodded at the rifle in the man's hand — "and you might as well tote a sign around your neck. Mighty few people carry a Henry in town with them."

Johnson looked down at the rifle in his hand, nodding. "Well, reckon that's so. But sometimes a man finds a rifle or pistol that just fits right in his hand. Kind of like a part of him, y'know? Leave that behind and he ain't whole."

"I've heard that's so," Hood said. "Of course, I imagine it all depends on what kind of man a person is."

Johnson opened his mouth to answer, but closed it as Mother came through the door with a plate of steak and fried potatoes in hand. She glanced at Johnson, eyeing him shrewdly, then said, "You just have a seat and I'll be right with you."

"Maybe later," Johnson said. He nodded at Hood. "Be seeing you, preacher man."

"I'm pretty busy," Hood said. "But if a man looks hard enough, he usually finds what he's after whether he wants it or not once he finds it."

Johnson pulled the door open and walked out.

Mother placed the steak and potatoes in front of Hood. "What was that all about?"

"A man looking for a reckoning," Hood answered. "Steak looks good."

"Humpf," Mother said. "You finish up

and I'll bring you a slab of pie. You want more coffee?"

"Please," Hood said.

He began eating as Mother hurried back into the kitchen with his cup. A feeling of foreboding and resignation slipped over him. The past from Tennessee had caught up with him, and Walker would soon follow. Tom Cade would soon be resurrected. He was as certain of that as the sun was hot.

23.

Hood stepped out of Mother's with Sam, gripping the bone tightly between his jaws, beside him. Then Hood paused to let his eyes adjust to the brightness. He felt better with a full meal under his belt, but knew his strength had not fully returned yet. He saw Peterson half-heartedly sweeping the walk in front of his store, and walked over.

"Hot enough for you?" Peterson asked. He leaned on the broom and pulled a handkerchief from his pants pocket and wiped his face. "I don't know how much longer we're going to be able to hold up under this if'n we don't get some rain soon. Worst drought I can remember and I been here ten years."

"It's hot," Hood said. "How's business been?"

Peterson made a face. "Not good. Nobody comes in unless they're down to scrapings. And less will come if crops don't come in.

'Course we always have a few cowboys in and around buying supplies, but that's only every two weeks or so. People just don't feel like moving much in this heat. Can't say I blame them. I don't feel like doing much either." He grimaced. "Even the beer down at The Cattleman's isn't that cool anymore. Heat just seems to have settled in all around. Even in the corners. Things don't get better, I'll probably have to pack up and go elsewhere. Don't know where," he mused. "I've pretty much run out of places to go."

"I know how you feel," Hood said.

Peterson gave him a bitter smile. "I imagine. I figure you came here for the same reason as I did. This is a place that God forgot about."

"I can't believe that," Hood answered.

"No?" A distant look came into Peterson's eyes. "I had another store. Back in Pecos. I was pretty happy there. Had a wife, three kids — two boys and a girl. I thought I had the world in my pocket, but then yellow fever came and took them. I couldn't stay there with the memories. So I moved. I went up to Fort Griffin and put in another store. One night some soldiers got drunk and went on a rampage and destroyed it. When I tried to stop them, they broke my arm and a couple of ribs. So I moved again. West, this time, to a small town called Shake-speare. But the mine was almost played out and I nearly went bust. So I moved again. This time here." He shrugged. "It's not much and I'm not gonna get rich, but I was making a living. Until now." He sighed. "Maybe I'm just fooling myself about moving. Maybe God has decided he needs another Job and I'm it. I just know I'm tired of trying to find a place to fit in again. No, I guess I'll just stay and let the chips fall where they will." He looked closely at Hood. "I figure you're the same way. You don't say much about your past. No one does here. But I figure you came here because you had no place else to go." A wry smile crossed his face. "There are other places where a parson's needed that would be a whole lot better than this."

"Maybe I'm needed here," Hood said distantly. "Maybe I'm supposed to be here for a reason. We're not given to know God's ways or reasons. Maybe He has a plan for me."

"Maybe," Peterson said, unconvinced. "But He'd better be getting on with His plans or Jericho's gonna dry up and blow away."

Hood nodded and walked away, back to the hotel. When he entered, Statler gave him a strange look and hurriedly placed a key on the counter.

"I take it my room's ready," Hood said.

"Yes. It is."

"And Barth told you to get it ready."

The cleric's eyes dropped to the counter.

"I figured as much," Hood said, collecting the key. "Now, go on down to the blacksmith's and get my saddlebags. The rest of my gear will come later."

"I'll send a boy," Statler said, his eyes remaining fixed on the counter.

"Now," Hood said gently, turning and making his way up the stairs, Sam on his heels.

He opened the door to his room and entered, giving the key a half turn in the lock. The room looked like he'd left it. He hung his hat on a hook next to the door and shrugged out of his coat. He crossed to the bed and dropped down on it gratefully. Sam settled on the hooked rug and began to worry at his bone. Hood closed his eyes and dropped into a light sleep, half-awake, thinking but not realizing that he was thinking, dreaming the words, the sentences, the questions and doubts.

What now? What are you going to do? God, I wish I had an answer. I feel like I'm being drawn back to what I was and do not want to be again. But is Tom Cade gone, drifting somewhere with the wind? I know that he isn't; he's just inside me, waiting to come out. And a part of me wants him to come. I want to smash those who have been causing all this trouble. You cannot reason with evil. It has a mind and a way of its own. I guess there comes a time when you have to descend into the pit and battle evil there at the source, for trying to reason and to guide evil to the right path doesn't work. Fight fire with fire when the water of salvation doesn't quench the fire.

A discreet knock came at the door and he awakened immediately, his tongue thick in his mouth. He swallowed dryly.

"Yes?"

"It's me. Statler. I have your things."

He rose and went to the door and opened it, standing automatically to the side should danger be there beside the clerk. But Statler was alone. Hood took the saddlebags and closed the door without speaking. He crossed to the table, placed the saddlebags on it and removed his Bible. He sat in the overstuffed Belter chair and began reading, seeking comfort, seeking answers.

Shadows lengthened in the room as the sun began to drop over the red mesa, taking the heat with it but leaving traces behind. Hood closed his Bible and placed it on the table. He stretched and looked down at Sam.

"Supper? Or are you satisfied with what you have?"

Sam growled, still gnawing on the bone.

"Well, come on. You can keep me company anyway," Hood said, rising.

Sam dropped the bone and rose, pausing to look wistfully at it before following Hood out the door.

Outside, Hood hesitated, then walked across the street to The Cattleman's. He entered, pausing just inside the door. He saw Barth at his usual table in the back, playing poker. Hood crossed to the table and stood beside Barth as the man laid down his hand and raked in the pot.

"A pair of aces and eights. Jack kicker," Barth said.

"Too much for me," one of the players said, throwing in his hand with disgust.

"I wanted to thank you for the room," Hood said.

Barth glanced up at him, then down as he began to stack his chips. "A man has to stay somewhere."

"Especially since the hotel was full."

Barth looked up again, a half smile on his lips, but didn't say anything.

Hood looked at the unshaven man to

Barth's left. He wore his hat pushed back off his forehead, revealing a thin face with a nose shaped like a hawk's. His eyes were hard and black like obsidian.

"You're Will Hardesty," Hood said.

The man gave a curt nod. "And you're the parson." He smiled mockingly, but the smile never touched his eyes. "Leastways, that's what I understand you be now."

Hood ignored him and looked around the room. "Where's your partner?"

"Johnson?" Hardesty shrugged. "Somewheres, I imagine. You want him for something?"

The challenge was inherent in his words, but Hood disregarded it.

"I thought I might invite the two of you to Sunday service."

"I don't take much to preaching. Had my belly full of it when I was a squirt and made to go. Didn't have much use for it then and don't have much use for it now. Fact is," he said, giving Hood a hard look, "I don't have much use for preachers either. Seems to me like they're always poking their noses into others' business whether they're wanted or not."

"The invitation's still open," Hood said, moving away from the table. "Whether you want it or not. The choice is yours. Fact is,

330

man must always make a choice. What happens to him comes when he makes the bad one."

"Doesn't that go with everyone?" Barth asked, looking up as he gathered the cards.

Hood paused. "Yes," he said softly. "That goes with everyone."

24.

Hood rose late and dressed carefully before leaving his room and making his way down the street to Mother's for breakfast. He moved slowly, feeling the heat of the day working hard upon him. He entered the café and paused, seeing McQuade and Johnson sitting together at a table in the corner. He removed his hat and nodded at them, then walked to his usual table and sat.

Mother came out of the kitchen, a cup of coffee in her hand. She placed it in front of Hood and smiled.

"You look a little better than you did yesterday," she said.

"It's your cooking," Hood said.

"Probably," she answered. "Man has to eat right. You want another steak?"

"You get the Chinaman to where he can cook it?"

"No. But it's still meat."

Hood felt himself smiling despite his

mood. "All right. I'll chance it anyway."

"Coming up," she said. She nodded slightly toward McQuade and Johnson and gave Hood a knowing look. "Don't get into any trouble while I'm gone."

"I won't," Hood said, leaning back in his chair with cup in hand. He sipped, keeping his eyes on the pair across the room from him.

McQuade looked boldly at him. "Something I can do for you, Parson?"

Hood shook his head. "Nope. You've been right accommodating lately. I appreciate that. Sometimes fences make good neighbors, I reckon."

A red-black flush mottled McQuade's face. "And sometimes fences just gotta go."

"That's true," Hood said. "I guess it depends on the time, though. And the man. Sometimes maybe the fence isn't worth the effort."

"I'm used to going where I want," Johnson interjected. "I want to go someplace and a fence's in my way, why, I just cut it down and move on. Never saw no reason to change my trail 'cause someone's ignorant enough to try and range me out."

"Could be a bad habit," Hood murmured. "Someday someone's likely to take offense at that."

"You, for example?" Johnson sneered.

Hood shrugged. "Who knows? A man has to do what's right. A person has the right to fence in his own range. Now, public range, why, that's another matter. I imagine someone would have the right to cut his way through. But private land? That's something altogether different. Besides, there's no reason to go out of your way to make trouble. Why not ride around it?"

"I don't ride away from anything," Johnson said. "Kind of an obligation."

"And I don't like being fenced off from water," McQuade growled.

"It's not your water," Hood answered.

"I need that water."

"What a man needs depends on what a man is," Hood said.

"What's that supposed to mean?"

"Maybe if you'd be a better neighbor, folks might be willing to accommodate you. Even if it means shorting themselves. But, McQuade, you have a tendency of running over people. You can't expect them to greet you with open arms. You catch more flies with honey than vinegar."

"You learn that from y'daddy?" Johnson asked.

"Pure fact," Hood answered, refusing to rise to the bait. "But you do what you want.

A man should. But a man shouldn't complain when others do the same. McQuade, you stay away from the Bar S."

"You telling me what to do?" McQuade said, his voice rising with anger.

"Yes, I am," Hood replied as Mother came out of the kitchen, arms laden with steak and eggs and apple pie. She glanced at McQuade and Johnson, her lips thinning.

"You want anything else?" she asked.

"No," McQuade snapped and rose. Johnson followed. He dropped two dollars on the table.

"I'll be going over the Bar S land whether that fence is up or not," McQuade said icily. "And anyone in my way will have cause to regret it."

He stormed out. Johnson paused at the door and gave Hood a small smile. "Be seeing you, Parson," he said.

The door closed behind them while Mother placed the food in front of Hood.

"You watch yourself," she said. "McQuade means what he says."

"I didn't think otherwise," Hood replied. "Food looks good."

She sniffed and walked away.

Hood had just finished eating and stepped out of the café when Mary came racing into town in a buckboard. She saw Hood and reined in beside him.

"I need you," she said breathlessly. "Charlie's been shot! His horse came back to the house. I rode out and found him by the north fence. Next to the mesa!"

A cold chill ran through Hood. "You see anyone?"

She shook her head as Hood stepped down to the buckboard and looked in the back. Daniels lay white-faced on a blood-stained quilt. Hood climbed into the buckboard and knelt, his fingers going to Daniels's throat, feeling the pulse beating faintly. Daniels had been shot three times and had lost a lot of blood.

"He's hurt bad," she said.

"We need to get him to the doctor," Hood said grimly as Mother leaned over the buckboard. Gently, he rolled Daniels over. Two of the bullets had exited.

"He won't last," Mother said. "Take him to my place. I've dealt with bullets before. At least, we can care for him until we get the doctor over from Trent."

Hood nodded. Mary goaded the horses and drove down to Mother's house. Peterson followed, and helped Hood carry Daniels inside and into the spare bedroom as Mother directed.

"Now, leave," she said, making shooing gestures. "Mary, you boil up some water while I get some bandages ready."

Reluctantly, Hood left the house and stood indecisively on the porch. Peterson came out and took a handkerchief from his pocket, wiping his forehead.

"Any idea what happened?" he asked.

Hood shook his head, his lips drawn in a thin line. "No," he said abruptly.

"You think it's McQuade? Or," Peterson said, clearing his voice, "those men he hired?"

"They're in town. Maybe Rawlins, but this doesn't feel like him. Rollie would have come at him straightforward. Daniels's no gunman and Rollie knows that. It could have been his brother, but I doubt it."

Peterson furrowed his brow. "Then who?"

"That's what I mean to find out," Hood said grimly.

He stalked off, his back stiff. He walked down to the stable. Bert was carefully turning iron in the fire.

"Saw Mary Riley come into town like demons were on her trail," Bert said. "Everything all right?"

"Daniels has been shot," Hood said abruptly. He walked back to Sheba's stall, lifting his saddle from the wall.

"What? Where?"

"Out by the mesa," Hood said. "Can you ride over to Trent and bring the doctor back?"

"Sure," Bert said, laying the iron aside. He wiped his hands on his leather apron and slipped it off. His face hardened. "Any idea who shot him?"

"Not yet. But I mean to find out. It's time we put a stop to this. I appreciate you doing this."

Bert shook his head as he walked to the back of the stable. "I reckon you're right. A man has to stop hiding his head in the sand sometime. I'll see you when I get back. Anything else I can do, you let me know then."

Hood led Sheba from the stable. "You're doing enough right now. Tell Mary I'll be back in a little while. I want to check out where he was shot."

He climbed into the saddle and rode out, turning Sheba toward the mesa. Sam loped at Sheba's heels. A quiet fury settled in Hood.

It took him nearly three hours to find where the shooter had waited, back among a jumble of boulders that marked the entrance to the small silver canyon leading back into the mesa. He found three .44-40 cartridge cases not far from the tracks. A half-smoked cigar lay near them. He frowned. Barth smoked cigars. But many others did as well. McQuade among them. But McQuade had been at Mother's with Johnson, and the tracks were too fresh to allow one of them time to shoot Daniels and make it back to town. So, who?

Painstakingly, he followed the tracks back to where the shooter had tied his horse. He studied the hoofprints carefully, but could see nothing unusual about them. Frowning, he went back to Sheba and mounted. He followed the trail as it wound along the side of the mesa, steadily south, losing it at near the turn to Hoffman's spread. He sat in the saddle, thinking. This made no sense at all. Why would the shooter come this far south instead of heading into town? Or over to Trent? Or, for that matter, anywhere else, unless he wanted to throw suspicion on Hoffman? And that didn't make sense either as Hoffman had shown his willingness to help Mary out of her predicament by agreeing to the cattle exchange. Rawlins? He doubted that. Rollie Rawlins fancied himself with a pistol and would have met Daniels straight on in town where others could witness a shoot-out. Rawlins didn't seem to be the type to want to hide a shooting that would add to his reputation.

So who could it have been? Hood thought grimly. There must be another party involved besides McQuade. And was there a connection between the man who shot *him* and Daniels? They had to be two different men. The tracks were different; the man who shot Hood had worn low-heeled boots, but the one who shot Daniels wore a rider's boots, high-heeled and narrow-toed.

Suddenly, unbidden, he remembered who he had seen wearing low-heeled boots, and the piece in the puzzle fell together. He turned Sheba and rode slowly back to Jericho.

The sun beat down, hotter than the hinges of hell, as Hood led Sheba back into the stable. Bert was gone, on his way to Trent, Hood thought as he unsaddled his mare and spilled a bait of oats into her bin. Maybe that was just as well. Bert might mean well, but he was no hand with a gun. Enough people had been hurt in the past few weeks.

Hood crossed the street to The Cattleman's. He shoved the doors aside with his shoulder and walked in. Barth stood at the bar, drinking a glass of whiskey with an egg in it. Hardesty and Johnson stood beside

Barth, a bottle of whiskey between them. They glanced up as Hood walked in.

"Well, Preacher, come to save some more souls?" Barth asked.

Hood came to him, his eyes flat and hard.

"Daniels has been shot," he said flatly. "But I figure you know that."

Barth's eyebrows rose. "Really? Any idea who?"

"I thought you might have some idea about that," Hood said.

"Me? Why would I know who shot him?" His eyes held Hood's mockingly.

Hood's eyes shifted to Hardesty, then Johnson. "And you," he said quietly.

Johnson stiffened. "Careful, Preacher," he said, turning slightly from the bar. "You better not be running your mouth off. A man could get himself into a lot of trouble flinging words around like that."

Hood backhanded him and he staggered back, his rifle clattering to the floor. In the same motion, Hood grabbed the bottle of whiskey and swung it across Hardesty's face. The bottle broke and blood spurted as Hardesty went down. Barth stepped hastily out of the way.

"You son of a bitch!" Johnson snarled, coming forward.

Hood swung from his hip, catching John-

341

son on the chin. Johnson's eyes crossed and he fell as if poleaxed, senseless. Hood turned as Hardesty began to rise. His boot caught Hardesty in the face. Stunned, Hardesty flew backward. His hands twitched as he lay on the floor.

Hood turned to Barth. "Now, tell me what you know," he demanded.

Barth's eyes flared. "You've overstepped your line," he said in a low, hard voice.

"Have I?" Hood challenged.

Barth glanced at Hardesty and Johnson. "I think you've just dug your grave, Parson. Those two aren't going to take this. You'd better leave town now."

Hood glanced down at Barth's boots — flat-heeled, highly polished.

"Doing much riding lately?" he asked softly.

"I don't ride out," Barth said. "I told you that before."

"But you keep a mount down at Bert's place," Hood said. "Why keep a horse if you don't ride?"

A dull red mounted in Barth's face. Carefully, he placed his glass back on the bar, his eyes steady on Hood's face.

"Turn the other cheek, Parson," he said. "You don't want to go any further with this."

"I've seen the tracks of a man wearing flat

heels by the mesa," Hood continued. "Not the one who shot Daniels, but one who took a couple shots at me a couple weeks ago. Funny thing is that you're the only one I've seen wearing flat heels. The size of the tracks would be about a man your size."

Barth's hands curled into tight fists by his side. "A lot of men wear boots like mine. Your friend Peterson. Most of the farmers. That's no proof."

"Maybe not," Hood said. "But I have a hunch you're a part of everything that's been happening with the Bar S."

Barth forced himself to relax. He laughed curtly and glanced down at Hardesty and Johnson. "Like I said, you have no proof. I think it'd be best if you left Jericho now. Those two aren't going to listen to reason."

"No, they aren't," Hood said. "But I think it's time we ended the fight for the Bar S."

The saloon doors opened behind Hood, and he turned to see Hoffman enter. Dust covered his clothes. The rancher stood for a moment, looking at Johnson and Hardesty lying on the floor. Then his eyes shifted and took in Barth and Hood.

"What's going on?" Hoffman asked.

"Daniels has been shot and the preacher here thinks I had something to do with it," Barth said. "But I've been here all day." He nodded at the bartender. "He's a witness. Along with a few others in town who might have seen me. When," he taunted Hood, "would I have had the time to ride out and shoot Daniels and get back?"

"Why do you think Barth was involved in the shooting?" Hoffman asked Hood.

"He might not have been the one who shot Daniels, but he knows who did. I'm certain of that."

"You have any proof?" Hoffman asked quietly.

"I saw his tracks before elsewhere where a bit of shooting was done," Hood said.

"That's nothing," Hoffman said. "You know that. The range is full of cowboy tracks."

"Not in some of the places I've seen," Hood said. He looked down at Hardesty and Johnson. Hardesty was beginning to move, his hand coming to his face and smearing blood. "You tell them to get out of Jericho when they come to."

"And what will you do if they don't?" Barth demanded.

Wordlessly, Hood turned and left. He paused for a moment, looking at Hoffman's horse, a piebald, standing hitched. Then he directed his steps toward Mother's house and walked in without knocking. Mary walked from the kitchen.

"How is he?" Hood asked.

"Holding his own," she said. "He's conscious now."

Hood walked into the bedroom. Mother stood beside his bed, wiping his forehead with a wet rag. Daniels looked up at him and grinned weakly.

"Looks like someone's got it in for both of us," Daniels said.

"You see who shot you?" Hood asked.

"No. I saw him leave on his horse, but couldn't tell who it was."

"What kind of horse was he riding?"

"A piebald," Daniels answered.

"I think that's enough," Mother said firmly. "He needs his rest now."

"Old harridan," Daniels said. His eyes fluttered shut. "Funny thing that piebald," he muttered.

Hood looked at Mary. She frowned.

"That doesn't make any sense," she said.

"I think it does," Hood said softly.

He walked toward the front door. Mary came after him.

"Where are you going?" she asked.

"To end it," he said, opening the door.

25.

Hood stood for a moment outside Mother's house, breathing deeply. He looked at the red mesa. Thunderclouds were beginning to build over the mesa, and flash lightning appeared beneath them. The day was beginning to cool subtly, although heat could still be felt. Dust hung in the air, making it hard to breathe.

Hood clinched his fists, willing the anger inside to settle. Beside him, Sam whined, sensing the turmoil running through Hood.

Hood glanced down at him. "I know, boy," he said softly.

He stepped down from the walk and crossed over to the hotel. He stepped inside and saw Statler standing behind the counter, writing in an account book. Statler looked up at him, then put down the pen and quietly went into the back room, shutting the door behind him.

Hood's lips thinned into a slight smile.

He went up the stairs to his room. He removed his coat, hung it carefully over the back of the Belter chair, and picked up his saddlebags, resting them on the table. He removed the Schofield from the bottom of a saddlebag and sat in the chair. Methodically, he broke the pistol down and cleaned it, wiping each part with a small oiled patch.

He rose and buckled the holster around his waist, settling the belt carefully around his hips. The weight of the pistol felt familiar, as if it had never been off his hip. He slipped the Schofield from its holster. It came naturally into the curve of his palm. He returned it and flexed his fingers. Slower than before, he thought automatically. He tried again, the pistol sliding smoothly, quickly from its holster, his thumb snapping the hammer back as the pistol came level.

Better, he thought. He tried again. And again, feeling the old quickness and instinct coming back as if it had never left him.

Drops of rain were beginning to splatter in the thick dust of the street as Hood stepped out of the hotel. October, he thought automatically. Almost November. The time for change.

He looked down the street. People were

coming out, looking at the heavy thunder-clouds building in the sky. Yet the buildings and objects seemed bright and sharp to Hood. He looked across the street at The Cattleman's. No one stood on the walk. He took a deep breath and relaxed, tension slip-ping from him. He stepped down from the hotel walk, and Tom Cade walked across the street, arms swinging freely, Hood for-gotten.

The saloon doors opened as Cade nudged them and stepped inside, taking a step to the right to put his back to the wall. Hoff-man and Barth sat at the table in back. Johnson stood at the bar, drinking a glass of whiskey, while Hardesty pressed a towel against his face to stop the bleeding.

They looked up as Cade entered, their eyes dropping automatically to the Schofield, then warily back to Cade's face.

"Well," Johnson said grimly. "You've come out of hiding."

Cade ignored his words. A tiny smile slipped over his face.

"What do you want now?" Barth de-manded.

"A reckoning," Cade answered. His eyes flickered to Hoffman. "I see you rode your piebald in."

A puzzled but wary look came over Hoffman's face.

"That supposed to mean something?" he asked.

"A man riding a piebald shot Daniels," Cade said. "I haven't seen any other horses like that in the country."

Hoffman's face cleared. "And you figure it was me?"

"It fits," he said. "I didn't know which of you discovered that silver canyon up on the Bar S, but that doesn't matter. At first, I thought it was McQuade who had found the old Indian mine and was using the need for water to disguise his real reason for wanting the Bar S. But I was wrong. You two were the ones after the Bar S, and not for water. You pushed McQuade as a cover for yourselves, even to hinting that he should bring in a couple of hard cases to help." Cade's eyes shifted to Hardesty and Johnson. "I don't know how he found out about you two, but it doesn't matter. McQuade brought you to Jericho." He glanced back at Barth and Hoffman. "What I don't know is the connection between you two."

Hoffman grinned and said, "We rode together for a while back in Texas. I had a little spread on the Trinity. Not much. Pretty much a single-loop outfit. But times were hard. Especially after the war when the Union boys came in. We" — he nodded at Barth — "decided a little Union gold would help matters along. But unfortunately, a couple of soldiers got themselves killed when they tried to stop our 'tax' collection. We came here. Halsey used his share to start this place. I took up ranching."

"And discovered the silver," Cade said.

Hoffman shook his head. "Nope. That wasn't me or Halsey. You were right the first time. One of McQuade's riders found the canyon while rounding up strays. 'Course, he came into an accident shortly after."

"You?" Cade asked quietly.

"No, me," Barth said coldly. "It was easy. I caught him cheating at cards."

"Was he?"

Barth shrugged. "People don't say much from boot hill."

"How did you find out about me?"

"Easy," Barth said. "I had Statler search your room after you had that confrontation with Rollie Rawlins. I thought it mighty strange that a preacher would act like you did. Statler found your pistol."

"A lot of men carry a pistol."

"Maybe. But a Schofield's not all that popular. And Tom Cade carries a Schofield. But Cade disappeared from sight after he left Walker. I had a hunch." He spread his hands on the table in front of him. "You can figure the rest. Ed here remembered you from Kansas. He'd driven a herd back there and went through Walker. He's the one who finally recognized you after I mentioned the Schofield. And he remembered your little problem with them." He nodded toward Hardesty and Johnson.

"And brought you down," Cade said softly, directing his attention to the two beside the bar.

"That's so," Johnson said. Without warning, his hand stabbed down toward his pistol as Hardesty took a step away from the bar. Cade drew quickly, thumbing off two shots. The first struck Johnson in the chest, turning him. His hand convulsed, sending the bullet intended for Cade into the floor before he dropped. The other shot hit Hardesty in the belly, and his pistol fell from his hand as he grabbed at the sudden pain, doubling over.

A bullet slipped past Cade. He took a step to his right, crouching as another bullet snapped by where he had been. He snapped a quick shot at Hoffman as the cattleman rose from his chair, aiming his pistol. The bullet hit Hoffman in the head, turning him. He sprawled over the table, upsetting it into Barth as the gambler tried to bring his pistol to bear on Cade.

"Don't!" Cade warned, but Barth ignored the warning. As he raised his pistol, Cade shot him, striking him in the shoulder, turning him. He tried to lift the pistol. Cade waited until it came level, then put his next bullet in the middle of Barth's chest.

Cade swung his pistol toward the bartender, Kelly, who froze, his hands below the top of the bar.

"Lift your hands slowly," Cade ordered.

White-faced, Kelly inched his hands from under the bar, raising them above his head.

"For Christ's sake!" he said, his voice rising to a squeak. "Don't shoot!"

"Come out from behind there," Cade said.

"I'm coming! I'm coming! Don't shoot!" Kelly said, a terrified look on his face. He scurried around the bar as Hood broke open his pistol and replaced the cartridges. He closed the action and slipped the Schofield back in his holster.

"Don't worry," he said calmly. "You're going to jail. As a witness," he added as Kelly appeared ready to faint. "Let's go."

They walked out of the saloon. A crowd was beginning to gather. Faces looked from Cade to the pistol and back. Shock appeared on their faces.

"Pastor," Peterson began, wetting his lips

nervously.

A shot sounded and Kelly folded at the hips, hands clutching his belly.

"Hood!"

Cade drew quickly as he leaped down from the porch into the street. McQuade stood by the stable, rifle shouldered. He fired again and missed as Cade leveled the pistol and shot three times in rapid succession. The bullets drove McQuade backward. He dropped into the street, legs twisting against the pain. Then, he lay still.

Slowly, Cade turned, the pistol still in hand. The crowd backed away from him.

Rain began to fall steadily as he walked across the street to the hotel.

26.

Kelly lingered for two days after giving his story to Bert and Peterson. Hood filled in the rest, and when the sheriff appeared at the end of the week, he ruled that Hood had acted in self-defense after hearing what the two had to say. But word of what happened quickly spread to the farmers, and few attended services the Sunday after. Mrs. Haddorn was conspicuously absent, but Hood knew that her wagging tongue had done its damage.

Two weeks passed, and Jericho began to grow as men flocked to town when news of the silver started to spread. Mary hired three of McQuade's cowboys to keep prospectors off her land, and rode over to Trent to add McQuade's land to hers on Hood's advice. The deed was registered shortly before the Rawlins brothers came into town. Ugly words passed between them and the county clerk when they heard that Mary Riley had already deposited surety money for the Box M, pending the purchase from any relatives of McQuade who could be found if they were willing to sell. None showed as time passed.

Daniels made rapid improvement, but was still too weak to return to the Bar S. Hood made daily visits to his sickbed, and one day found Mary with him when he walked into Mother's house.

"You're looking better," Hood said. "Must be the nursing."

Mary blushed and said tartly, "We're glad you came by. We have something to ask."

"What's that?" Hood asked.

She looked down at Daniels and took his hand. Daniels smiled up at her and turned his attention to Hood.

"It seems that this woman has finally come around to my way of thinking," he said.

"Your way," she said. "You men think you're the only ones to have ideas."

"All right," Daniels said. "She proposed to me and I accepted."

"I did no such thing!" she said, turning scarlet.

"We thought you wouldn't mind doing the honors," Daniels added.

"I'd be pleased," Hood said.

They were married the following Saturday.

After the services, Hood went to Mother's for dinner. Mother grinned when she saw him.

"Steak?" she asked, setting a cup of coffee in front of him.

"You get that cook so he can fix it proper?" Hood asked.

"He hasn't had time to practice much, but I think he can do a respectable job," she answered.

"Then, let's give him a try," Hood answered.

"Rollie Rawlins is in town," she said.

"Oh?" Hood asked. But a coldness settled in his stomach.

"Says he's looking for you," she said. "Thought you would like to know. He's probably up at The Cattleman's."

"Better hold that steak," Hood said, rising. Sam whined and rose reluctantly from the floor to follow him out.

"You be careful," Mother called after him.

He smiled at her as he shut the door behind him.

He walked down to the hotel and entered. The lobby was empty. He climbed the stairs to his room. The Schofield hung in its holster from the back of the Belter chair. He studied it for a moment, then sighed and strapped it around his waist. He checked the cylinder and slipped the pistol back into his holster.

He felt the darkness descending upon him as he went back down the stairs and crossed over to The Cattleman's. The saloon was half empty as he walked in the doors. Rawlins stood by the bar. He turned to face Hood when he saw his reflection in the mirror.

"Well, well," he said mockingly as he turned to face Hood. "Look who's here." He glanced down at the pistol at Hood's waist. "I reckon I know who you are today. That's good. I wouldn't want to kill a preacher."

"There's no need for this, Rawlins," Hood said. "None at all."

Rollie smiled lazily and his hand blurred as he went for his pistol. The gun came up when Hood's bullet struck him. He staggered back against the bar, disbelief in his face.

"You . . . you . . ." But he never finished what he was trying to say. The pistol dropped from his hand and he crumpled to the floor. He tried to reach the pistol, but a film came over his eyes and he shuddered once and died.

Hood's shoulders sagged as he walked to

him and stood looking down at him.

"You should have stayed on the ranch with your brother, Rollie," he said softly. "You should have let things be."

He turned and walked out, feeling the weight of the sky upon his shoulders.

That Sunday, only three families appeared for services, and the next day, Tannin rode into town to see Hood. He found him at the church, sweeping.

"Good to see you," Hood said, pausing and leaning on the broom. "Not many have been coming in lately."

Tannin shook his hand. "I know," he said, looking ill at ease. "That's why I came in. To talk," he added.

"Oh?" Hood raised his eyebrows.

"Yeah." Tannin removed his hat and began to turn it in his hands. "People are having second thoughts about you as the preacher."

"I see," Hood said dryly. "Missus Haddorn, I'd guess."

"She's part of it," Tannin said. "Most folks know her gossipy ways, but that don't seem to make any difference. The fact is, they know what happened. The saloon, Barth and Hoffman. McQuade."

"And they don't want a man like me as their minister," Hood said gently.

Tannin looked up, embarrassed, but relief showing in his face as well. "I figure every man has the right to look for a new life and to change. But," he sighed, "I'm just one voice crying in the wilderness. And Parks," he added. "Parks almost got into a fight with a couple others who got to flapping their lips about you. Fact is, though, there are only a few of us and I don't know how many will stay with you down the road." He ducked his head. "I don't even know about us. The boys," he started to say and stopped. He looked up at Hood. "You know how it is."

"I understand," Hood said. He leaned the broom against one of the pews. "I guess it's time that I moved on. Don't think badly of the others. I guess deep down I knew it would come to something like this eventually. A man can't hide from his past forever."

"I'm sorry," Tannin said.

"So am I," Hood answered. "But the walls of Jericho only come down in the Bible."

The sky was gray with the promise of rain when Hood rode out of Jericho, Sheba stepping lively, glad to be free of her stall. Beside her, Sam trotted. The land was still brown, but traces of green were showing beneath the mesquite, and when Hood passed the

Bar S range, the grass was standing heavy and tall. Steers moved lazily in the pasture, but things didn't feel right in the world for him as he rode north, away from the town where he thought he'd have a new beginning. In one saddlebag rested his Bible and his father's silver cross and watch. In the other, the Schofield, buried at the bottom beneath white shirts and the Wesley collar.

The red mesa loomed on his left, high and forbidding. He rode steadily north, and soon came to the high flatland that stretched out endlessly in all directions. He rode on into the barren wasteland.